KNOCK OUT

A MASON SHARPE THRILLER

LOGAN RYLES

INKUBATOR
BOOKS

Published by Inkubator Books
www.inkubatorbooks.com

ISBN (eBook): 978-1-83756-463-7
ISBN (Paperback): 978-1-83756-464-4
ISBN (Hardback): 978-1-83756-465-1

In memory of Janet...
Who loved, laughed, and left the best kind of mark.

1

It wasn't a fistfight. It wasn't even a brawl. It was an absolute beat-down, and by all appearances it had been so from the start.

I laid on the brakes and brought my Harley to a squealing stop at the mouth of the alley. From twenty yards away details were obscured, but the key facts were perfectly evident—it was one against three, and the one was a skinny teenage kid, while the three were big, beefy guys in leather vests. Sweat and tangled beards, prison tattoos and heavy leather boots that landed in the kid's shins, knocking him off balance. He fell, one arm colliding with the edge of a metal dumpster on his way down. Flesh tore. The boots kept falling.

I deployed my side stand and hurtled off the bike—then I was on them. The guy in the rear never saw me coming. I grabbed him by his long greasy hair and yanked his skull back, exposing a sweaty black snake tattoo on the left side of his neck. One foot to the backside of his weight-supporting knee knocked him off balance. A shove to his right shoulder capitalized on his instability, hurtling him face-first into the same dumpster the kid had crashed against. His nose met the metal with a sickening crunch, and then he went down, leaving me to pivot toward the next guy just as he was pivoting toward me.

Wide eyes flooded with outrage and violence. His right fist cocked back, readying to knock my lights out. Long before he could swing, my knee rocketed into his groin just as the flat of my palm landed against his nose. He screamed and stumbled, semi-disabled and fully disoriented. I slid past him, driving my elbow into his eye on my way to the third guy.

My final target was the only one of the three who had any time to prepare for my assault, but his tactical intelligence was poor. He should have run, gaining space down the alley before wheeling on me and drawing the nickel-plated 1911 shoved into his waistband. Instead he stalled, surprised by the speed and savagery of my assault. He spun to face me, one meaty hand dropping toward the pistol just as my elbow blackened the second guy's eye.

Fingers closed around a checkered grip. His thumb flailed for the 1911's hammer—it was carried uncocked, another mistake. The pistol rose, the muzzle reaching my knees as he fumbled for the weapon's safety.

And then he was out of time. I grabbed the top of the gun with my left hand and wrenched it backwards against his trigger finger. The finger snapped with an audible crunch of bone. He shrieked like a child and stumbled. I kept wrenching the gun, then I was yanking it. The grip had circled one-hundred-eighty degrees and now faced me. I grasped the handle and tore the weapon free as he stumbled for balance.

I could have shot him—I didn't bother. I belted him over the face with the pistol's butt instead, shattering his nose. Then I flat-palmed him in the sternum, and that was enough to bring the bleeding tower of Pisa to a total collapse. He fell. I flicked off the pistol's safety, cocked the hammer, and spun.

Just in time to place the muzzle dead in the face of the second guy, who was even then clawing for his own weapon.

"*Don't*," I said, breathing easily.

He froze, staring down a half-inch hole of death, his disoriented mind grappling with immediate thoughts of eternity the same way all his animal ancestors had done when faced with a similar predicament.

"Drop it," I said. "Right now."

He complied. A Charter Arms Bulldog clattered to the alley floor. I surveyed his companions. The first guy was just beginning to recover from his collision with the dumpster, sitting up and gazing around with the dazed expression of a kid fallen off a trampoline. The third guy was still whimpering, holding his nose and kicking backwards.

The kid—the actual kid—sat wide eyed, his bloody arm wrapped in his t-shirt, his nose running like a faucet into a half-open mouth.

I evaluated my options, thoughts racing quickly through a list of possible questions. The who, what, when, where, and why of it all. The explanations. The guilty verdict. The possibility of calling the police and turning over the investigation to the relevant authorities.

It was logical, maybe even moral. But the thing is, I've lived in the kid's shoes before, crossing the wrong people on the bad side of town. There's no excuse for beating a kid—not ever. At the same time, there might be an explanation, and calling the cops might only worsen the victim's situation.

Also, I didn't feel like filling out a witness statement or arguing the justification of my actions. So I went for option B —the simpler approach.

"Beat it," I said. "All three of you."

The guy whose eye I'd elbowed blinked, tears streaming down his face. He seemed confused. He looked to his buddies. I jabbed with the pistol.

"Move!"

That was enough. The second guy helped the first guy to his feet. The third guy pulled himself upright against the alley wall. Then they were all stumbling away from us, shooting ugly glares and raising middle fingers, but it was all just empty angst. At the end of the alley they turned a corner. A moment later the familiar growl of V-twin motorcycles thundered across the street.

Then they were gone. I flicked the 1911's safety back on, bringing it to *Condition One.* I wiped sweat off my nose, noting with satisfaction that my heart rate was barely elevated.

Fruits of my recent cardio labors.

Lowering the pistol, I spat across the grimy concrete. Then I finally turned back to the kid.

"So who are you?"

2

His name was Spencer Meyers, and the moment I heard his voice I was forced to reduce my estimations of his age from late-teens to mid-teens. He was big for his age, nearly six feet tall, and very well built. Brown hair reached down into his face and over his ears, blood speckling a worn St. Louis Blues t-shirt.

An average-looking kid. And yet, he wasn't average. He was in over his head and behind on his payments, by the look of it. A *stupid* kid.

"Let me see your arm," I said, sliding the pistol into the small of my back.

"I'm all good. Thanks."

I snorted. He was anything but, yet I couldn't help admiring his bravado. Once again, it reminded me of myself at his age.

"How much do you owe them?" I asked.

Spencer squinted. "Owe them?"

"For the drugs they advanced you. The ones you're selling at school."

Spencer looked back down the alley in the direction the three thugs had fled. He shook his head.

"It's nothing like that, man. There ain't no drugs."

Sure. So they were wrecking you for the fun of it.

I thought it, I didn't say it. I motioned again for the arm.

"Let me see it."

At last he extended his arm, unwrapping it from the makeshift t-shirt bandage. I took it gently in one hand and used my other to probe the wound. It was long, about five inches, and jagged. Flakes of rusty metal rested in the flesh. Blood seeped out.

"You need stitches," I said. "You know how to find the nearest hospital?"

Spencer shook his head. "Nah, man. Can't do that."

I cocked an eyebrow. "So there *are* drugs."

He gritted his teeth, replacing his arm in the t-shirt tail. "*No*. I told you. No drugs. It's—" He stopped. His head ducked, face flushing a little. "I don't have insurance. I can't afford the hospital. It'll be fine."

No insurance. It was a story that resonated with me on a personal level. I didn't carry medical insurance either, and I was very familiar with the outrageous cost of emergency medical care. Sure, you can bum it, if you want. Show up at the ER, acquire the required treatment, promise to pay, then disappear.

But there's no honor in theft, and I could admire a man who would suffer his injuries before he made promises he couldn't keep. Even as Spencer clamped down on the wound, pain racing across his face, he lifted his shoulders in a man's stance and offered me a nod.

"I'm much obliged to you."

Much obliged. He sounded like an old man. I simply

nodded as Spencer turned away from the dumpster and started down the alley, limping a little, but keeping his head up. Carried on by the pride.

"Wait," I called, kicking myself even as I said it. Spencer looked over his shoulder. "You need a tetanus shot," I said. "There's rust in that wound."

"Got one a couple years back," Spencer said. "They're good for a while."

"And the stitches?"

He shrugged. "I'll wrap it up. Don't mind the scar."

That brought on a smile. *Tough kid.*

I shot a thumb over my shoulder, back toward my Harley. "Scars don't win the girls, kid. Not anymore. Come with me."

I turned for the end of the alley, stopping along the way to destroy the abandoned Charter Arms revolver with a quick smash of my heel against the open cylinder. I tossed the warped and ruined weapon into the dumpster and glanced back. Spencer hadn't moved, his face clouded with suspicion.

"I was in the Army," I said, tone relaxed. "Combat medical training. I know all about stitching."

He still didn't move.

"It's *free*," I said, a little sarcastically.

Another glance at his arm. A bite of his lip. Then his better senses overcame him, and he followed me to the end of the alley where my 1994 Harley-Davidson FLSTF Fat Boy sat glimmering in the afternoon sun, handlebars cocked, giant headlight pointed at the ground. Thirty years had worn the jet-black paint into something approaching a matte finish, corrupting the shine on some of the chrome, and leaving a permanent haze in the solid disc front wheel. But for all that, the bike looked good. It was a classic, a style I had loved since watching *Terminator: Judgement Day* as a kid. The Arnold bike.

"Hop on," I said, handing him my helmet. I slung a leg over and fired up what had once been an 82-cubic-inch Evolution motor. That original power plant had enjoyed substantial modification under the expert touch of the previous owner. Bored out to displace 88 cubic inches, with a nasty cam and a tune to tie it all together, the Fat Boy ran like a scalded dragon under full throttle. I couldn't confess to my top speed without incriminating myself, but it was much faster than any cruiser had any business traveling.

The bike was a rocket.

From the sidewalk Spencer chewed his lower lip while blood dried on his upper. He cradled the helmet, but still seemed to hesitate. I sighed.

"Look, kid. Take it or leave it."

That was enough. Spencer slung his leg over the Fat Boy's pillion and propped his feet on the passenger pegs. He knew enough not to wrap his arms around my waist, opting to brace himself against the low-profile sissy bar instead. I found first gear and enjoyed the wind in my uncovered hair as I hit the street, aftermarket exhaust snarling.

To his further credit, Spencer kept quiet, allowing us both to enjoy the ride. We wound our way out of North St. Louis, hopping up onto I-70 and racing up to highway speeds. I whipped the bike in and out of traffic, relishing in the pull of the modified engine even under excess load, and crossed the Mississippi River using the Stan Musial Veterans Memorial Bridge. In mid-November it was cool in Illinois, but not yet cold. We worked our way out East St. Louis, migrating through increasingly quiet suburbs until we reached a little spot about ten miles northeast of town, situated right on the eastern bank of the mighty Mississippi—the Purple Crane Campground.

I was clueless as to the origins of the name. Purple cranes —whether they be the metal kind or the winged kind—were nowhere to be seen. But curiosities of nomenclature notwithstanding, I had to admit that "the camp", as owner/manager Dottie Brooks called it, was just about the quaintest little spot I had called home in years. Comprising two dozen slots nestled under towering red oak trees, at least half of the lots faced the water, and half of those came pre-equipped with vintage campers, permanently installed, ready to be leased.

Slot 12, my slot, was one of those pre-equipped rentals. My home of the moment was a 1966 Airstream Caravel. Seventeen feet long, battered and worn with age and use, but suitably refurbished for my vagrant bachelor needs. It included a bed, a postage-stamp kitchen, and a compact shower just big enough to turn around in. All things considered, it was perfect.

I turned the Fat Boy into the slot, raising a hand to Ms. Dottie as she appeared across the street outside her permanently installed fifth-wheel. The RV was surrounded by stacks of car tires filled with dirt and flowers, a makeshift garden that Ms. Dottie watered with a little metal can no less than six times per day. At eighty-four, the years were creeping up on her, and her short-term memory was sketchy at best.

Long-term memory, however, was razor sharp. She often regaled me with stories of her husband, the Korean War hero, her daughter, a retired mathematician who now helped her run the old campground, and, of course... her son.

"Hey, Ms. Dottie!" I killed the bike and lifted a hand. Ms. Dottie grinned a denture smile and waved back, as cheery as the sunflowers being drowned under her watering can.

"Toddy! Come see me later. I got some fresh pork chops from the butcher."

I swung off the bike and stretched beneath the afternoon sun. Despite the physical exertion of pounding three guys into the pavement, I felt spectacular. My daily swims in the Mississippi, combined with long nights of good sleep and leisurely evenings spent practicing my violin were working their magic. My physical, and even mental, condition was better than it had been in...years. I felt like I was on vacation.

"I thought you said your name was Mason," Spencer spoke for the first time as he stood awkwardly alongside the bike, still clutching his t-shirt-wrapped arm.

"It is."

I stepped inside the Airstream, drawing the captured 1911 from my waistband and rolling it over in my hand. It was a Springfield—one of their "Garrison" models equipped with a skeletonized trigger and brown checkered grips. Not a bad handgun to keep around, although concerns of its potential illicit history—to say nothing of Illinois's aggressive gun laws —left me half-inclined to chuck it into the river.

Considerations for a later date. For the moment, I tucked the weapon into a kitchen cabinet and turned toward a bin of camping gear resting on the counter. Among a makeshift complement of cooking utensils and fishing paraphernalia, I kept a diverse first aid and trauma kit. I couldn't recall if I'd packed any stitching equipment, but I knew I had a sewing kit used for re-affixing rogue buttons. That would suffice.

"Why did she call you Toddy?" Spencer seated himself at the rickety wooden picnic table outside the Airstream, a glint of suspicion in his eyes. I glanced back toward Ms. Dottie who was busy swamping her petunias, talking with animation to the pink flowers.

"Don't worry about it," I said. "Let me see your arm."

Spencer extended the arm with a grimace and I tore the t-shirt away. Uncapping a bottle of hydrogen peroxide, I unceremoniously dumped it into the open wound. Spencer yelped and yanked the arm back. I smacked him across the face, not very hard, but hard enough to get his attention.

"Man up. This gets worse before it gets better."

Spencer gritted his teeth and replaced his arm on the table. I whistled my latest violin tune as I strung black thread onto a sewing needle. The melody was a complex advancement in my hitherto pedestrian fiddling skills—an attempt to depart from my affinity for folk music and classic rock covers in favor of "real" violin pieces. Namely, Vivaldi's "Four Seasons".

I wasn't sure if I was enjoying the change.

"Is that medical thread?" Spencer asked as I advanced with the needle.

"It's free thread," I said, and promptly stuck him. He winced and shut his eyes. I pulled one side of the gash toward the other, keeping my work tight and uniform, and lubricating the wound with antibiotic ointment along the way. Spencer required twenty-six stitches in total, which likely wouldn't impress any girls, but I couldn't deny he impressed me with his steady silence.

I knotted off the last stitch and flicked the blade of my Victorinox Swiss Army Knife to sever the thread. Then I grunted.

"There you are, sir. Wait a couple weeks, then pull them out with tweezers."

Spencer opened his eyes and inspected my handiwork, rolling his arm. A slow smile crept across his face.

"Hey...that's not half bad. Were you a nurse?"

I thought of Afghanistan. Racing bullets, bursting grenades, shrapnel-infested IEDs. Lots and lots of stitching, more than a little of it self-inflicted.

"Something like that," I said, repacking my equipment. Spencer started to stand.

"I really appreciate it. Saved me a chunk!"

"Hold up there, partner." I raised a hand, bending at the waist to fish through a nearby cooler. The ice was all melted, leaving lukewarm soda cans bobbing in three inches of water. I set a pair of Dr. Peppers on the tabletop and pushed one toward Spencer.

"Have a seat," I said.

The suspicion returned to his face. I motioned again. He sat and cracked open the soda, slurping a long drink. I set my can down.

"So you don't deal drugs, huh?"

Spencer shook his head. "No. Never."

"Okey-dokey, then. How about explaining to me why three sweaty dudes were pounding you into breakfast sausage?"

3

Spencer didn't want to answer, avoiding my gaze and taking protracted sips of his drink to stall for time. It was an obvious tactic, and given his current predicament—sitting at my picnic table, miles from home with no transportation, slurping my Dr. Pepper—a useless one. I had him over a barrel, as they say. Eventually, he was smart enough to acknowledge it.

"I...I fight," Spencer said.

I laughed. "Not very well."

The kid flushed. "It wasn't what it looked like. It was supposed to be one-on-one. An audition. They dog-piled on me."

"An audition? What kind of audition is a street fight?"

Spencer looked at his soda can, stalling again. I raised my eyebrows.

"Look," he said. "You can't say anything, okay? They'll knock my teeth out."

"They were doing a pretty good job of that already."

"Yeah, well. For real. You can't talk about it."

"What the heck is this? *Fight Club?* Spill already."

Spencer didn't get the reference—too young, no doubt. But he spilled anyway, leaning forward and lowering his voice.

"It's legit, man. Like, not legal, but official. Out in that old industrial district north of the city they've got this whole fight ring going—a real underground operation. Anybody can take a turn, just buy a ticket and hit the ring. There's a gauntlet, they call it. Like, five of their best fighters. You beat all five and you win. *Big.*"

I squinted. "Are you kidding me?"

He raised both hands. "I swear. I've been there! Never to fight. Just snuck in to watch. It's real protected, obviously. The cops would bust it all up. But it's a thing. People win thousands!"

I snorted, swallowing warm Dr. Pepper. It wasn't the underground fight club that surprised me. Foolishness like that occurs in every corner of the globe, including America. I was more taken aback by Spencer's obvious naiveté. Maybe it had been too long since my teenage years. I was starting to forget how moronic a half-formed human can be.

"Take a nickel's worth of advice for free," I said. "If there's a house, the house will win. You don't want any part of their game—not unless you want a lot more of those."

I pointed to the stitches. Spencer glanced down, then shook his head.

"Nah, man. This was just a misunderstanding. My fault, really. They got pissed because I talked about..." He stopped. Lowered his voice. Leaned forward. "The *club*. Right? In broad daylight. They don't like that."

"I imagine they don't. So why did you?"

"I..." He hesitated. Rubbed his wounded arm. "I wanted a shot. Like, a chance to fight."

"You said that happens at the club."

"Right, right. But to get into the ring you got to put up some money. A lot of money, really. I didn't have it, but I thought if I auditioned and proved myself, maybe they'd make an exception. I knew they liked to hang out north of downtown, so..."

"You jumped them."

"No. I mean...well. Not exactly."

I laughed again. I couldn't help it. Spencer flushed darker red.

"It's not as dumb as it sounds. I'm a blue belt, you know. Been taking karate classes at the rec center since junior high. I can handle myself!"

The bluster was laced with more than a little indignation. I felt the warmth of it, registering the embarrassment and desperation in his eyes, and my smile faded. A more subdued reality replaced the humor.

He was an idiot, yes. But a bold idiot. A confident idiot. An idiot very much like myself, at his age.

"Look," I said, tone growing serious. "I want you to listen to me. I know a lot about violence. More than most. And it's not a sport—not even close. It's pain. It's damage. It's the worst thing humans can do to one another. I'm telling you, it's not something you want any part of. Not for fun, and definitely not for money. Okay?"

Spencer's tongue darted out over his lips. He was fidgeting with the trailing end of one stitch, apparently unfazed by the pain. Working something over in his mind, wrestling with it. Calculating.

Then a light bulb clicked on behind his eyes.

"*Dude*. You took those guys apart! They never stood a chance."

I frowned. "They were beating the snot out of you. It was justified."

"Right, right, I know. That's not what I mean..." He leaned forward. "*You* could fight in the club! Win big—serious money. I could take you there, introduce you. Maybe earn a commission."

"What?"

"Like ten percent! Call it an agency fee. You'd tear that place apart!"

I shook my head, once again blown away by the stupidity, but this time less frustrated and more exasperated.

Kids. Nobody could tell me anything at sixteen. Nobody was going to tell Spencer anything, either.

"I don't fight for sport, kid. Never have. Never will."

"But you're so good!"

"Exactly," I snapped, voice cracking like a bullwhip. Spencer flinched, recoiling a little. I glared him down, not moving.

Then I caught myself. I took a breath. I deliberately softened my voice. "Exactly."

Spencer slumped on the bench, a cloud of defeat descending over him. I drained the Dr. Pepper and pitched the can into a nearby bucket. Hauling myself out of the picnic table I looked out over the Mississippi River, regarding the sun as it sank toward the distant St. Louis skyline. The day was almost spent. In another three hours it would be nightfall, and I had someplace to be before then. I checked my watch.

"Where do you live?" I asked.

Spencer shrugged as if it were a flexible question. I realized he was pouting, and I snapped my fingers.

"Hey."

"Jennings," he muttered.

"I don't know where that is."

"North St. Louis." Now Spencer was rolling his eyes. The expression irritated me. The answer was also incompatible with my current obligations, which lay south of the city.

"You got money for a cab?" I asked.

A shake of his head. I sighed and turned back through the open Airstream door. Digging through the cabinet beneath the sink, I located the battered metal cashbox that had served as my bank account for the past two-plus years living as a vagrant bumping around the country in a beat-up pickup truck. About sixteen grand lay inside—all that remained of my savings following recent expenditures in South St. Louis. Enough to keep me freewheeling at the Purple Crane Campground for months.

I peeled off a hundred bucks, replaced the box, and stepped outside the Airstream. I locked the door and passed Spencer the bill.

"See Christine at the camp office. She'll call the cab for you."

Spencer mumbled his thanks and pulled himself out of the picnic table. He turned to go, that hurricane look of jumbled thoughts still swirling in his eyes. Teenage confusion, adolescent turmoil.

I remembered it well...and it hurt to witness.

"Hey, Spence."

He looked over one shoulder. I offered a smile. "It was great meeting you. Roll easy, okay? Stay on the right side of the tracks."

Spencer shot me a peace sign. Then he was headed toward the camp office, walking in a loose roll that defied his recent physical abuse.

I shook my head, flipping the Airstream keys in my hand. Then I bungee-corded my violin in its case to the Fat Boy's sissy bar, slung a leg over, and fired up the engine.

4

Paciello's Custom Restorations may not have been the best antique auto shop in the Midwest, but it was certainly one of the best. Ten weeks into an eight-week, frame-up restoration of my 1967 GMC pickup, I had to admit that going over time and over budget was paying off. Arthur Paciello, a perpetually greasy-handed Italian-American in his late sixties who chain-smoked Marlboros and preferred to go by "Arty", was most certainly a wizard in the craft of breathing fresh life into abused and neglected classics.

His shop sat in South St. Louis, a six-bay building with several dozen rusting antiques baking under the late afternoon sun in the gravel parking lot outside. Crewed by five restoration experts as passionate as Arty himself, the shop smelled of grease and motor oil, had never been air-conditioned, and was perpetually serenaded by Italian opera music—a necessity of Arty's "creative process".

I parked the Fat Boy in the lot, unable to resist a grin as I saw my pickup hoisted on a vehicle rack, sparks flying from a stick welder hard at work on the undercarriage. Arty's crew had done *wonders* for the old GMC. More than a fresh coat of paint or a reupholstered bench seat, they had stripped the truck down to its bones and blasted away every spec of rust, coating the undercarriage with protective sealant, rebuilding the entire front end, rebuilding the inline-six engine, replacing the brake lines and swapping the aged drum brakes for modern disks. The dozens of dents left by neo-Nazi thugs with baseball bats—another story—had been pulled, the scratches polished out. There was a new wind-shield, new windows, and brand-new mirrors. The cracked and faded head and taillights had been swapped, the faulty radio replaced with a modern unit designed to look like an original.

Even the interior of the extended bed had been sand-blasted and coated with a spray-in bed liner, per my request. The windows of my camper shell had been replaced, the crooked hinge on the rear door swapped out. Arty's crew had disassembled the tailgate and rebuilt the latch assembly. They did the same with the crank window mechanisms and three-speed shift linkage.

All that remained *was* the fresh coat of paint. Light green for the body, bright white for the cab and the camper shell. Practically a brand-new truck.

Arty met me at the open roll-up door, sparking up a cigarette and jabbing a thumb toward the flying sparks.

"Installing the winch mount, as requested."

I bent to admire the handiwork as the welder stepped out from beneath the truck. It was a custom job—Arty's man had taken special care with his work. The welds were nothing short of beautiful.

"Should get me out of the mud," I said.

"A hundred years bad luck if you put this beauty in the mud," Arty snorted. "If I had any sense, I wouldn't give her back!"

I had a feeling that Arty said that to all his customers, but I laughed anyway. He guided me around the body of the truck, pointing out little improvements and apologetically highlighting even the slightest imperfection his crew had been unable to correct. I wouldn't have noticed any of them on my own.

"You got those tires coming in?" I asked.

"Yeah, yeah. Be here tomorrow. I still say you shoulda gone with white walls. Lower the old girl...cruise!"

"Not my style, Arty. I like ground clearance."

Arty dismissed me with a grunt, lowered the rack and introduced me to some weather seal improvements to the windows and door frames—enough to keep the rain out, hopefully. He'd even managed to fix my broken righthand windshield wiper, which hadn't worked since I'd bought the truck.

"A new ride!" Arty declared with a smoky smile. "I'm a saint for this, Mason. Shoulda charged you twice as much. Some of my best work!"

I shook his greasy hand as I turned for the parking lot. "You're a magician, Arty. And a scoundrel."

"Ha!" He snorted a laugh. "Hey, you tired of that Fat Boy yet? Another rip-off—I gave her away!"

I slung my leg over and hit the starter. "Not even close, Arty."

"Not close to being tired, or close to being a rip-off?"

I grinned. "You decide."

Then I goosed the throttle, throwing gravel as I hurtled out of the parking lot and back into St. Louis.

BEYOND BASEBALL AND GATEWAY ARCHES, the virtue I associated with St. Louis was barbecue, and the legend had most certainly not disappointed. My favorite BBQ shack in the city was Rusty's Rib Bar, a dilapidated old cedar-sided building situated west of town. Real firewood burned in the smoker, a column of black as dark as the inside of Arty's lungs pouring from a brick chimney. The floors were dirty. Only half of the overhead lights worked, leaving the place dim and hazy. Rusty himself worked the grill, a four-hundred-pound artisan who most certainly got high off his own supply.

Who could blame him? Rusty cooked the best rack of ribs I'd ever tasted.

I ordered my usual—a full rack with a side of potato salad and collard greens, washed down with unsweet tea. I'd pass on the pecan pie, given that I'd missed my afternoon swim while dealing with Spencer.

The food came out piping hot and I ate next to the window, watching as the sun slipped ever closer toward Kansas. Rusty sang while he cooked, old blues tracks by the likes of Howlin' Wolf and John Lee Hooker. His voice was terrible, but the joy in it couldn't be denied. It relaxed me better than three fingers of whisky, the sweet barbecue sauce slowing my heartbeat to a lazy thump.

It was the strangest feeling. Deeper than relaxation, or even calm. It was...not quite peace. I still had the nightmares on occasion. I still drifted into memories of two years prior, both the good and the bad. They twisted my stomach in the same way, unearthing the deep pain of irreversible loss.

But for the first time since those gunshots cracked down

the long hallways of an elementary school in south Phoenix...I felt I could accept them. Accept myself *for* accepting them.

And just listen to Rusty sing.

With a belly so full I felt that the bike was named after me, I ran the Fat Boy onto the highway and turned east. The sun was warm on my back, the November wind cool in my face. I kept the RPMs low, not rushing, now very familiar with the route. It had become something of a routine—I did it once, then I did it again a few days later. Now I completed this ritual of barbecue and sunsets at least three times a week, enjoying it just as much every time.

I crossed into Illinois south of East St. Louis and turned the bike north—not for the Purple Crane Campground, but for Malcolm W. Martin Memorial Park. It sat on the outskirts of the city, running right along the Illinois side of the Mississippi River. There was a parking lot and a multi-level ramp structure that offered an observation deck built with a stellar view of the St. Louis skyline just across the river. I'd enjoyed that view on many an afternoon, but it was frequently populated by tourists and locals, and my introverted soul sought a more secluded spot.

Accordingly, I parked the Fat Boy and unstrapped the violin case. Slinging it over one shoulder, I crossed out of the park, reaching three parallel sets of railroad tracks, followed by a low concrete wall and another three sets of tracks.

Then at last I arrived at the eastern banks of the river, a patchwork of uncut grass and muddy sand stretching out for miles to either side. Barges pulled up against it, various industrial mechanisms plunging into the slow, murky water at intervals between them.

And standing directly in front of me, seven hundred

yards distant, reflecting the slowly fading glow of the sun, was the Gateway Arch itself—the St. Louis skyline spread out behind. Just like a postcard.

I settled onto the bank and unpacked my violin, taking my time to tune it up and rosin the bow. I started with Vivaldi, but quickly gave him up in favor of some of the same blues riffs Rusty sang back at the rib bar. Sad songs about love lost, jobs oppressing, life flowing on as slow and inevitable as the mighty Mississippi. Those melodies crooned from the strings of my violin as the setting sun shone over my face, the city spilling out before me, the river slipping by, my body perfectly relaxed.

No...it wasn't peace. Not quite. But it was something approaching peace, and I'd never been more thankful for it.

I completed my ritual with three chapters from my late fiancée's Bible. After several months of stumbling through the Psalms and Proverbs, two of Mia's favorites, I did what felt like the rational thing and started at the beginning with the book of Genesis. The origin of all time. I was now nearing the end of the book and only a little less confused about the meaning of life than when I started, but I found the words comforting. I read a chapter or two before closing the book, closing my eyes...and doing the thing that perplexed me most—speaking to God.

Talk to Him, child. Talk to Him just like you're talkin' to me.

It was the advice of an old lady from Arkansas. A golden woman. I'd spent many an hour since unpacking the meaning of her simple directions. I still felt like I was over-complicating it, but I did talk to Him. I thanked Him for the day—for the blessing of life, food, and freedom. I asked Him for guidance.

I hoped He was listening.

The cool air flooded my lungs as I rumbled back to the Purple Crane Campground, shooting a two-finger salute to Christine, Ms. Dottie's sixty-year-old daughter and the property's manager. Then I was back in Slot 12, killing the motor. Stretching. Wishing I'd ordered a slice of pecan pie to go as I twirled my keys and headed for the Airstream's door.

Then I stopped. I squinted in the light of a neighbor's campfire, body turning rigid.

The Airstream wasn't as I left it—specifically, the *door* wasn't as I'd left it. It hung open in inch, the locking mechanism distorted by the marks of a pry bar.

I set my violin case down and glanced over my shoulder. My neighbor was the only person around—some hairy guy from Minnesota who was usually a six-pack deep by this hour. Judging by the empty bottles piled around his chair, tonight was no exception.

I eased the Airstream's door open, quickly clearing the interior.

Nothing appeared out of place. There was dirt on the floor, but that could have been me. The bed, my clothes, the toiletries in the shower stall—all was undisturbed.

I stuck my head out and called across the campground. "Hey, Gerry! You see somebody come around here?"

My inebriated neighbor craned his head. "Eh?"

"Did anybody come around here? Anybody go inside my camper?"

He chugged Miller Lite. Then something seemed to dawn on him. "Oh, yeah. Your cousin came by. Said he forgot something."

"My cousin?"

"You know, the kid."

The kid?

Spencer.

I pivoted back inside, stepping to the kitchenette. Digging beneath the countertop, locating the cash box. Knowing the truth before I even opened it.

The box was lighter than it should have been. I flipped the lid open and confirmed the truth all the same.

Not all the cash was gone—about six thousand dollars remained. But the largest band of Benjamins, the bedrock of my stash, was missing. *Ten grand.*

I smacked the box shut and pivoted for the door. In another moment I had the bike fired up. I was roaring back toward the highway.

And toward North St. Louis—because I knew exactly why Spencer had taken the money. And what he would do with it.

5

With Spencer's description of my target in mind, it wasn't difficult to track down the underground fight club. I gunned the Fat Boy back across the river and wound into North St. Louis, gravitating naturally toward a point just southwest of Mosenthein Island on the western bank of the Mississippi, where I instinctively knew the industrial district would lie.

Sure enough, warehouses, rail yards, shipping depots, and a plethora of abandoned brick buildings constructed in an early twentieth century style lined the waterfront, most of them dark, only a few of them secured by chain-link fences. I wove amid them, rumbling back and forth across railroad tracks and edging gradually northward until I first detected the lights. Tail lights, specifically. A line of cars edging into a gravel parking lot secured by a pair of beefy bouncers. The converted brick warehouse resting beyond that parking lot was marked as a rave club, which didn't surprise me. It wasn't like the criminals responsible would erect a neon sign advertising an illegal fight club.

No, this operation was covert. Discrete. The armada of three dozen black motorcycles lined together near the club's entrance reminded me of the three guys who pummeled Spencer, then escaped under the throaty roar of oversized V-twins.

Okay, then. So this circus was run by a motorcycle gang —terrific.

I parked the Fat Boy amid the lineup of beefy Harleys and sleek Indians, taking a moment to survey the competition for any indicators of specific gang affiliation. I'd learned the hard way in Phoenix just how destructive and ruthless biker gangs can be, but not all fat guys bound together by a mutual affinity for chicken wings and loud motorcycles are created equal. There's some difference between the hardcore biker gangs of the west coast and the average club of obnoxious wannabes who pride themselves in ignoring parking tickets.

Judging strictly based on the patch-covered jackets slung over handlebars, I estimated this group to fall somewhere in between the two extremes. Their logo—a snarling dog head covered by the Gateway Arch—featured no indicator of national affiliation, but I also detected none of the oversold bravado so common amongst amateurs. No cheap stickers bragging about how tough they were, or how they were riding home to have carnal relations with somebody's mother.

It doesn't matter. Whoever was running this show, I wasn't here for them. I was here for my money, and maybe to ram my boot up the posterior of a dumb kid who needed a lesson in prudence.

I slung my half-helmet over the sissy bar and was starting down the lineup of cruisers when fresh lights appeared at the entrance of the parking lot—not the blue and green neons of the rave club sign, but the blinking red of an ambulance. It took me by surprise, because there was no siren. Even so, the driver was in a hurry. He barreled up to the entrance of the club and ground to a stop. Two paramedics bailed out, rolling a stretcher from the back of the vehicle. As the club's doors opened to allow them passage inside, a storm of screaming-loud techno music burst over the parking lot.

I slowed, glancing back to the ambulance as my mind sorted the pieces and jumped to an obvious conclusion.

Please, no...

But my assumptions were right on the money. The stretcher reappeared through the double steel doors just as I reached the entrance. One paramedic pushed it, the second jogging alongside with an oxygen mask pressed over the patient's face.

The patient was a kid. The kid was Spencer Meyers. And he was *wrecked.*

I stalled five yards short of the ambulance and watched as he glided by. Stretched out with one arm twisted backwards and one foot pointing directly perpendicular to the other, Spencer looked like he'd been run through a cotton gin. His nose was smashed in, blood ran from his left ear, and his open mouth exposed two missing teeth. His eyes were already so swollen I wouldn't have known whether they were open or not, but he was clearly unconscious. The stitches I'd installed only a few hours before now looked like the healthiest part of his body.

My jaw closed as the stretcher slid inside the ambulance. The paramedics jumped aboard. The doors slammed.

Then the vehicle roared out of the parking lot as the

greasy-looking guy standing next to me calmly inserted a stick of gum into his mouth, lips stretched into a smirk.

"What happened?" I demanded. Of course, I already knew. Greasy turned my way and cocked an eyebrow. The smirk never faded.

Then he turned for the club door, calling over his shoulder. "Break dancing. Kid fell down a flight of stairs... Bad luck, huh?"

If he'd been ten feet closer, I would have knocked the gum right out of his head. As it was, I watched the ambulance disappear toward St. Louis, then turned to follow Greasy into the club.

"Hold up there, partner." One of the bouncers cut me off, planting an open palm into my chest. I stopped cold, looking down at the hand and then back into his face. He was big, young, and likely spent more time in a gym than he did in bed. But the moment my iron gaze reached his, the hand fell away from my chest.

"Cover's twenty bucks," he mumbled.

I drew my wallet. Jammed a twenty into his hand. Then I was headed through the doors. They swung back, admitting me to a world that felt like another planet. Flashing strobe lights, concussive techno music blaring from invisible speakers, and enough haze in the air to obscure my vision beyond twenty feet.

There was a dance floor. A forty-foot bar that stretched the length of one wall. A raised platform where a DJ jerked and twitched like a demon-possessed maniac while he operated a turntable. About three hundred people packed together across the concrete, mostly twenty-something guys and girls dressed in skin-tight clothing that left precious little to the imagination.

Weed smoke hung heavy on the air—a metric ton of it. Two inhales past the door and my head went a little light. Glass bottles rocked toward the ceiling as liquor streamed into plastic cups by the gallon. Cash passed across the counter, cards swiped at machines. In one corner a guy made out with a girl so drunk she could barely stand.

His hand was up her shirt. Nobody was paying any attention.

I tuned out the chaos and swept the crowd for any signs of Greasy. He was long gone, faded into the morass like a rat into a garbage heap. The only club employees I could find were waitresses balancing drink trays, bartenders mixing drinks...and two guys standing either side of a single metal door all the way in the back of the room.

Iron faces. Bulging shoulders. Black biker jackets featuring a snarling dog face inside the Gateway Arch.

Bingo.

I pushed through the crowd, heedless of the sweaty bodies swarming around me like a mess of tangled earth-worms. I bumped into a guy and he cursed me. I brushed past a girl and she pivoted wide, drunken eyes on me, reaching for my belt.

I broke free and made it to the door. The two guys guarding it eyed me with frigid glares, then one of them simply extended a hand.

No comment. No explanation.

He wanted a pass, probably. Some form of authentication for entry. I had nothing.

"I want to see the boss," I shouted.

He couldn't hear me over the music—or at least, he pretended not to hear me. I leaned forward and screamed a little louder.

He glared and shook his head. "Scram!"

Scram? I squinted. He folded his arms and eyeballed a passing waitress, acting as though I had vanished.

That pissed me off. I turned to follow the waitress, observing the drink tray she carried. There was one beverage—something pink in a clear plastic cup, with a cherry floating on top. I swept it off the tray and backhanded it into the nearest guard's face, so quick and accurate that he never had time to close his eyes.

The big guy shouted and raised both his hands into a desperate shield—too little, too late. I drove my shin into his crotch, and he toppled. Then the second guy was on me, but not nearly fast enough. His muscle-bound body required precious time to get moving, and long before he reached me I had a sidewinder cocked back and ready to go, my point of aim dropping beneath his ugly face to his unprotected windpipe. I struck it with the web of my hand, smashing hard enough to send his head snapping backward.

Then I shin-kicked him the same as the first guy, a strike to the groin that would suspend any opportunities of scoring with the waitress. He staggered and choked, falling into the crowd. I reached for the door and pushed my way through.

The rave club behind me was Venus, the room I stepped into was Mars. The temperature spiked an instant ten degrees and the strobe lights vanished. In their place blackness gave way to a pool of concentrated light twenty yards ahead, the space between clogged by bodies that were all faced away from me—toward that pool of light.

The music was also gone, and in its place were the throaty voices of perhaps a hundred people, heads thrown back as cheers and cries broke toward the ceiling. Amid them I detected the heavy *thunk* of bone against flesh, matched with a muted cry. The crowd thundered louder, and I looked between their shoulders into that pool of spotlight.

I could barely make out the ropes of a boxing ring, not elevated on a platform but sunk into the ground, like the bottom of an arena. Whatever other persons occupied that ring, I could only make out one—he was big. He was shirtless and bloody, bent down, his left arm locked as he pinned something to the ground, right arm raining blows like a chugging machine gun.

The crowd roared. I stood transfixed by the spectacle for only a moment before I remembered the two groin-kicked men behind me. Far from permanently disabled, they would barge through the door shortly enough. I wanted to finish my business before then.

Sliding into the crowd, I worked my way right as a bell rang and the bloody guy lifted both arms, throwing back his head and howling like an animal. The army of spectators gathered around him returned the howl, jumping into the air.

It was madness. Anarchy. Total blood lust. And it only served to further infuriate me.

I reached the long bar at the back of the room where a duet of products were available for sale—alcohol, and wagers. For the moment the spectators were focused on their bloody champion and there was no line. I advanced to the bar and laid my palm down with a meaty smack.

"What'll it be?" The bartender asked. Unliked the curvy waitresses in the rave club outside, this guy was the furthest thing from attractive. He wore the same dog-and-arch leather vest as the two ball-busted dudes outside—no shirt, sweaty chest hair protruding. Cue-ball bald, with a bandanna wrapped around his skull.

No, this guy was designed to draw attention. He was designed to transact—as quickly and efficiently as possible. That worked just fine for me.

"Get the boss," I snapped. "*Now.*"

He blinked. "Excuse me?"

I leaned across the bar, speaking through my teeth. "*Your boss.* Get him."

Momentary indecision played across his face. He looked to the door and must not have seen his bouncers. That was enough to tilt him in my favor.

"Wait here."

He disappeared through a curtain behind the bar and I checked over my shoulder to make sure I wasn't about to be clobbered. The entrance burst open and the two guys limped in, eyes bulging as they swept the crowd. The spectators were finally breaking, splitting into lines as they headed toward the bar. Providing a screen of bodies behind me.

I had a few minutes.

The curtain parted again and the bartender returned. He was not alone. Behind him walked a guy every bit of six-three, maybe six-four. Broad shouldered and overly muscled —the kind of muscles that gym time alone can't deliver. Clothed in a leather biker jacket sporting the now familiar snarling dog logo. His thick arms gleamed with sweat. A coarse beard and a patchwork of tattoos completed the look.

His eyes were cold and absolutely lifeless.

The bartender said nothing. He simply jabbed a thumb at me, as though that was introduction enough. The boss squinted. Then he lifted a random glass of clear liquor off the counter and drained it. It landed with a smack.

"What do you want?"

From behind me the swarm of spectators crushed in for drinks and bets. I ignored them, speaking loud enough to be heard over the melee.

"The *kid*," I said. "I'm here about ten thousand dollars."

6

The bouncers arrived the same moment I spoke. A heavy hand landed on my shoulder and I wrenched around, ready and willing to reengage. His fist closed and arced back. My shoulders bent and I twisted at the hips, driving with an open right palm straight to the sternum. The blow carried the momentum of my body weight and threw him completely off balance. He toppled backward, his blow flying wide, his bulk crashing straight into the chest of his companion. They both staggered. I pivoted to follow up.

Then the boss interjected. "Wait!"

I kept my eyes on the bouncers, still ready. They recovered their balance and looked ready to rip me limb from limb. Hands dropped into pockets and the usual accouterments of gangster violence appeared—brass knuckles and a switchblade. I would have laughed if I weren't so pissed off.

"I said *wait!*" the boss roared, now. The two guys hesitated, looking like angry dogs straining against invisible chains. I twisted halfway back, keeping the bouncers in my peripheral vision. The boss's teeth gritted. His face flushed. With a jerk of his head, he directed his men toward the curtain. The bouncers closed, and this time I let them take me. Rough hands around my upper arms propelled me around the end of the bar. I stumbled through the curtain and into a small office occupied by a scarred metal desk, two chairs, a haze of cigarette smoke…and a woman. She sat slouched on a couch, dragging on the source of the smoke. Dressed like the others, about my age.

And absolutely stunning. Dark hair. Crystal blue eyes that reminded me of a mountain spring. Lithe but curvy beneath a leather jacket. A rose tattoo on her left arm featured thorns that wound down to her wrist.

She looked dead into my face and exhaled smoke. I stumbled as the bouncers shoved. The boss thrust his way through the curtain and grunted at the woman.

She stood without comment, smashing the cigarette into an ashtray and never breaking eye contact with me. She smirked—it was a *poor fool* look. Then she flicked dark hair over her shoulder and slipped through the curtain.

The boss circled his desk and sat down with a crunch of worn chair springs. He poured himself a glass of straight vodka and swallowed it. The glass slammed as before. Behind me, the bouncers bristled. I could feel the angry tension radiating off them like nuclear reactors.

Finally, the boss looked up. "Who are you?"

"He jumped us!" one bouncer broke in. "Forced his way in—"

"Shut up." The boss wrinkled his nose in disgust. The bouncer obeyed. The boss raised both eyebrows at me.

"The kid," I said. "He left in an ambulance."

The boss thumped his chest with a closed fist. Burped vodka fumes. Then nodded.

"So what?"

"So *somebody* beat the tar out of him."

That brought on a sarcastic grim. "This look like preschool to you?"

"No. It looks like an illegal gambling operation."

The grin faded. He ran his tongue in front of his teeth and sat forward. "If you've got a point, you better get to it."

I thought quickly, evaluating my options. I was tempted to burn this place down—to pound every smug face and smash every liquor bottle. Certainly, Spencer's abuse warranted that much. But on the other hand, I wasn't a superhero. I had lucked out with a couple of muscle-bound brutes with mud for brains. I couldn't expect to out-gun them all—especially if literal guns entered the mix.

And besides. I hadn't come here to start a war. I'd come here to recover what was my own.

"The kid paid you ten grand," I said. "Cash."

No answer.

"It was my money. I want it back."

A soft snort. The boss rotated his glass and seemed to be measuring me up. Those lifeless eyes ran from my boots to my shoulders. He sucked his teeth. Then he shrugged, just a little, as though his body were spontaneously responding to a mental tick. A decision—a conclusion.

"You new around here?"

I thought it was an odd question. St. Louis is a big city. Lots of people are new.

"So what if I am?"

"Well. If you're new, I'd be inclined to make an exception."

"What sort of exception?"

"The kind where you get thrown out on your ass instead of having your throat slit."

There was no hint of bluster in his voice. No hint of theatre, either. He meant every word, I could tell. But I wasn't cowed.

"Look," I said. "I really don't care what sort of racket you're running. I'm not a cop, I'm just a guy who's missing ten grand and takes issue with seeing a kid beat to a pulp."

"Maybe that kid had it coming."

"Maybe he did," I admitted, remembering Spencer's hardheaded stupidity. "So why don't you hand over the money and we'll call it a night?"

That brought back the sarcastic grin. The guy opened his mouth.

Then the curtain tore back and another sweaty body barged into the room, already speaking even before he saw me.

"Hey boss, we got—"

The speaker broke off. I twisted toward him, our eyes locking, and my stomach fell.

I recognized his ugly face. The snake tattoo on his neck. His crooked teeth.

His busted nose.

It was one of the guys from the alley—one of the mud brains I had pounded while rescuing Spencer.

"*You!*" the guy barked. He threw himself at me, not waiting for permission. I ducked right and prepared to pile-drive him with my right fist, aiming for the nose I had already broken. Before my arm was halfcocked the boss was shouting, and the bouncers sprang into action. I was wrestled backward. The guy kept lunging at me, shouting curses and spraying spittle.

"That's him! The guy from the alley! Let me at him!"

"*Shut up!*"

The boss's command was just loud enough to reclaim control of the situation. He orbited the desk and drove a hand into the newcomer's shoulder, knocking him into the wall. Faux wood paneling shook and a picture frame dropped, shattering. The boss ignored it, turning back to me. His gaze swept me head to toe, and this time the lifeless eyes finally illuminated with a cold, smug light.

I didn't like it.

"You?" he asked. I knew what he meant. I didn't answer.

"He got all three of us," the new guy snarled. "Let me at him!"

The boss snapped his fingers. One of the bouncers gut-punched the newcomer hard enough to drive the wind out of him. He choked and doubled over. The boss simply smiled—not at his idiot henchmen, but at me.

"Three against one," he said. "That's impressive."

I made no answer. The grin grew wider, and the boss returned to his chair. He poured himself another glass of raw vodka. One boot landed on the desktop. He sipped. Winced with the burn. Lowered the glass.

"I tell you what, hot shot. You want your money back? Maybe we can make that happen."

I knew what was coming next. The distant chants of the crowd outside were as clear an indicator as my own intuition.

"*Next! Next! Next!*"

"I don't fight for sport," I said.

He laughed. "Oh, this isn't sport. This is a blood fest."

I didn't answer. He dropped his boot off the tabletop.

"Here's the deal. I'll offer you the same gamble your little runt friend made—ten grand against the gauntlet. That's five of our best fighters, *in a row*. You beat them all, you win ten-to-one. A hundred G's, cold hard cash. I'll even waive your entry fee, seeing as the kid already paid it."

"And if I lose?"

A smirk. A shrug. "You join the kid."

It was a setup. I knew that by the boiling venom in his gaze. The sly, snake-like cunning.

If there's a house, the house always wins.

Unless.

Of course there was an *unless*. An exception. A cheat code to the endless war of the masses against the machine. I hadn't shared that cheat code with Spencer because I knew he couldn't execute it. In this context, I wasn't sure if I could either.

But there was something else, also. Something hot and angry. Something that started in my bones and leaked into my blood, boiling in my gut on its way up my spine. Thicker than fire, sharper than jagged rock.

It was more than indignation; it was outrage laced with disgust. I pictured Spencer in the alley, overwhelmed and pounded into the dirt. And then rolling out of here on a stretcher, the brutalized victim of an obvious scam. That made him a fool, certainly. But it didn't make him the villain.

The villain had been this smug prick—because he had *taken the money*.

"You know what?" I said. "You've got a deal."

The boss's smirk spread to a toothy grin. I broke free of

the bouncer and closed on the desk. Outside, the crowd continued to chant, calling for the next round. The next display of gratuitous violence to blow their money on.

And I was going to give it to them.

"Get me some gloves," I said. "And start counting my money."

7

I stripped out of my shirt on the way to the ring, kicking off my boots as a buzzer sounded overhead and red and blue lights flashed like the strobes on a cop car. From high in the darkened ceiling a voice thundered from a loudspeaker, heavy with manufactured drama, like a bad used-car commercial.

"Ladies and gentlemen...we bring you *The Gauntlet!*"

The crowd went nuts. I reached the edge of the fighting ring, escorted on either side by the bouncers, with the boss himself on my heels. I dropped my pants atop my boots, now stripped down to boxer shorts—the closest thing I had to fighting pants. From every side the crowd crushed in, a perpetual roar of drunken glee echoing off the walls.

The sound made me sick. It conjured up mental images of Ancient Rome, the Colosseum, and thousands of blood-thirsty spectators overlooking a sandy pit of gory death. The basest of human desires, an animal expression of contorted lust.

And here I was ready to feed it—except I didn't plan on

delivering much of a show. I'm not and never have been a sport fighter.

I was a soldier.

"No holds barred," the boss said with a grin. "Fish-hook 'em, eye-gouge 'em. Break their knees...or maybe they'll break yours."

He tugged a gap between the ropes, allowing passage. I held his gaze, unblinking.

"Get my money," I said again. Then I slipped through the ropes and hit the mat. The building erupted with fresh roars. A few jeers. Plenty of lewd comments.

I ignored them all, bouncing on the balls of my feet. Stretching to limber up dormant muscles, testing my balance.

This was going to be quick—as quick as I could wreck five guys. It would have been easier with a tool. On the streets I would have used a two-by-four, a brick, or—my favorite—a tire iron. Added some leverage. Cheated.

But I could make do with my hands. I wasn't worried about what these thugs would throw at me. If they were anything like the muscle-bound morons I had already confronted, this would be the easiest hundred grand I ever made.

"What's your name?"

The referee wore a skin-tight black shirt and sported a glass eye. It was out of joint with his natural eye, leaving him with a wild, cross-eyed look.

"Sharpe," I said, not even hesitating to use my real name. I had nothing to hide.

"Good name. Where you from?"

"Phoenix."

The ref grabbed my arm and lifted it toward the ceiling. He flicked on a microphone and barked into the night.

"Ladies and gentlemen, all the way from the great western deserts of Arizona, I give you *The Scorpion!*"

Seriously?

The resulting screams hurt my ears. While the referee kept my arm up, spotlights pivoted down to focus on the center of the mat. The glare was so bright I was forced to drop my face. Sweat popped out on my spine and forehead. The ref released my arm and stepped to the side. He spoke into the mic again.

"Tonight's challenge involves five rounds of our toughest fighters. If The Scorpion wins them all, he takes the jackpot. Ladies and gentlemen, you know the rules. No holds barred. No move too dirty. No assault too vicious. For our first challenger, we bring you a new fighter, straight from the streets of the Windy City...*Coyote!*"

I squinted through the lights as the ropes parted. A form appeared, stepping onto the mat with an unsteady stagger. Not a big guy. Not a particularly muscular one, either. Average size, average weight. I outweighed him by no less than thirty pounds, and nothing about his awkward stance conveyed the confidence of a fighter.

What?

I looked to the edge of the ring, again making eye contact with the boss. He only smirked, a knowing glint in his cold eyes. I shook my head in disgust and tugged on a pair of open-finger gloves. Not boxing gloves—no, these were MMA gloves, designed for grappling as much as striking. They were already stained with dried blood.

I advanced to the middle of the mat to face off with my opponent. He lifted his face to make eye contact, revealing an expression of abject fear. The crowd thundered. The bell chimed. He fell back on his right foot, already off balance, and threw a sloppy right hook. I ducked it with ease, sidestepping. He recovered his balance and went for a left jab. This time I accepted the blow on my right shoulder, as much out of curiosity as laziness.

It felt like a slap. Like a fly swatter. The gloved first bounced off my shoulder and I looked at the guy—no, the *kid*—with a disbelieving squint. He was sweating. Flushed.

Then he gritted his teeth, anger taking over. He launched himself at me. I sidestepped, grabbing his left arm and wrenching it behind his back, up toward his shoulder blades. He cried out in pain, but in another second I had my right forearm hooked around his windpipe, pressing down. Cutting off airflow. Lifting his feet off the mat as he thrashed to break free.

There was no breaking free. I had implemented this move on a hundred rowdy non-coms in Afghanistan. People I didn't want to kill, but had to subdue. In seconds his brain burned through an expiring supply of oxygen. His body went limp. His eyes rolled back. I dropped him on the mat and pointed to the ref.

"Next."

The crowd exploded. The bell rang. The kid did not get up. Two of the motorcycle gangsters rushed in to clear away his unconscious body as the announcer roared my name.

"The Scorpion *strikes!*"

The blue and red lights returned, so bright I could barely see. I looked out of the ring, still confused. Searching for the boss.

And then I understood. It was the crowd—they were

surging toward the wager counter, cash in hand. Eager to place their bets.

On me.

I laughed. I couldn't help it. It was such an obvious ploy, yet everyone was falling for it like cattle to the slaughter. I finally found the boss, and this time his smirk spread into a grin. He rubbed his fingers together in the universal *money* signature. I simply shook my head.

You're going to regret this.

The next man into the ring—*Congo*—was everything the first kid wasn't. Light on his feet, poised and focused. A real fighter. Or, at least, a real boxer. He knew his moves and closed on me with precision, always guarding his face, always balancing his weight on his front leg as he struck.

He'd spent some time in a ring. But he'd never spent any time on the streets.

I let him strike, dodging his blows with catlike grace and not bothering to return fire. I let him tire out even as the crowd screamed for action. I circled. I faked. I drew him close to the wall, feigning as though I was backing into the corner.

Then I darted left. I circled as he failed to follow. I cocked my right foot and drove it straight into the side of his right knee—hard enough to shatter the joint. Bone snapped and Congo went down shrieking, face pointed toward the ceiling. I straddled his body, grabbing his left arm and wrenching it up to his shoulder blades. Then I choked off his windpipe, the exact same move as before.

Ten seconds. Twenty. He went limp, and I let him drop.

Never fails.

"Next!" I shouted.

The building shook. The lights blazed. Even the

announcer seemed semi-stunned. I didn't bother to look for the boss. I beckoned toward the edge of the ring where fighter number three stood. A skinny guy covered in tattoos with a shaved head. A real grappling MMA fighter, by the look of it. Somebody who liked to get low, to throw his opponent off his feet.

Somebody who took a pile-driving right hook straight to the jaw the split second the bell rang. He never saw it coming, and he dead sure wasn't ready for the follow-up left hook to his ribcage. Stumbling back, he scrambled for footing and escaped my shin-kick to the ribs. I stayed on him, suffering a kick of his own across my kidneys. Pain erupted up my back even as blood sprayed from his lips in a crimson shower. I knew he would go for my waist next, and I was ready for it. I let him come, not even fighting. His arm circled my back. His left leg wound around my right. He jerked to throw me off balance and bring me down.

I flat-palmed both his ears—hard. Even as we toppled, he screamed in agony, blood draining from both busted eardrums. We hit the mat and the pain broke his focus, just for a moment. That moment was long enough for me to break his grapple, twist my hips left to throw him sideways onto the mat. I landed on top and decked him in the jaw again, driving his teeth together and slamming his head backward. The blow stunned him. He was disoriented.

I went for the throat. A one-handed squeeze while I pinned his left arm with my knee and his right arm with my free hand. Twenty-six seconds. Lights out.

Screams exploded from every side. I drew myself to my feet, winded and a little dizzy. My kidneys ached. The bell chimed and the announcer babbled. A tide of spectators surged to the wager bar, eager to place more bets. Liquor flowed. Drums pounded from overhead speakers.

I made eye contact with the boss, and this time the grin was gone. He stared at me with those cold eyes, something between rage and confusion twisting his features into a snarl. I extended my left hand toward him and pinched my bloody thumb and forefinger together.

I made the money sign. The crowd lost their minds. The boss flushed a dark shade of crimson and shouted an order. The bell chimed again.

I turned to face my next opponent...and found not one, but *two*. A big guy and a lithe guy, both moving easily on their feet, weight balanced, stance perfect. As graceful as hawks gliding in for the kill, breaking apart even as the crowd packed in. The announcer thundered, projecting names I didn't recognize and didn't care about. I could see the ambush coming in real time, closing in from both sides.

Then snapping toward me like the jaws of a bear trap.

8

I pivoted left, choosing the big guy by default. He might be the slower, but his body weight would crush me quicker. I needed him off his feet, and I landed a blow to his ribcage even as I ducked his first swing toward my face.

Then the second guy struck from behind, landing on my back like a cat. One arm encircled my face, one thumb gouging into my right eye even as his free arm closed around my windpipe. I gasped precious air and stumbled. The guy ratcheted his arm tighter, crushing my airway. Ramming his thumb deep into my right eye. I screamed and jerked, fighting to throw him off.

He clung on like a brier, and then the bigger guy was back. He grabbed my left shoulder to hold me steady, then wound up a ballistic missile of a haymaker. Grinning. Eyes blazing.

I choked, blackness closing around my vision. I saw the right hook coming, launching from his shoulder, orbiting toward my face. I jerked, unable to break free of the big guy's grasp as the parasite on my back clamped down on my throat. In another second those closed knuckles would smash into my nose, obliterating the expensive nasal reconstruction surgery I was still paying for.

No chance.

At the last moment I jerked left, drawing the big guy's elbow inward. Closing the gap. Bending at my waist.

And drawing my head a half inch beneath the rocketing fist. It kept coming, but my head was no longer there. The skinny guy's head became the bullseye.

Bone shattered and the barnacle on my back screeched. The arm around my throat loosened, the thumb in my eye fell away. I thrashed left and slung him off, blood spraying across my face as he fell.

Then I was on the big guy, driving hard. Throwing my body ahead with no thought of self-preservation, no attempt to dodge or deflect his blows. I didn't have time. My *only* hope was violence of action. To hit him with more force, more speed, more savagery than he could manage in a constrained period. To overwhelm his training, his fancy spin kicks and grapple moves, and crush him with brute force.

It worked. I felt the initiative sliding my way as I plowed into his chest, head down, ramming the air out of his lungs. He choked and stumbled back. I stole a play from the parasite and rammed my right thumb toward his eye—not a permanent move, but enough to distract him a second longer.

The thumb missed. My knee did not. I obliterated his unprotected crotch with a strike so hard I thought I heard his soul depart his body. He didn't even scream. He just choked and fell backward. We reached the ropes and I pushed once with my left arm, knocking him further off balance. His middle back dropped over the ropes, his legs snapped up. I grabbed an ankle and heaved.

His whole body toppled into the crowd, and I spun around just in time to catch the bloody face of the parasite hurtling toward me like a charging bobcat.

I sidestepped. I lifted my forearm in a clothesline sweep for his throat. He slid to dodge the blow and caught my shin in his gut instead. That threw him backward. His head struck the mat. My knee landed on his stomach, my right fist crashing into his already smashed faced. His eyes rolled back. I didn't bother with the choke move.

I kept pounding—once, twice, three times. On the fourth blow the guy went limp. I heaved, nearly falling over myself, so dizzy that the mat around me felt like the rocking deck of a ship. The uproar from the crowd was ear-shattering. The lights blazing bright enough to blind me.

But I didn't hear the bell. I registered the absence with a confused squint. I gasped as a unified voice called out to me —not one spectator, but all three hundred of them.

"*Behind you!*"

I turned. The big guy launched himself back through the ropes, hurtling toward me with an awkward lurch that betrayed his shattered balls. He was two paces away, already winding up his next blow. I was still on my knees, still gasping. No time to get up.

I didn't try. I rolled right instead, landing on my back, bunching up my knees. Gritting my teeth. Watching as that hurtling side of beef closed in slow motion.

Then kicking out with both feet, aimed straight for his already wounded crotch.

He saw the legs coming and struggled to turn, but momentum is a wicked thing, and it was all bent against him. He caught my feet straight to the pelvis and fell flailing backward, arms windmilling.

I rolled again. Back on my feet. Circling even as he fought to pick himself up. Tears streaming from his face. Hands clawing the mat.

I shin-kicked him straight in the face. His head snapped back. His eyes spun. I drove my foot down on his spine and he collapsed. I almost collapsed myself, but I maintained my footing by digging my toes into the mat. I stepped back. I wiped blood from my face. I gasped for air as the scream of three hundred voices pounded in my skull.

His face lifted, blood draining from a shattered nose. I looked to the boss, barely visible through the lights and haze. I thought of Spencer. I gritted my teeth.

I struck with my foot again, straight to his jaw. The bone snapped. His eyes rolled back.

He went down, the bell chimed, and the crowd went *wild*.

9

I took my time leaving the ring. It wasn't a victory lap, it was a desperate attempt to regain my breath. I was staggering. Gasping. The world swam around me as the bell continued to pound, mixing with roars of "*Scorpion! Scorpion! Scorpion!*"

I wasn't flattered. I was closer to enraged. I would have paid half my winnings for everyone to shut up. But there was no silencing the crowd, and most of them had already forgotten me, anyway. They were swarming the wager bar, eager to cash in winning bets.

I staggered to the ropes and accepted a bottle of water from a stranger. Half of it coursed down my bruised windpipe, the other half washed the blood from my face. I tore the gloves off.

Then I looked for the boss. He stood at the edge of the ring, and this time there was no doubting the wrath in his eyes. That cold was gone, now replaced by magma-hot rage. He was quaking with it, muscled arms crossed. Jaw locked.

We stared each other down for what felt like a perfectly still minute.

Then I raised a hand and made the money sign one more time. What spectators remained exploded into cheers. The boss simply turned and headed for his office.

I clambered out of the ring and collected my clothes, tugging on my pants and slipping my feet into my boots before I followed him through the swarm of sweaty humans. We circled the bar even as the muscled gangsters waged a losing battle against a crush of angry betters. Apparently, there wasn't enough cash on hand to settle the wagers. That wasn't an acceptable answer for the mob. Things were spinning rapidly out of hand.

I pushed through the curtain and found the boss standing alongside his desk, pouring himself another glass of vodka. He didn't offer me any. He didn't speak. The three bruised gangsters from the alley all stood in the backdrop, arms folded, glaring at me.

And this time, they were all armed—pistols in leather holsters, the retention straps unsnapped.

So it's like that.

"You owe me a hundred grand," I said.

The boss swirled his vodka. Knocked back the glass, gulping it down. Then he tilted his head.

"Follow me."

He routed around the desk and through another curtain. I narrowed my eyes, every combat instinct won over a few dozen brushes with death now ignited to full alert. It was wrong, all of it. The maddened outrage I'd witnessed as the boss stood just outside the ring was gone. Now he seemed almost subdued.

He'd made a plan, and that knowledge didn't reassure me.

"Let's go," one of the background thugs spoke, hand on the grip of a polished revolver. His right eye was still bloodshot from my pummeling earlier that day. I couldn't imagine it hurt worse than the throbbing blur of my own right eye, still oozing blood from the gouging of the parasite.

"He getting the cash?" I said.

A smile. But no answer. I set my jaw.

Right.

I pushed through the curtain, arms loose at my side. The three gunmen followed me at a healthy distance into a storage room packed with beer kegs, a makeshift boxing gym, and heaps of cardboard boxes. I didn't see the boss, but there was another door. It stood open, the black Missouri sky visible above an armada of glistening black motorcycles.

I stopped. My fists tightened. I looked over one shoulder. The guy with the bloodshot eye gripped his revolver.

"*Move*," he snarled.

I sighed, shaking my head. I looked through the door, back to the motorcycles. Then I proceeded, because I didn't have a choice. If there was going to be trouble, I'd rather face it outdoors, anyway.

I passed through the door and stepped onto black asphalt. The moment my boots crossed the threshold, a chorus of thunder ripped from the bank of motorcycles—a dozen or more engines firing at once, modified exhausts snarling, headlights glaring into my face. I shielded my eyes and looked across a semi-circle of black-clad riders swinging legs off their bikes. Leaving the machines running. Closing the distance between us until I stood with my back to the door, surrounded on three sides by menacing meatheads in black leather vests, handguns visible at their hips.

Blanketed by *plenty* of sound cover.

My fight hand closed into a fist as an orange flame sparked beneath the shelter of somebody's palm. A cigarette ignited. Then the boss appeared from the semicircle, closing to only a yard away from me, dragging on his smoke. He blasted a cloud of gray into my face, breathing between his teeth and staring me down with those miserable eyes.

I didn't so much as flinch. I kept my fist closed at my side, my shirt rolled up beneath one arm. Then I spat—a wad of phlegm right between his feet.

"You owe me a hundred grand," I repeated.

The boss's lips lifted in an angry snarl. "I don't owe you a *dime.*"

I glanced around the perimeter of silent thugs, observing their focused eyes boring into me. Daring me to make a move.

I looked back to the boss. "Five fights, a hundred grand. That was the deal. You're going to pay up for the same reason you're going to pay all those bettors. You've got a reputation to uphold. What happens if the people learn you're just a cheap scam artist?"

It was a bold accusation, but I knew it was true. His snarl exaggerated to expose clenched teeth.

"I'm gonna pay those bets because my high rollers are all judges and prosecutors. *You...*" he jabbed with the cigarette, bringing the red hot ember to within inches of my bare chest, "...are nobody."

Dead silence. I waited. He drew the smoke back to his lips. Inhaled a long drag.

"You sure about that?" I said.

His lips lifted into a grin. He tilted his head. In unison, the dozen-odd gangsters spread out in a semicircle around me drew their handguns. Battlefield instincts informed me that the three men behind me had also drawn their firearms. The message was clear.

The boss spelled it out for me all the same. "Now you're gonna get out of here while you're still in one piece. You're going to leave my city and I am *never* going to see you again... because if I do, I'll carve out your organs and dump your rotting corpse in the river. *Am I clear?*"

He was. Every word brought my blood closer to a boil, but nothing he said surprised me, and a quick inspection of the gaping handgun muzzles directed at my chest sealed the arithmetic of the situation.

There was no play, here. I'd been cheated by the house, and really, it was my own fault. I'd let anger get the best of me. I'd *wanted* to pound some flesh after watching Spencer get carted away on a stretcher. Now I was sporting a brutalized right eye and who knew what other invisible injuries.

I thought about the money Spencer had stolen—ten grand. Then I remembered the lines of bettors demanding cash from empty drawers, and I knew I would never get that money back. I'd cost this operation enough cash for one night.

It was time to leave.

I pushed between the leather vests, arriving at my Fat Boy. It sat parked amid the bikes, my half-helmet still riding the sissy bar. I tugged my bloody shirt on. Rested the helmet on my head and left the chin strap dangling. Then I looked back.

"If I ever see you pound a kid again," I said, "I'll dump you *all* in the river."

Nobody answered. I slung a leg over and hit the starter. The bike rumbled to life, barely audible over the perpetual thunder of twelve other V-twins. I kicked backward out of the parking spot.

Then I twisted the bars and headed for the exit, not bothering to look back.

10

The nearest hospital to the rave/fight club was Homer G. Phillips Memorial—a one-building complex situated off North Jefferson Avenue with a parking lot half the size of a Walmart. Despite being small, the facility was bright and clean, appearing almost brand new. But that wasn't why I knew the ambulance had taken Spencer here. That deduction was made based simply on his mortal condition. The paramedics would have rushed him straight to the nearest emergency room, and judging by the bright red neon sign displayed over a pavilion on the hospital's north side, that emergency room would be the twenty-four-hour facility at Homer G. Phillips.

Running the Fat Boy into a slot near the back of the lot, I ignored my throbbing muscles and still-aching kidneys as I cut the motor. My admonitions to Spencer about sport fighting echoed in my mind as a self-condemnation, and I muttered a curse under my breath.

I was too old for this foolishness.

"Good heavens, what happened to *you*?" The nurse at the

emergency room counter spoke with a heavy southern accent, looking up from an iced coffee as I entered. A quick glance around the empty waiting room confirmed that I was the only one there. I didn't see another nurse, either.

"I'm here to see somebody."

A short laugh. "No kidding. How about an MRI machine?"

"No. Not for me. I'm here to see the kid—Spencer Meyers."

That was enough to melt the smile from her face. The nurse set the coffee down and beckoned me forward. She requested ID. I handed her a worn Arizona driver's license that read *Sharpe*, not *Scorpion*. She lifted a phone and spoke to somebody in the back, referencing my name. She hung up.

"Mr. Meyers has been transferred to a room. Give us five minutes. He'll see you."

So he's conscious. Well, that was good.

I fed quarters into a vending machine and wolfed down two candy bars and a Coke while I waited. The sugar helped to mask a little of my exhaustion, but did little for the burn in my kidneys. The nurse kept glancing my way, semi-confused and semi-alarmed, but not asking any further questions. At last she waved me back, and I plowed through double doors into a large triage bay. She handed me off to another nurse who led me through winding halls and up one level to a bank of hospital rooms. Every inch of the place looked as clean and polished as the outside, and mostly empty. I got the feeling that the facility had recently opened and was not yet operating at full steam.

The nurse stopped outside a closed door and peered up at me. She seemed to consider. Then she shook her head, dismissing her thoughts, or maybe me. She pushed the door open. I stepped inside.

Spencer Meyers lay stretched across a hospital bed, looking exactly like a movie prop from a film about underground fighting. He was bandaged head to foot, one leg encased in a cast and held in a sling, his nose placed in a brace, one eye covered in a patch. Another few bandages and he might as well have been a mummy, but for all the obvious damage, he was conscious. His one good eye rolled lazily toward me as I entered, displaying all the hallmarks of heavy medication.

Our gazes locked, and his eye widened in surprise— maybe a little fear. His lips parted, but he wasn't the first to speak, because he wasn't the only one in the room. There were two others, a woman and another kid. The woman stood next to the bed, tears in her eyes. She might have been thirty-five or close to fifty—I couldn't tell. The marks of a hard life covered her like tread marks on a worn road. Wrinkles, thinning hair, faded tattoos.

And the needle scars on her arm. Most of them old. All of them a dead giveaway.

The kid was a girl, maybe six or eight years old, and sadly she looked no better than the mother. Seated in a wheelchair, wrapped up in a pair of thick pajamas with a pale face fixated on Spencer, it was no more difficult to solve the riddle of her suffrage than that of the woman—it was cancer. I could see it in the way her skin clung to her bones like tissue paper. The pale wateriness of her eyes. The fuzzy knit cap that covered her skull, nothing but bare skin visible beneath its edges.

Chemotherapy, I thought. A lot of it. She looked barely alive.

"Who...are you?"

The woman's question faltered. She was sweeping my body head to toe, looking mildly alarmed. Her gaze switched to Spencer. Her mouth fell open. She pivoted back, now suddenly flushing.

I held up a hand. "I didn't do it. I tried to stop it, for what that's worth."

Her mouth closed. I could tell she was unconvinced. I cocked an eyebrow at Spencer, waiting. Seeing if he would man up.

He did. He ran his tongue over his dry lips and spoke in a rasp. "He's a friend, Mom."

The woman looked at her son. A tear slipped down her cheek. Her lower lip trembled. "Do you know who did this?"

The question was directed at me, but I didn't answer. I couldn't be sure what web Spencer had already woven, and I wasn't eager to interject myself into a potential lie. I simply approached the bed, hands in my pockets, and surveyed Spencer's busted body.

He looked terrible. Even worse than he had on the stretcher outside the fight club. I doubted that he'd lasted through even the first round of the gauntlet—the bait round, designed to get the wagers flowing.

They had pummeled him like a volleyball.

"Not your best day, huh?"

Spencer looked away. His lips tightened. He seemed to be wrestling with something. I made no effort to fill the silence, happy to let his conscience do the work for me.

This was a lesson he needed to learn—permanently.

"Mom, why don't you get Lily something to drink?" Spencer's voice was a rasp.

His mother frowned, placing a hand on his shoulder.

The hand trembled a little, and I didn't think it was due to emotion so much as nerve damage.

"*Mom.*" Spencer's voice dripped with teenage angst. To my surprise, his mother held up an apologetic hand and retreated to the girl's wheelchair. The child shot me a weak, bashful smile as she rolled past. In another moment the two of them were gone and I was alone with Spencer.

I kept my hands in my pockets. Waiting. Spencer met my gaze with his one good eye, then looked quickly away. He shifted in the bed. I thought he might cry.

I sighed and dragged an armchair away from the wall, settling down next to him. I folded my arms.

"Okay, kid. You better start from the top."

11

A heavy tear slipped out of the bloodshot eye, and Spencer turned his face away. His cheeks flushed. His right fist bunched around the hospital sheets, twisting and contorting them. His jaw clenched, all the medication in his blood stream failing to overcome the waves of frustration.

I thought it was guilt at first, but then I saw something deeper. Something that felt a lot more intrinsic.

"Why'd you do it, Spencer?"

No answer. I relaxed the best I could with an aching body and contented myself to wait him out. At last Spencer mumbled, still looking away: "A hundred grand...a *hundred grand.*"

"Bad answer," I said. "Money is the worst possible reason for violence. What does a dumb kid need with a hundred grand anyway? You wouldn't even know how to spend it."

Spencer's face pivoted toward me. The cheek beneath his good eye was wet with tears. He looked confused. Even wounded.

"You thought the money was for me?"

My lips parted. Confusion deadlocked me—but only for a moment. Then the truth of the thing hit me like a right hook to the face, something Spencer and I both had intimate knowledge of.

"I don't have insurance." It was what Spencer had said when I recommended a hospital for the gash in his arm. He couldn't afford medical care.

My gaze snapped toward the empty door where the mother and the little sister—the very *sick* little sister—had disappeared. And then I understood.

"What does she have?" I said.

The question unleashed a hardness over Spencer, a sort of anger I had yet to witness—even when he was freshly pummeled by three thugs in an alley.

"Neuroblastoma," he said. "Cancer."

The name was unfamiliar to me, and I knew that couldn't be a good thing. When it comes to cancer, rare usually means *worse*. And more expensive.

"Your mother doesn't have insurance," I said. "Your sister doesn't have insurance."

Spencer snorted a humorless laugh. He didn't answer. I sighed.

"Look, kid. Believe it or not, I didn't come here to kick your ass. I want to help you. But you gotta meet me halfway."

Spencer's lip twitched. The hardness returned. "No, there's no insurance. My mom look like the kind of woman who holds down a steady corporate job? She bags groceries at the discount supermarket. She's only been clean a couple years."

"Father?" I asked.

"What do you think?"

I sighed. I ran one hand over a bruised face, rough with unshaven razor stubble. I was suddenly so tired I could barely sit upright. It wasn't just the physical exertion of wrecking five guys in a row—and taking a few hits myself. It was deeper than that. It was the slow, steady drip of heartache and tragedy that I had witnessed over the past two years during my ramblings around America.

Not the big stuff—not the stuff that makes headlines. This pain was the everyday sort. The lost jobs, broken marriages, abused children, ravaging diseases.

Consuming addiction.

Spencer didn't know it, but he and I had even more in common than I first thought. My mother, a long-term substance abuser, had died of an overdose when I was only fifteen. And my father? I'd never met the guy. Never had the chance to meet him. He split while my mother was pregnant, or so she claimed.

Regardless, I knew a lot more about Spencer Meyers' predicament than he would ever give me credit for. But proving my bona fides would do nothing to assuage his situation.

I looked up to see Spencer squinting at me. He seemed to understand my physical condition for the first time. His lips parted. Temporary hope lit his eyes.

"Wait...you fought."

I grunted. "Against my best judgement."

"Did you..." He sat up, grimacing but coming alive with hope.

"Win?" I said. "Yes. I did."

"So—"

"No. There's no money. They never paid up. It's a scam,

just like I told you it would be. If there's a house, the house wins. One way or the other."

The defeat that crushed down on Spencer looked somehow heavier than all the abuse he had suffered up to that point. He fell back into the bed, and for a long moment neither of us spoke. I knew he was crying again but doing his best to keep it quiet. I could only see his eye patch, but his chest quivered with each breath.

I felt his pain in my very gut. Not because I know much about cancer, or have ever had a little sister to love. I felt the pain because I understand despair as well as anyone. The way it bores into your very bone marrow, eating you alive.

The thought of it brought to mind the first few chapters of Genesis from my late fiancée's Bible. A description of paradise on Earth where humans existed in tranquility.

Despair like this was something that no one—certainly no *kid*—was ever meant to endure.

"I'll pay you back," Spencer mumbled.

"What?"

"The ten G's I took from the camper. I know it was wrong. I just thought..."

His face pivoted again. He ran his tongue over his busted lips. "There's this treatment in Germany. Something about CAR-T cells...it's a therapy. I read about it on the internet, and they say it really works. We don't have it in America yet, but you can go to Germany and buy it...if you have the money."

If you have the money.

The words sank into my gut and twisted. I put a hand on Spencer's arm and squeezed.

He was still just a boy. A particularly stupid boy. But the burden crushing down on his shoulders and his reactions to it reflected courage beyond his years. If I put myself in his own shoes...yeah. I would have stolen that ten grand, also.

"Don't worry about the money," I said. "You've generated enough debts tonight."

I jabbed a thumb toward the cast around his leg and Spencer rolled his good eye. He didn't answer. We sat in silence a long while as I did my best to share his pain. I knew it couldn't be helping much. When a thing consumes you from the inside, nobody can ease that suffering.

At least...no person.

I finally stood with a gentle grunt, shaking my head at the pain radiating through my lower back. That single kick to the kidneys was going to stick with me. My right eye burned, also.

"I'll come back and check on you," I said. "Try to get some rest."

Spencer closed his eye, tears drying on his face. I orbited to the end of the bed, halfway to the door before I stopped. I looked back.

"You're the man of your house, aren't you?"

Spencer's eye opened. He faced me.

"You see anybody else?"

The words cut deep. I headed for the exit.

12

The ride back to the Purple Crane Campground was the least enjoyable I'd experienced in a while. Not just because the aches and pains of my recent stint as an amateur cage fighter made every jolt and rumble of the Fat Boy uniquely torturous, but also because I felt physically *heavy*.

The agony of Spencer's predicament resonated with me. I felt his desperation, his hopelessness, his abject frustration. And yes, I felt some guilt as well. I'd come to that hospital ready to kick his ass. A reckless, selfish, stupid kid who took what didn't belong to him to gamble on what could never be his.

But that hadn't been Spencer's story, and nobody was giving him the benefit of the doubt. Least of all, a small army of sweaty meatheads on motorcycles, only too happy to take ten grand from his pocket before watching him depart in an ambulance.

It was life—compliments of a fruit humanity was never supposed to consume. I wanted to help. I didn't have the first idea where to start. I was too tired and sore to think clearly. The best plan I could put together was to get back to the campsite, strip out of my bloody clothes and spend half an hour in a shower stall of the campground's bathhouse. The water never really got hot—lukewarm at best—but the water pressure beat the socks off the shower stall in the Airstream, and the ritual of a shower would ease my mind. Help me to sleep.

The problems would still be there in the morning.

I turned off the highway and rumbled up the busted asphalt drive, body sagging under somebody else's weight. The bouncing headlight of the Fat Boy cast shaking light over the automated gate at the entrance of the campground and I reached for the scannable access card dangling from the bike's handlebars.

And then I stopped. My left hand closed over the clutch. My right foot crushed down over the rear brake. Loose gravel popped as the rear tire locked.

The automated gate—a horizontal metal bar wrapped in reflective yellow tape—was missing. I flicked the Fat Boy's headlight to high beam and caught a glint of reflection in the ditch opposite the gate post. Rumbling forward another ten yards, I finally saw the gate resting in a drift of leaves. The bar had been ripped clean off the post and now lay bent in the ditch. I glanced to the campsite office, standing another thirty yards down the road to my left.

The lights were on, but I didn't see Christine. I didn't see anybody.

Releasing the clutch, I gunned the motor and rushed past the busted gate. I turned a curve, winding through thick trees.

Then I saw other lights—red and blue, flashing steadily

just beyond the trees. I accelerated, heart thumping as the Fat Boy's exhaust snarled. I hopped a speed bump without slowing, and then I reached the mouth of the actual campground.

There were emergency cars—two fire trucks, two police cars, one ambulance. I smelled the smoke long before I identified the source. It was the camp's general store, a small portable building where Ms. Dottie sold outdoor essentials —mostly ice cream and bug spray. The structure had been about fifteen feet square, but now it was gone. Nothing but an ashen heap with a firefighter still pumping Mississippi River water onto the wreckage.

I hit the brakes again and ground to a stop, surveying a mass of loitering campers, some gathered in knots, some collecting trash from overturned garbage cans.

It wasn't just the general store—the whole place was wrecked. Camp chairs were thrown around, string lights ripped down. A nearby pickup truck had two of its tires slashed, while the camper next to it sported a busted window. The place had been smashed, the damage both random and severe. It was as though a giant had crashed down Purple Crane's main street, randomly kicking over trashcans and punching out windows.

Only, this had been no giant. My headlight revealed tire marks burned into the asphalt—*single* tire marks, wide and dark.

I gritted my teeth, killing the bike as Christine approached. She wore a dirty Purple Crane t-shirt, her face blackened by soot. The left side of her curling brown-gray hair was singed. A bandage enclosed one forearm.

"Vandals," she said. "It was—"

"A motorcycle gang," I finished.

Christine stopped. She nodded. "Yeah...three guys, anyway. Loud bikes."

There was no anger in her voice, just more of the same crushing defeat that blanketed Spencer. That was okay, because I was already the willing custodian of any necessary outrage. It was boiling in my very blood, cauterizing my injuries and smothering my weariness. I'd gone five rounds in an underground fight ring, but given the opportunity, I would have thrown myself in for another five.

Or at least another three.

"You know them?" Christine squinted. It must have been something in my face that gave it away. I deployed the side stand and swung off the bike. I stood alongside her for a long moment, watching Ms. Dottie orbiting around her over-turned truck tire flowerbeds, sobbing as she scrambled to rescue her ravaged petunias.

"I know them," I said. "And they're about to know me."

13

I parked the Fat Boy alongside my rented Airstream, which had survived the reckless sacking of the campground, then spent the next two hours helping the others to clean the place up. Nobody awaited instructions or blamed management for the late-night disturbance. They simply pitched in, like all good travelers do, collecting trash, banging dents out of metal garbage cans, sweeping up shattered glass, and doing their best to comfort Ms. Dottie.

Meanwhile, a quartet of cops collected witness statements, inquiring about the make and model of the three motorcycles, the race and general appearance of the men riding them, etcetera.

I knew it was all an act. Not because they were bad cops, or incompetent ones, but because this fight was well beyond the capacity of any local sheriff's department. They already knew who was responsible. A gang this large and dominant would have a reputation. The very fact that they hadn't already been shut down was proof that they had both leverage and intimidation on their side.

I remembered what the boss had said about his high rollers—all prosecutors and judges—and I wished I'd punched his lights out.

"You got insurance?" The lead deputy was conversing with Christine as I approached. Dottie's daughter nodded absently, watching with heartbroken eyes as her mother continued to scramble between the columns of toppled tires, scooping up soil with her bare hands.

Ms. Dottie was beside herself, seeming as much confused as distressed.

"We'll put a report together so you can file a claim," the deputy said.

"How about an arrest?" My suggestion carried more than a little venom. I was tired, bruised, and amply pissed off. The deputy turned exhausted eyes on me, and I knew he felt the same—minus the bruising, anyway.

"We'll need to coordinate with the St. Louis PD on that," he said. "These guys are almost certainly from across the river. You don't have any security cameras, do you?"

The last question was directed at Christine. She shook her head.

"No. They all wore helmets, anyway. The full-face kind, with dark visors. Nobody could see their faces."

"What about license plates?" I asked.

Another shake of her head. "Couldn't see them either. They were, like...folded in."

"Outlaw brackets," the deputy said. "Plates mounted on a hinge. All they have to do is kick them and they fold against the frame...it's a getaway tactic."

I was familiar with the design—I'd seen plenty of such brackets back in Phoenix, not only as a cop but also as a self-destructive, orphaned teenager "borrowing" sport bikes...my first introduction to the motorcycling hobby.

"Your best bet is an insurance claim and a new gate," the deputy said. "Maybe a stronger one."

"How about an AR-15?" My tone continued with the venom. The cop made no reply, simply closing his notebook. I departed the pair and met Ms. Dottie next to her fifth wheel. When she saw me, her tearful eyes ignited in hope. She wrapped both arms around my body and buried her face in my chest.

"Toddy, you're home! Oh, my gracious. If you'd been here, this never would have happened. Did you bring your gun?"

She peered into my face, trembling hands clenched around my arms. I simply smiled, but didn't answer. I reset the tires on top of each other and used a neighbor's shovel to scoop the dirt back into them. Christine helped Ms. Dottie replant the salvaged flowers while the firemen and the cops packed up and left. By two a.m. the campground was pretty much put back together...but nobody could relax. Quite a few "golf bags" had appeared from inside pickup trucks. Old guys sporting veterans' hats and law enforcement tattoos sat beside campfires with beer bottles in one hand, those nondescript bags lying next to them.

Too bad they hadn't been quicker on the draw.

"She should sleep," I said. "So should you."

Christine nodded, her face creased with deep stress. She kept glancing back toward the busted gate, which had now been barricaded with a pair of one-ton pickup trucks.

"They won't be back," I said, offering a smile. "You can get some shuteye."

"Are you leaving, Toddy?" Ms. Dottie's voice cracked with emotion. I turned my smile on her.

"I'm just headed to my place. I'll be here in the morning."

"You're not going back to Kuwait?"

I exchanged a glance with Christine. Her eyes were apologetic. She took Ms. Dottie by the shoulder and guided her toward their shared fifth wheel, speaking softly to her about a bath and a cup of tea.

"Oh, I do love a cup of tea. You know, your father used to make me a cup whenever he wanted a little *somethin'-some-thin'*. I guess he must have drugged it. You know what I mean!"

Christine didn't even blush as she helped her mother into the camper. I shuffled back to my Airstream. Stripping out of my clothes, I showered in the cramped confines of the camper's stainless steel bath closet, resigning myself to the convenience of pitiful water pressure.

Dressed in gym shorts and a t-shirt, I contemplated my bed for only a moment before opting for my hammock, stretched between trees with a partial view of the mighty Mississippi. I cracked open a lukewarm Miller Lite and sipped it as I watched the dark expanse of water, allowing my body to wind down slowly. Counting the figures in my head.

Ten grand stolen from my lock box, plus the hundred grand in deprived winnings from the fight ring. Then there were the expenses of repairing the campground and flying a cancer-stricken child all the way to Europe.

I reached a total. I rounded the number for good measure. Then I relaxed into the hammock, my beer still jammed against my thigh, and fell easily to sleep.

I didn't dream. I didn't stress. I rested easily in the knowledge that accounts would be settled in the very near future.

14

I was up at sunrise, having slept only five hours but feeling good. I stripped down and swam two miles through the river—an easy mile downstream, and a brutal one back upstream—then I cooked a heavy breakfast of eggs and bacon on my camp stove.

With a full belly and a clear mind, I locked the Airstream, fired up the Fat Boy, and guided the bike around the barricade of one-ton pickups. In short order I was pointed west, crossing the river, headed back into the city. A target already defined.

I didn't bother with the police station. I knew it would be a waste of time. The sheriff's department from Illinois would already be in contact with the SLMPD, and if any serious action was to be taken—which I doubted—my further testimony would do nothing to aid it. At best, the St. Louis cops would make a trio of arrests and extradite those suspects to Illinois, where presumably corrupt prosecutors, bought off by the gang, would plea down the charges to a slap on the wrist.

Even if those three thugs went to prison, nothing would be done about the root of the problem—the *real* core of the gang. After sleeping on it, I thought I had unraveled the mystery of who had sacked the campground, and how they had known I lived there. The latter question was betrayed by the quick access gate card I kept dangling from the handlebars of the Fat Boy. It was printed with the Purple Crane Campground logo, and one of the meatheads back at the fight club must have noticed it as I departed.

As for the *who* of the matter, that question was even more obvious. It was the three guys I had pounded in the alley while rescuing Spencer. Low-level soldiers with Mississippi muck for brains who were acting out of vengeful impulse—and no doubt *without* the approval of their bosses.

Even though it would likely cost him nothing in the long run, there was no way the leader of a highly profitable, highly organized criminal enterprise would knowingly permit three soldiers to sack a random campground out of spite. It was foolish and needless. He'd already run me off.

No. This had been unsanctioned aggression, which meant it was unlikely to be repeated. Yet it was going to cost the boss a heck of a lot more than it cost his three meatheads. He was going to answer not only for the damage to the Purple Crane, but for the damage to Spencer Meyers. The damage to my own body.

And the financial damage to my lockbox.

I began my day at the St. Louis visitor's center, where I acquired a colorful map of the city. Then I migrated to a hardware store for a cigarette lighter, a pack of oil rags, a red marker, a compact pair of bolt cutters, and a pair of cheap binoculars.

The cashier squinted at the peculiar assembly of items,

but made no comment other than to pitch me on a store credit card. I declined, packed the gear into the Fat Boy's saddlebags, then headed next door to a supermarket where I purchased a brand-new burner phone, a prepaid debit card, dark sunglasses, a St. Louis Cardinals baseball cap, and a six-pack of fancy root beers in fat, glass bottles. I sipped one as I headed back to the bike. It was a little sweet, but not half bad. I dumped the rest out and crammed all six bottles into what remained of my saddlebag storage space.

Then, at last, I was ready to go to work.

The business of a police stakeout is anything save glamorous. Reclined in the filthy, sagging seat of an old sedan with Coke bottles for urinals and potato chips for breakfast, lunch, and dinner is about as exciting as watching paint dry. The job is even harder on a motorcycle with a modified exhaust and no tinted windows to hide behind. I ended up abandoning the bike in another supermarket parking lot in North St. Louis and doing much of my work on foot—ball cap pulled down over my ears, sunglasses sheltering my face like a movie star. Burner phone and binos close to hand.

I began at the rave club, because I expected to find somebody counting the cash from the previous night's take. I was right. Several bikes were present, including a few I recognized. Seated across the street at a diner, I ate lunch and took notes. License plate numbers and descriptions of persons entering and exiting, all recorded on the burner phone's note-taking app.

I observed the woman again—the one I'd seen in the fight club's office when I first entered. Tall and trim, with dark hair held back in a ponytail, she departed the rave club astride some kind of squat little bike with a nasty twin muffler, screaming down the street as though the dragons of hell were on her very heels.

She handled the bike well. She looked good on it. And somehow...she didn't seem to fit. Not only because the muscle-bound rocket she rode looked nothing like the over-built cruisers the rest of the gang rode, but also because she was...

Well... Attractive, if I was being honest. In shape. Put together. Composed. Not all sweat and blubber.

Interesting.

I tapped down another note, then I returned to the supermarket for my bike. The next phase of my operation would be riskier. I needed to trail some of these guys across town to uncover what I was certain would be a more diverse network of criminal entrepreneurism. Back astride the Fat Boy, I drew just close enough to the rave club to observe the exit of the parking lot, then waited for a pair of thick guys dressed in those faded leather vests with the dog and arch logo to throw their legs over twin Road Kings—beautiful machines that reflected a lot better hygiene than their riders. The two guys turned out onto the four-lane, an SUV passed, and then I swung into traffic.

It wasn't difficult to keep up. Road Kings are powerful but not necessarily quick. The Fat Boy was modified to be very quick. I kept my distance but never lost sight of the pair as they wound deeper into the seedy neighborhoods of North St. Louis. I'd never ridden here before, but nothing I saw was unfamiliar.

Sun-bleached old houses, their siding falling off, their roofs poorly patched. Overgrown yards. Cars on blocks. Mailboxes rusted and leaning. Trash blowing across the street. All the hallmarks of economic hardship and social abandonment. A sad neighborhood.

But not a forgotten one—not completely. The motorcycles stopped at a house on the corner with a slouching front porch and late model Cadillac Escalade parked in the busted driveway. I left the Fat Boy a block away and approached through what once had been a park and was now just an abandoned expanse of high grass with a rusted arrangement of playground equipment littered amongst it.

I used the binos to survey the house for the next two hours. People came and went. The Escalade departed, then returned. I observed bags—mostly grocery sacks—half loaded when the Escalade driver left the house, but bulging with irregular, brick-like shapes when they returned.

I made notes on the phone, grunting in semi-disbelief.

Too easy.

Back on the Fat Boy I continued my trek throughout the city. The operation consumed the entirety of an afternoon. The two guys on the Road Kings led me to a prostitution operation amid the rat trap motels near I-70. A dozen odd girls working one grungy room to the next and occasionally traversing to the truck stop next door for business in the sleeper cabs of out-of-town semis. I marked out the pimp and took record not only of his physical description but also his license plate. I recorded two more drug houses, what might have been an electronics fencing warehouse, and a motorcycle garage that was most definitely serving as an alternative headquarters.

Six addresses. Three dozen suspects. Just as many license plates. By sundown I had enough information to keep an arrest squad and a district attorney's office busy for the rest of the year—which itself was a brutal form of ancillary evidence.

These guys were operating with impunity, only half-heartedly covering their tracks. Yet they hadn't yet been busted, which could mean only one of two things. Either every cop in the city was as crooked as scoliosis, which I seriously doubted, or a few powerful judges and prosecutors had been bought off and were hamstringing the entire police force by refusing to take any meaningful legal action against the gang.

Which I didn't doubt in the least.

Fair enough. I'll use the feds.

The last item on my stakeout checklist differed from the others. It also took less time and effort to find, because I already knew exactly where to look. Three blocks from the SLMPD headquarters, well within easy walking distance, but also with a large gravel parking lot with plenty of room for squad cars. The cop bar sat on the outskirts of the tourism district, a sagging green pub sign advertising cold beer and hot sandwiches. I ducked inside just long enough to drink a glass of water and confirm the number of St. Louis cops inside—fifteen, and it wasn't even happy hour—then I was ready for dinner.

Rusty sang Howlin' Wolf's "Smokestack Lightning" as he slathered spicy barbeque sauce over my ribs. I retreated with my tray to a corner booth and tucked in to fresh collard greens washed down with sweet tea. I took my time, watching as the sun evaporated over Kansas.

Then I drew my brand-new burner phone like a sidearm and went to work. Two calls to the Drug Enforcement Administration—different offices, one in St. Louis, one in Jefferson City, just for good measure. I altered the pitch of my voice for each call, reporting on a drug den I had barely escaped. Armed men, cocaine and heroin *everywhere*. Guns? Yes, lots of guns. Piles of cash, also.

Did I have an address? As a matter of fact, I did. It took me a moment to recall it. I was still emotionally distressed from my brush with death. I choked, but got it out. I begged them to send agents. I hung up and chowed down on a rib just as Rusty launched into "Baby How Long"—one of my favorites.

The ribs were extra spectacular that evening. I suspended my phone calls long enough to polish off another three. Then I dialed the St. Louis police department. I reported a hooker at the truck stop off I-70 who had ripped me off. I hung up and dialed them again, miming the voice of a lethargic cashier at the truck stop counter.

There was a fight going on at the motel next door. I described the pimp I'd witnessed earlier that day, even listing his license plate. He was wasting a girl—the cashier thought she might be a prostitute. Wait...was that a *gun*?

I hung up. Rusty called from behind the bar.

"Hey, brother, you want some pecan pie? It's fresh and hot."

I restrained a burp. Wiped my mouth. Then I grinned.

"You know what, Rusty? Make it to go. I've got an appointment."

15

I made it into the outskirts of North St. Louis just as the Fat Boy's fuel needle dropped into the red, marking an empty tank. Pulling off at a nondescript fuel station with a slouching pavilion and foggy convenience store mirrors, I parked the bike on the far side of the pump furthest from the store, casting a quick glance around for any sign of security cameras.

I saw none. I paid at the pump with the pre-paid debit card I'd purchased at the grocery store and filled the bike first. Then I retrieved those six fat root beer bottles from the saddlebags and dispensed their sugary contents into the trash can before trickling ten ounces of eighty-seven octane ethanol-laced fuel into each one.

I left an inch of empty space at the top, hung up the nozzle, then went for the oil rags. They were thick and rough, fitting into the mouth of each bottle with a little effort. Sufficiently sealed, I repacked them in the saddlebags and buckled the covers.

Then I was back on the bike, winding toward the river...
and the rave club.

The place was bumping exactly as it had been the night
before. The crowd of motorcycles was there. A pair of ugly
bouncers stood at the door, and a surge of young and reckless humanity stood lined up waiting to gain access.

I circled beyond all of it, heading another hundred yards
down the busted riverside street until I reached the backside
of the structure. I rumbled across gravel and through a couple
of wide mud puddles before reaching the building's tail end
—that section closest to the river, where the fight club lay.

I killed the bike. I stretched my fingers and back,
popping the joints. I thought of Rusty's pie, and despite the
gorge-fest of a rib meal I'd just consumed, my mouth
watered. Had Rusty thought to include a plastic fork with my
takeout carton? I wasn't above eating the pie with my fingers.

Swinging off the bike, I dug out a root beer bottle and my
camp lighter. I turned the bottle sideways as I approached
the rear of the rave club, where the flat-topped roof featured
a pair of massive, industrial AC units that chugged steadily
despite the early November chill.

By the time I rocked the bottle upright again, a trickle of
gasoline had saturated half the cloth, and it ignited with a
momentary pass of the lighter's flame. Not a rush, not an
explosion, just a healthy hot burn.

I burped into my fist, tasting Rusty's famous BBQ sauce.
Then I flipped the bottle overhand, straight over the top of
the fight club's wall, smashing down only a yard outside the
intake grill of the nearest AC unit. Glass shattered against
sheet metal, and a second later a hot *whoosh* signaled the
ignition of the raw fuel contained within. A hot fireball

exploded toward the sky, unleashing with it a cloud of thick, black smoke.

That smoke was instantly inhaled by the AC unit, which only served to aggravate the flames and produce additional smoke. I strolled back to the bike and retrieved the carton of root beer bottles, still thinking about my pie. At the base of the fight club's back wall I held a bottle in one hand and a lighter in the other, cocking my head and waiting for the alarm.

A minute ticked by. The AC unit continued to snort black smoke even as the flames began to die against the metal roof. From the front of the building I heard voices—the laughter and clamor of those revelers still eager to enter the rave club.

Another sixty seconds. I was just thinking I would have to apply the second bottle when the alarm finally sounded as a prolonged shriek, followed by multiple shouts of *"Fire!"* exploding from the rave club's entrance.

They could have spared the panic. Nobody was even remotely close to being in danger. But actually, I didn't mind the desperation. It encouraged a maddened stampcdc, which was exactly what I wanted. I lit the next bottle and pitched it. Bottles three through six arced like artillery shells to burst across the metal roof, each launching a temporary fireball that lit the sky as additional shouts erupted from the far side of the building.

Engines roared. Tires spun. Cries of confused frustration sounded from the bouncers. I retreated to the Fat Boy and fired up the engine, rumbling back through the muddy gravel lot to the riverside street now clogged with cars. A siren of a different sort rang in the distance, accompanied by red flashing lights. I eased my bike into a vacant lot about two hundred yards removed from the rave club. Once more I killed the motor, and this time I finally reached for the takeout carton.

Oh, Rusty *had* included a fork. An extra-large slice of his famous pie, also, heavy with cinnamon sugar sprinkle. It seemed my generous tips were paying dividends. I sliced off a bite and entered nirvana as the first St. Louis fire engine rumbled to a stop outside the rave club and firemen bailed out.

The flames were already dying, much as I expected. Metal roofs and concrete walls don't burn. The flames were all fear factor, very little actual threat. But the damage was done, nonetheless. The rave club was empty for the night, and the fight club was falling dangerously close to an unwelcome sort of exposure...all thanks to sixty ounces of gasoline and some cheap rags.

Touchdown.

I was just finishing the pie—and committing myself to a double-time river swim the next morning—when the thugs responsible for the entire operation rolled out of the building to move their armada of motorcycles out of the fire engine's way.

They were furious, both red-faced and obstinate with the firefighters, which certainly amused me. I relaxed into the seat and licked the last of that sticky pie filling off my teeth. I waited until I saw the big cheese himself, that burly guy with the lifeless eyes and the coarse beard, appear next to the fire engine.

He was shouting at the first responders. Gesturing angrily toward a rooftop now safely extinguished of flame, appearing to deny the firefighters entry into the building. He wanted them to leave. He wanted them to skip the interior inspection.

They weren't having any of it. They barged right past him and entered the club. He spun to follow, face passing across the parking lot, the street...and me.

I lifted a hand and shot him a two-finger wave. The boss froze, face contorting into a confused scowl...and then a white-hot, *enraged* scowl. He recognized me. His lips parted. He started toward the street.

I hit the starter and dropped into first gear. I motored lazily out of the lot and onto the street, taking my time as I passed within fifty feet of his bullish bulk. We made eye contact, and I winked.

Then I gunned the motor and faded into the night.

16

The boss's goons were better at trailing me than I would have guessed. Long before I exited North St. Louis I detected them on my tail, roaring along on a pair of beefy Harley Street Glides that I could have easily lost with enough twists and turns but even the bored-out muscle of the Fat Boy struggled to outrun on an open highway.

I selected an exit and faded onto surface streets, breezing through a few stop signs and not slowing until I had reached downtown—that little spot at the intersection of the business and tourism districts, only two blocks removed from the police station. I parked the bike in a narrow parallel spot right in front of the cop bar. I took my time dismounting, giving my tails plenty of opportunity to rumble down the narrow street and pinpoint my destination.

Their faces contorted in disgust. One of them spat tobacco juice at me, but fell well short of his mark. I strolled into the cop bar and inhaled a deep lungful of beer fumes and cigarette smoke. I selected a booth in a darkened corner.

I sat with my back to the wall and ordered a Miller Lite—nothing too strong; I expected to be back on the bike soon.

Then I relaxed, picking at the bottle's label with one thumb, watching the door. I didn't have to wait long.

The boss himself appeared just as the waitress arrived with my second beer. He was sweaty, his face a little blackened by smoke, his lips twisted into a perpetual snarl. One of his goons flanked him like a bodyguard. I waved to draw their attention, denying myself the smirk I so desperately wanted to indulge in.

I'd poked the bear enough—at least for now.

"Couple more for my friends," I said, signaling the waitress. She shot a suspicious eye at the newcomers, then departed without comment. The boss slid in first. His compatriot—some bulky guy with a twisted nose and eyes the color of river water—slid in next to him. They both glared at me, not so much as blinking as the waitress slid two more bottles of Miller onto the table.

Then the boss spoke through his teeth. "A cop bar? Really?"

I shrugged, swigging beer. "You can't pay them all off. There's got to be at least a few honest guys in the room, happy to gun you down if you try anything. I'm guessing you'll make the smarter choice and indulge in some good faith business negotiation."

"What the hell are you talking about?"

"I'm talking about the little blue house with the yellow shutters, for a start. That drug den of yours where you warehouse the good stuff. I heard it was raided today...a real mess."

I grimaced. The boss's teeth ground. He didn't answer.

"Or maybe we should discuss the pimping operation

over by the highway…you know, at the truck stop. Seems St. Louis's finest made some sterling arrests today. It'll be a week or two before that operation gets back on its feet. That's a lot of lost revenue."

Now the veins in his forehead were bulging, turning a darker shade of violet with each thump of his angry heart. He spoke through pinched lips.

"I'm going to beat your body into a pulp before I wrap a chain around your neck and dump your lifeless ass in the river."

I laughed. Shook my head and retrieved a golf pencil and a trivia scorecard from the condiment basket at the end of the table. I flipped the card over and wrote on its blank back.

"No, you're not, big man. Because if you try, I'll bring your entire circus crashing down around your ears—one federal bust and flaming fight club at a time. What you're going to do is settle out of court, the gentlemanly way. A one-time payment to rid yourself of a world of hurt."

I pushed the card across the table. I swigged from the bottle. The boss eyed the penciled figure and the vein in his forehead looked ready to explode. His face snapped up, a mortar shell's worth of vitriol cocked and loaded behind his tongue.

I cut him off, uninterested in the outburst. "It's a fair figure. The one hundred grand I won in the ring, plus fifty grand for the damage to the camp ground—a replacement general store, and new trash cans. I called Home Depot for quotes. It's a solid estimate. I added twenty percent for labor, and an additional ten percent because, well, you pissed me off. Call it a pain-and-suffering surcharge."

"Are you out of your *mind?*" he growled.

"Usually. But not tonight. At the moment I feel quite

reasonable, which is good news for you. I could have burned that fight club to ash, and I probably should have, but I didn't want to risk any innocent lives. Whatever you lost in drug money and hooker fees, trust me when I tell you that it's a drop in the bucket compared to what I'm capable of costing you. Look at that number and multiply by ten. Not all at once, of course. But over days. Weeks. An endless harassment that leaves you without a pot to piss in. Of course, that's a lot of trouble for me, but I've got nothing better to do."

I leaned close, speaking just loud enough to be heard over the blare of a Linkin Park track. "You *don't* intimidate me. Neither does your third-rate army of beer-gut thugs."

The boss said nothing. His teeth clenched. I could see the calculation in those dead eyes. The consideration.

It wasn't a mathematical calculation, but a strategic one. Like playing chess. He was wondering how he could wiggle his way out of check before it became checkmate.

"I know people in this town," he growled. "You have no idea who you're messing with."

"Judges and prosecutors?" I laughed. "So call them. Have me arrested. I'm sure there's a cop around here someplace."

I gestured to the growing crowd of SLMPD officers gathering in the bar. Half of them were watching us. The boss never broke eye contact.

"Go ahead," I urged. "I'd love to see a courtroom. Boy, do I have a story to share. You'll need to pay off federal judges before I'm finished."

Dead quiet. The bodyguard with the broken nose eyeballed his boss, looking confused and overwhelmed, as though his rudimentary brain circuits were melting down under the strain of all this unexpected complexity.

I tapped the trivia card. "In cash," I said. "Clean bills. No funny business. I *will* know."

At last, the boss reached for his beer. He took a long pull, draining half of it. He set the bottle down.

"It'll take some time."

"You have until tomorrow at lunch," I said. "Don't make me add a late charge."

His fingers tightened around the bottle. His jaw clenched so hard I thought his molars might bust. Then he jerked his head, and the bodyguard slid out. The boss followed. He stopped at the edge of the table.

"The campground was a mistake," he said.

"Rogue action," I confirmed. "I know. But they were still your guys, and you're still going to pay for it."

Another bulge of the vein in his head. He leaned close enough that I could smell the Miller on his breath.

"You better pray we don't catch you in a dark alley."

I swallowed beer. And smiled.

"No, buddy. *You* better pray."

17

The boss and his bodyguard departed amid a roar of cammed V-twin engines. I paid my tab and stepped out, watching their tail lights fade. Then I looked the other way, deeper into the darkness. I squinted amid the shadows, searching.

I saw nothing, but I knew it was there. It was a scientific certainty for a pair of reasons. First, because there was nothing in the boss's lifeless gaze that convinced me he was truly ready to accept the fatality of his situation.

And second...because he hadn't asked me where to deliver the payment.

Fair enough.

I fired up the Fat Boy and headed out of town, this time turning west, farther into Missouri. And this time, I rode slowly, signaling at every turn and not stopping until I reached a twenty-four-hour Walmart on the outskirts of a St. Louis suburb. I strolled inside and found my way to the hardware section, where I purchased fifty feet of half-inch twisted nylon rope. It was black, with a test limit of seven hundred pounds. Only forty bucks for the coil.

In the patio section I purchased a quad-pack of fireplace logs, the manufactured kind that light easily and burn for a long time. A little camouflage grease from the hunting department to darken my face and hands.

My last stop was the Walmart's automotive department, where I hefted a trio of tire irons, measuring each for weight and balance. I liked the crooked kind best, with a lug wrench built into the tip. Eighteen inches long, about four pounds in weight. The model I chose came with a rubber grip near the end opposite the lug wrench, a luxury I had yet to encounter but certainly enjoyed.

I grabbed beef jerky and bottled water at the checkout, then I was back on the Fat Boy with the fire logs strapped to the luggage rack, the lug wrench slid between the saddlebags and the frame. I headed deeper into rural Missouri. I didn't have any particular location in mind. I was mostly looking for a rural spot with a few trees around. Someplace with no lights or houses nearby. A quiet, romantic spot.

A place to get personal.

I found the battleground of my choosing at the intersection of a hundred-acre cornfield and a stand of planted pine trees about half that size. A dirt road provided access to both, running along the border of the pines before turning into a wide curve that led directly through the trees for a mile or two, and eventually exited onto a paved county road.

The last house I had passed was two miles back. The only light to join the glow of the Fat Boy's headlamp was that of a half-moon and a few hundred twinkling stars. Parked at the edge of the field, I killed the motor and listened to the whisper of the wind drifting through the pines.

It smelled amazing, a little cool on my skin but still relaxing. Almost soothing.

I looked over my shoulder and listened for the sounds of cars rumbling down the distant two-lane state highway. All was quiet, a near-perfect calm.

But I wasn't fooled. Not for a second.

About twenty yards into the cornfield, I found a clear patch of tilled soil with nothing save random dead cornstalks poking from the dirt. I cleared them away and erected a t-pee structure with my fireplace logs. An application of my lighter ignited all four, and a moment later a healthy blaze burned in the darkened field. I gathered enough stalks and loose dirt to build a body-sized mound next to the fire, then I was back astride the bike and rumbling down the dirt road.

I selected a spot just around the bend in the road where the planted pines were nearly ready to be harvested, about twelve inches in diameter and fifty feet high. The nylon rope looped easily around a trunk on the righthand side of the road. I tied it off about five feet above the ground, then ran it across the road and tied it off the same way on the far side, as tight as I could pull it. I thumped the rope to test the tension, and was rewarded with a dull hum as it vibrated like the G string on my violin.

Good enough.

I rumbled out of the trees and crossed into the edge of the cornfield, two hundred yards from the now-blazing campfire. I killed the motor and switched off the ignition to cut off the headlight, but remained straddled in the saddle, watching.

And waiting.

This time the wait dragged on for nearly half an hour. As engine heat evaporated from the V-twin between my legs I found myself longing for the comfort of the camp fire. It was still going strong, the dense constitution of the artificial fireplace logs holding up nicely. It looked warm. I was starting to shiver.

But I didn't move and I wasn't stressed, because if there's one thing I know about dogs, it's that they *always* lunge for the tasty morsel in the end. They can't help themselves. It's in their very nature—their animal bones.

And I knew a pack of dogs had followed me out of St. Louis. Maybe they'd taken time to bring in reinforcements. To map out a battle plan. To lay a perfect ambush. Whatever the delay, I didn't doubt for a moment—they were coming.

Bring it on.

The first crackle of a motor finally coughed from down the dirt road ten minutes later. Double headlights appeared from over the crest of a field terrace, the burble of distant exhaust joined by the throaty voices of several additional bikes.

The lead machine was a Dyna Fat Bob, a handsome bike that I would regret wrecking. Next in line were a pair of Road Kings, a couple Softails, and then...was that a V-Rod?

Well, how about that. It looked like a special edition model, also, although I couldn't be sure at a distance. The bikes rumbled into a tight pack at the edge of the road. Engines and headlights died, and the crowd of six men dismounted with angry intentionality. Helmets slung down, voices calling in subdued growls that they must have thought very covert.

If I really *had* been sleeping alongside that campfire, I would have heard them coming from a mile away. As it was, I only shook my head in disgust, plucking a long stalk of dead grass and chewing the soft end.

The meatheads marked the dimming campfire with fat, pointing fingers. I observed baseball bats and sidearms. Even a shotgun. They approached with shoulders low, backs bent. Only one of the six seemed to have any clue what he was doing—that was the guy with the shotgun. He walked on the balls of his feet, or tried to.

He was overweight and struggled to maintain his balance in the uneven soil, but he managed the shotgun well. He kept his head up, both eyes open, sweeping his surroundings. I wondered if he had ever been deployed to some violent battlefield on the far side of the planet.

Probably not. If this guy had any semblance of experience in a firefight, there was no way he would be venturing into an open field without a shred of cover to hide behind.

I flicked the kill switch on the bike to *run* mode and clamped down on the clutch. My finger hovered over the ignition switch. I waited until they reached the firepit and the first guy hurtled forward with baseball bat cocked back over his right shoulder. He actually slammed it into the pile of dirt and cornstalks, howling like some kind of coked-out maniac plowing through a wall.

"*Got 'im!*"

I rolled my eyes. I flicked the ignition and mashed the starter button. The Fat Boy thundered to life with a bark so loud I winced. The reverberations of the snarl carried over the open earth and reached my enemy as the bike's giant headlight washed them in an incandescent glow.

18

The reaction was a thing of beauty. Complete confusion descended over their ranks, one man crashing into another, the fool with the bat wheeling around and whacking a buddy straight in the chest. The buddy fell, landing in the fire. He shrieked and thrashed. The other five men pivoted on me as I dropped into first gear and eased out on the clutch.

It was a four-hundred-yard ride to the tree line. The parked Harleys were closer to that bend in the road than I was by a factor of half, but I had the head start. Gunning my bike, I hurled up a rooster tail of loose soil, and then I was off. The shotgun thundered, but at two hundred yards I was perfectly safe. Through my peripheral vision I tracked the progress of all six men now racing for their bikes. One of them looked to be still smoking from the campfire he'd fallen into. The guy with the shotgun was screaming orders.

My front tire crossed off the tractor trail and onto the dirt road just as the voice of six overbuilt motors rumbled to life. I hit third gear and ramped up to forty miles per hour, slinging sand and now leaning into the turn. Pines swallowed me on either side. My headlight bounced, but when I looked ahead I couldn't see the rope.

Black nylon had blended perfectly with the night. I was left with nothing save memory and instinct to time my next lean, throwing my bodyweight into the lefthand grip. The Fat Boy leaned on command, dropping hard toward the packed orange clay. I mashed down on the rear brake, allowing the back tire to swing wide behind me. In the blink of an eye I turned perpendicular to the road, laying the bike so low that the clutch-side floorboard dragged the dirt. A cloud of sand erupted over me, and I passed beneath the rope with inches to spare. I saw it flash across my face as I rocked my head upward. I hurtled on another ten yards, pulling out of the lean and releasing the rear brake, ending the slide. I rose upright again and dropped the transmission into first gear.

Twenty yards farther down the road, I finally stopped. I thumbed the kill switch and deployed the side stand, heart hammering from a dump of adrenaline. I slung one leg off the bike.

Then the dogs were upon me. They roared around the curve in a thunder of exhaust, all rolling on the throttle and screaming into the trees as though their lives depended on it. Four of them led the pack—both Road Kings, the Fat Bob, and the V-Rod. The Softails drew up the rear, struggling through a Harley-generated sandstorm.

Blinded. Helpless. Hurtling headlong into a half-inch wall of nylon.

The rope caught the lead riders at shoulder height, throwing them backwards as bikes toppled sideways. In an instant headlights were bouncing, bikes colliding, voices shrieking. Half the motors died and the pair of Softails rocketed into the wreckage. One rider flew from his saddle, hurtling right over his handle bars, headed for the ditch. Another was run over, a Softail tire crushing his shin as a screech rent the air.

I watched from twenty yards away, a little overcome with the devastation of my own handiwork. I could have left them right there, hopping back aboard the Fat Boy and roaring away before they knew which way was up.

I could have—but I wouldn't. I'd made the boss an offer. He was properly informed of the consequences should he reject that offer. Now I had to honor my commitment.

The tire iron slid out of the gap between saddle bag and fender. I gripped it by the rubber handle and met the first meathead at the side of his mangled Road King. He was halfway to his feet, scrambling with the revolver in his belt when the tire iron struck. A blow to his jaw shattered the bone, sending teeth shooting into the trees. The next strike wrecked his left shoulder. He caught my boot to his nose, and then he was down. I spun to find the captain fumbling with his shotgun. Before he could reach the trigger, I caught the weapon by its barrel and shoved the muzzle straight into the ground. The gun thundered and dirt erupted in a cloud. He couldn't see a thing. I couldn't see a thing.

But I remembered where his temple was, and the tire iron found it. Two down, four to go. I clocked the guy with the busted leg in the back of his empty skull as he fought to escape. He collapsed into unconsciousness just as that baseball bat whistled toward me with the wrath of a dive bomber. I sidestepped it with ease, catching the guy off balance as he struggled to extricate his boot from beneath the V-Rod.

He was out of time. He knew it as my boot crashed into

the side of his knee. The joint shattered, and he toppled with a shriek.

Then the last two guys were on me just the way the final two contestants in the fight ring had been. One came from my left, the other from behind.

I side-stepped them both, raking the tire iron across the nearest guy's stomach. He fumbled with a knife as the second guy lunged for the fallen shotgun. He made it only halfway before my boot landed on his spine, hard enough to fracture ribs. By the time I had him pinned down, the gut-struck guy had recovered his wind and retrieved his knife.

He should have spent the time running. I broke his hand with the tire iron, and wiped the nose off his face with my next raking sweep. Clocking him in the top of the head as he tumbled, I then backhanded the guy beneath my boot with the crook of my weapon—straight against the temple.

I wasn't sure how much time had passed since the moment I first engaged. I was winded, and I used the still-taut rope to steady myself as I kicked free of the carnage and found my way to the V-Rod.

The air smelled heavy with a blended stench of blood and gasoline. I found the lone survivor still pinned down by his bike, body twisted awkwardly to one side. Somehow, the V-Rod was still running. I cut the motor with a jab of the bloody tire iron against the kill switch. I spat into the sand. Then I squatted.

The survivor scrambled, still fighting to get back to his feet. I rapped him in the back of the head, just hard enough to stun him. He turned desperate eyes on me, a short beard infested with dirt and blood splatter.

"Please, man! Don't kill me. It weren't my idea!"

I didn't recognize him. He was just another anonymous

stand-in for the universal face of greed, abuse, exploitation...corruption.

"Shut up," I snarled. "You don't want me to give you something to cry about."

To his credit, he obeyed. Still quaking with pain but no longer pleading. I placed the tire iron under his throat, forcing his chin up.

"You know who I am?" I asked.

He choked. "Not really."

"That's fine. But you know why they sent you?"

A nod.

"Terrific. So now I want you to listen closely. You're going back to your boss with a message. This is a legal matter, so details are important. Okay? I need absolute accuracy."

"O-okay."

"Tell him he has one more chance to settle out of court, otherwise this thing goes to trial. Tell him that my initial offer is off the table. I'm now doubling it. Okay?"

Wild eyes flicked left and right. Maybe he was looking for a friend, or a weapon. He found neither. I jabbed with the tire iron.

"Okay!" He coughed. "I hear you. Settle out of court. Double the amount."

I nodded. Stood. Twirled the tire iron. I looked down at the V-Rod, now covered in dirt, with a dented tank, but still a beautiful machine.

"Nice bike," I said. Then I turned back for the Fat Boy, holstered the tire iron next to the saddlebag, and roared toward St. Louis.

19

I made it to the outskirts of University City, riding east along I-64 before I picked up my next tail—and unlike the last one, this wasn't the slow plod of a distant meathead riding a heavy cruiser. The light first appeared in my rearview mirror as a blob of bright white, an LED glow accompanied by the nasty snarl of a high compression engine. I thought it was a lone crotch rocket at first, a late-night rider eager to tear up some empty highways. I moved to the right, offering an opportunity for the faster machine to pass.

But the blob in my mirror moved with me, closing until it was identifiable as an inky dark shadow leaning low over straight handlebars. A small figure. A fat front tire. A horizontal, rectangular headlight.

I didn't wait around for additional details. Dumping on the throttle, I gave the Fat Boy's modified engine full rein to run like the wind. The front suspension stretched as the rear tire dug in, and a moment later I was splitting lanes between semi-trucks with the speedometer clipping toward triple digits.

And still, that white-hot blob followed. With graceful ease, the unidentified motorcycle streaked between the semi-trucks and zipped past a minivan. The rider was right on me, matching the Fat Boy's speed with ease and gobbling up the ground between us.

Wind tore at my exposed face, flooding the half-helmet and tugging against my chin strap. My heart rate spiked as I checked my mirror, the mathematics of my situation boiling down to a simple inevitability. This maniac was going to catch up—quickly. Whatever happened after that, I liked my odds of surviving a hundred-mile-per-hour crash a lot less than my odds of pounding six fat guys into the dirt with a tire iron.

Get off the highway.

It was the logical answer, and my next opportunity was racing toward me in a blur. An exit led off the interstate, down a ramp and into an industrial district due west of downtown St. Louis. I saw the sign as a glimmer of green standing two lanes to my right and not technically within reach.

I took it anyway, not signaling, only glancing once over my right shoulder before veering hard right. I blazed in front of a semi-truck, hugging close to the bike's fuel tank as the truck laid on its air horn. It rushed by me just as I passed into the turn lane, missing the safety barrier by barely a yard. As my body ran hot with adrenaline, I downshifted and raced down the ramp toward an intersection marked by a red traffic light. An overpass streaked to my left, a four-lane city street blocking my path. Warehouses and manufacturing facilities surrounded by high chain-link fences stood on all sides. I squealed to a stop at the white line and looked instinctively upward and to the left—back toward the highway.

My pursuer had stopped on the overpass, modular helmet rotating upward as they peered over the crash barrier, down onto the four-lane. I couldn't make out the face through the haze of flickering street lights and distance, but I knew our gazes locked. I dropped back into first and goosed the throttle. The rider closed their helmet and spun their bike around—they were headed backward along the emergency lane, racing for the same off ramp I had taken.

I turned right on instinct, blowing through the intersection just as my light turned green. I opted for the inside lane, taking advantage of the break in traffic to ramp the Fat Boy back up to speed. I ran the next red light and hurtled across a pair of railroad tracks, now lost amid the industrial district. It swallowed me on all sides. I looked into the rearview mirror...

And there was the bike, rider leaned so low that they melted into the frame, helmet only inches above the handlebars, that flood of white LED glaring in my face. I'd gained half a mile of breathing room with my stunt at the off ramp, but that gap was evaporating right before my eyes, the blob of bright white sucking ever closer.

Fine, I thought. *You want some? Come get some.*

Half a mile ahead the open entrance of a gravel lot was marked by a white and red sign—it was a logistics company. A trucking yard. The gate stood open, and just beyond it I observed long rows of parked day cabs and box trailers, their noses pointed toward the street. A metal building stood next to them, maybe a warehouse or a mechanic's shop. There was a mobile office trailer. An American flag flapped atop a forty-foot pole.

Good enough.

I laid on the brakes and spun toward the gate, hurling gravel through the turn. In my rearview mirror I observed my tail slowing to follow, but I still had a couple hundred yards of breathing space to exploit. Roaring up to the entrance of the mechanic's shop, I cut the engine and deployed the Fat Boy's side stand. I pulled the tire iron from the rear fender, dry blood now crumbling around the grip. I swung off the bike and slipped between a pair of semi-trucks just as my pursuer growled through the gate.

The tail bike's RPMs had slowed considerably since I had turned into the trucking yard. The rider was taking their time, easing to a stop. The motor rumbled on for another ten seconds, a faster and higher-pitched tempo than I was used to hearing from the big, slow Harleys that had chased me before. I couldn't clearly see the bike as I rolled beneath a box trailer, passing to the next aisle between trucks and returning to my feet.

I listened. The motorcycle cut off. A boot crunched on the ground. Then a sickeningly familiar sound broke the stillness—the metallic *click-click* of a pistol being charged.

I pressed my back against the side of a box trailer, maneuvering my legs so that the trailer's rear wheels shielded them. I listened for footsteps.

I didn't hear any. The loudest sound was the methodic tick of the two motorcycle engines slowly cooling. At first I thought my adversary remained frozen in front of the trucks, but when I edged to the nose of the nearest semi and risked a glance beyond, nobody was there.

My Fat Boy rested right where I'd left it, front forks

cocked to the left. The pursuer's bike rested twenty yards farther on, a squat and muscular little machine with fat tires and low-slung handlebars. Inky black with bronze trim, twin tailpipes, and a Harley Davidson logo emblazoned on the tank. It looked nothing like the other bikes that had trailed me out to the cornfield, and yet I recognized this squat, muscular monster.

I'd seen it before, and the realization gave me a little jolt.

What?

I didn't have time to finish the thought. Just as positive identification cleared my brain, a thumping creak finally alerted me to my enemy's location. It came not from around me, but from *above* me. The sag of a box trailer roof under bodyweight, followed by the *pop* of fiberglass restoring its shape as that bodyweight was removed. I instinctively slung myself sideways, headed for the underside of the nearest box trailer as I envisioned that handgun raining death from above.

I never made it. My invisible foe appeared like a shadow from directly above, moving in a flash across the top of the same trailer I was scrambling for cover beneath. In a blink of black, they dropped, hurtling right off the edge of trailer's roof and bouncing off the side of the adjacent trailer on their way down.

It wasn't a human move—the stunt was more reminiscent of an acrobatic house cat, and it was executed so quickly that I never had time to roll beneath the trailer for cover. My mind computed the geometry and knew I would find myself on my knees just as that handgun orbited to obtain a clear shot.

I would be vulnerable, helpless. Riddled with gunfire.

I turned instead, launching out of my squat and pivoting

toward the oncoming blur of black. The tire iron arced in my right hand, slicing through the night air. The helmeted form of my attacker struck the gravel like a feather and bounced right off it. They were thin and lithe, operating just outside the reach of my tire iron as I fell back on my support foot, bracing myself against the side of the trailer. The tire iron missed my enemy's helmeted head by millimeters, and then they were on me. A gloved hand shot out and drove my striking hand left, ramming it into the side of the trailer. I almost lost my grip on the tire iron. The next strike came as a rabbit kick that landed hard in my right shin. The boot was steel toed and smashed easily through my swimmer's muscles, crashing into defenseless bone. I stumbled, caught off balance and toppling. I flailed for support but found none. The only option left to me was to stagger backward, awkwardly swatting with the tire iron.

The black shadow dodged the blow with ease. I regained my feet a yard back and braced myself for the lunge. The tire iron was cocked and ready. I was going to hurtle myself like a pouncing jungle cat, undermining my enemy's speed and agility with a battleship's worth of sheer weight and force.

But just as my muscles bunched, the gaping black muzzle of a handgun leveled with the bridge of my nose. The weapon didn't so much as twitch. The face behind the tinted helmet visor spoke in a dull, female snarl.

"Don't move."

I froze on the gravel, knuckles white around the grip of the tire iron, looking down the blackened steel slide of a Glock 19. The figure behind the weapon stood rock steady, breath whistling through the chin vent of her helmet.

"Drop it," she said.

I hesitated, noting her index finger curled around the

bladed trigger. Just a breath away from splitting my melon with a mushrooming copper-jacketed slug.

And yet she hadn't fired...not yet. *Why?*

I relaxed my shoulders, not advancing, and also not dropping the tire iron. The Glock's point of aim remained fixated on my nose, not wavering for a moment. The woman's breathing calmed, and I pictured the face back at the fight club.

Dark hair. Crystal eyes. A stunning beauty.

"We should talk," I said.

A snort of soft laughter, but no other response, and no repeated command for me to drop the tire iron. The woman wasn't moving at all.

"You gonna shoot me?" I said.

No answer. No directions. I squinted, lifting my hand to wipe away the sweat draining out from under the half-helmet I still wore. It happened to be the hand grasping the tire iron.

"*Don't* move!"

Now the voice snapped. The finger tightened. I froze, lifting my fingers in surrender.

"Okay...no problem."

I lowered the tire iron, observing the com unit mounted to the left side of the woman's helmet flashing green. She reached up with her free hand and mashed a button. Grunted something I couldn't quite hear, yet somehow felt that I recognized.

Was that a...

I never finished the thought. From a few miles away, a new sound arrested my attention. A soft whine. A rising wail mixed with a higher-pitched pulse.

My body relaxed, a self-deprecating grin stretching my

sweat-streaked face. I looked over her shoulder, beyond the fence, back toward the highway. I could already detect the blink of blue lights reflected against street signs.

"Seriously?" I said.

I couldn't be sure, but I thought the full-face helmet tilted just a couple degrees. I imagined the woman smiling, and when she spoke, I thought I heard the smile also.

"You're a lot of trouble."

I snorted a laugh. "I'm not even getting started."

The first SLMPD car growled to a stop on the street outside the gate, a doorpost-mounted spotlight washing over us with the wrath of the midday sun. Two doors popped open. Cops stepped out, moving with urgency but not emergency.

They hadn't yet drawn their weapons. They were speaking instead into radios. Waiting for the second unit to arrive...

Stacking mistakes upon mistakes.

The helmeted woman took a half-step back. She twisted her head, thumbing up the visor to call over her shoulder to the incoming cops. Taking her eyes off me for barely a second, a blink of time so minuscule that it was gone as quickly as it came.

But I'd seen it coming, and I exploited it accordingly. The tire iron flicked up, crashing leftward and arcing toward the side of the Glock. Even as her eyes caught the movement and those cat-like reflexes kicked into gear, I was already hurling my body to the right. The crook of the tire iron struck the slide of the handgun and shoved the muzzle to my left. Her finger constricted the five-point-five pounds necessary to deploy the striker, and the gun belched fire. A hot slug zipped past my left arm and slammed into the side of the trailer. The cops scrambled back toward their car, hands flailing for sidearms as I launched myself forward.

I struck the woman head-down, my half-helmet landing in her chest with the force of a battering ram. The Glock flew out of her hand. I dropped the tire iron and plowed right through her, not stopping even as she hit the gravel and my boots fell dangerously close to crushing her ribcage. I threw myself over her body, and then I was free.

From behind the open doors of the squad car, the voices of the cops shouted for me to stop. They threatened to engage.

I knew they wouldn't shoot. Whatever the woman had said during her 911 call, they couldn't have nearly enough information about the situation to engage an unarmed man. I reached the Fat Boy and was mashing the starter as soon as the side stand was up. The motor churned, and I released the clutch under half throttle.

Gravel flew. The back tire spun wide. From behind me a voice called "*Stop him!*"

But it was too late. In another second, I was hurtling toward the gate and the cop car parked across it. The two St. Louis policemen did the smart thing and dove for cover even as I exploded through the gap between their front bumper and the gatepost.

Then I was back on an open street. A second police car raced toward me and I easily swerved around it. Cold night air tore at my lungs...

And I was in the wind again.

20

It wasn't until I reached the highway and lost myself in a tangle of late-night traffic that I allowed myself to breathe easily. My body was so strung out on adrenaline and survival hormones that I hadn't processed any clear thoughts during those harrowing moments between my arrival at the trucking lot and my escape through the barricade of police cars.

No thoughts—just instinctual reactions. Fast and brutal enough to bring me out alive, although I couldn't deny that if the woman had wanted me dead, I would be. She had me in her sights. She had her finger on the trigger. It was checkmate.

But she hadn't fired. Why? The six meatheads I had pounded amid the planted pines certainly seemed eager to bury me. Were her orders different?

Or was there something else at play? Something more complex?

I had a pretty good idea, but as that supercharge of survival juices faded away, exhaustion was finally crashing in. I'd had a very long day, stacked on top of very little rest the night prior. I needed shuteye, and I needed it in a place where I could be reasonably certain of being undisturbed for at least six hours.

Motel.

It was the logical next step. The campground obviously wasn't safe, despite the posse of shotgun-toting ex-military guys begging for the chance to avenge Ms. Dottie's petunias. It was too predictable a spot. I needed something random, something nondescript. Something like one of the rat traps where I had busted the gang's prostitution ring.

I found what I was looking for south of St. Louis, nestled near the intersections of I-55 and I-270. It was certainly a rat trap, but the rent was fifty bucks a night and there was a parking spot next to a weed-infested swimming pool where my Fat Boy would be out of sight of either highway. I parked and took a room on the second floor, barricading my door with a cigarette-burned armchair before finally stripping out of my sweaty clothes and inspecting the shower for use. It was moldy—seriously so. I decided to pass and embrace my own stink.

I didn't think too hard about the problem at hand. I didn't feel that I needed to. I already had an inkling of the obvious, and even if I was wrong, clarity would come in the morning. I stretched out on top of the covers, trying not to consider how many seedy characters would have done the same, and turned out the lights. I stared at the ceiling and ignored the throb of my steel-toe-obliterated right shin, and the burn of my gouged right eye.

In three minutes flat, I was dead to the world.

I SLEPT BETTER than I had any right to, not opening my eyes until the clock on the nightstand read 9:21. The blackout curtains stretched across the motel room's front window had done their job, allowing only a slice of sunlight that revealed crimson stains on the blue carpet. I blinked the sleep away, reluctant to dismiss the comforting dreams that had so long enraptured me in contented slumber.

They weren't new dreams—at least, the subject wasn't new. Maybe the context was. I dreamed of my late fiancée, as I often had over the past three-plus years since I first met her. That glowing star of a creature, transcending from another world into a shabby Phoenix bar. All smiles, all bright eyes, all light on her feet. Not a girl, not naïve or stupid. Simply pure in a way almost no adult can be.

It was instantly attractive, a moment I will never forget. Yet that specific moment hadn't visited my dreams nearly so often as the moment that occurred several months later in the hallway of a Phoenix elementary school...amid gunshots and blood spray.

I closed my eyes and attempted to retreat into that bar, back to that first moment. I pictured every detail of the place, every particular of the music, and the drink in my hand, and the smell of blended perfume and cologne colliding with raw liquor.

It was *almost* real. Almost...resurrected.

I opened my eyes again, breathing out a long breath, resigned to the inevitability that it was only a dream—and from this moment forward always would be. I placed myself back in the present, back in the gritty reality of South St. Louis, and shelved considerations of the imaginary world for an inventory of the physical.

Fingers and toes? Present and accounted for. I could hear

and I could see despite the tender bruising around my right eye. Unfortunately, I could also smell. The room stank of sweat and cigarette smoke.

Now for the real questions, the inspection I knew would render disappointing results. I flexed my elbows and shoulders and experienced predictable stiffness. I rocked my hips and loosened cramped muscles.

Then I tested my right leg and bit back a curse. Pain coursed up from my shin, reminding me that the steel-toed strike from the night before had been anything but a dream.

Stupid jerk. A part of me regretted batting the woman's sidearm away instead of testing the integrity of her full-face helmet against the crook of the tire iron. I make it a rule to not fight women...but I hadn't picked this fight, and despite escaping, I couldn't consider myself the victor, either.

Planting both feet on the floor, I embraced the pain and flexed my leg to drive back a little of the stiffness. I breathed through my mouth, steady inhale-exhale patterns designed to calm my mind. I cleared the clutter of dreams and fantasies away and withdrew to the night before. To the conclusion that had entered my mind even as I screamed past that barricade of cops and broke for freedom.

Probable? I wasn't sure. But logical?

Definitely.

I splashed water on my face and redressed. The diner across the street offered a full menu but I passed on the breakfast, settling for coffee. I didn't have an appetite yet. I spent the time instead contemplating the problem and devising an experiment to test my theory. I could think of only one possible strategy, and I didn't like it. It was the kind of scenario that left my back against the wall, vulnerable if things spilled out of control. Or if I was wrong.

Then again, I knew I wasn't wrong, and I also saw no path forward except to confront the elephant in the room. I could keep smashing my way through the gang's soldiers, leaving one after another in a tangled mass of shattered joints and wrecked motorcycles. Eventually, I would probably get my settlement. Or take it by force.

But that plan only worked so long as the obstacles in my way were justifiably smashable at the crook of a tire iron. Cops—presumably innocent cops, legitimately engaged in the pursuit of their oath to protect and serve St. Louis—were no such obstacles. Not unless and until I knew for certain that they were crooked, and even then, there was a special procedure that required more nuance and care than my full-force dismantlement of the gang's meatheads.

For the moment, I found myself backed into a corner, with limited options to proceed. I could always cut bait, of course. Pick up my truck early and head out of town, leaving Spencer Meyers to his financial problems and the gang to their lucrative industry.

But that wasn't happening—no chance. Not only because Spencer needed the cash, and I was owed the cash, but also because I had been pushed. Manhandled. Threatened. *Bullied.*

And I don't tolerate bullies.

I left a five-dollar bill on the table for my coffee and returned to the street. My appetite was awakening, but I wanted to topple a few dominos before I indulged in an official meal break. Besides, Rusty's place didn't open for another ninety minutes, and I was unapologetically addicted.

First I needed a change of clothes—I was filthy and feeling it. A Walmart would suffice, with a bathroom where I could conduct a foxhole shower with wet wipes. Then I had a decision to make. A left turn or a right. Go with my gut, or play it safe?

It was an easy answer. I hadn't been born to take it safe, and by the time I was clad in a pre-washed pair of Walmart jeans complete with a t-shirt and a fresh application of deodorant, I was ready to roll the dice.

I phoned the St. Louis Police Department and turned myself in.

21

The woman on the motorcycle arrived outside of Rusty's Rib Bar just as a half rack slathered in spicy barbeque sauce with a side of potato salad and collard greens came to rest with a clack on my picnic-style table.

"Third time this week," Rusty scoffed. "You'll be ready fo' the slaughterhouse yo'self in a few weeks."

"It's a disease, Rusty. I'm the real victim here."

The big man broke into a raucous chuckle and headed back behind the counter, launching into a Charles Ray classic—"Hit the Road, Jack".

I sipped sweet iced tea, ignoring my meal as I watched the woman swing off the Harley. I had identified the bike the night before with a quick Google search on my new burner phone. It was Harley Davidson's brand new "Sportster S", an absolute rocket of a machine built around a twelve-hundred-fifty-two-cubic-centimeter engine which, according to the website, produced ninety-three foot pounds of torque and a hundred and twenty-one peak horsepower.

Well, that explained why I hadn't been able to outrun the crystal-eyed maniac now stopping to survey my parked Fat Boy. What it *didn't* explain was why she had been chasing me.

At the behest of a violent motorcycle gang? I thought not.

The woman tugged her helmet off, flicking her head to clear wispy brown hair from her face before she looked through the restaurant's open-air windows to my position at the picnic table. I lifted a hand in a casual wave, sipping tea through my straw.

Those twin pools of crystal turned icy cold despite the sunshine. She planted the helmet beneath one leather-jacketed arm and plowed through the restaurant's screen door, flatly ignoring the greeting of a cashier as she approached my table.

She stopped at the end of it. I was just distributing thick barbeque sauce over the length of my rack of ribs with the flat of a knife. Rusty was generous with his sauce, but not very equitable in its application.

"I should put my boot through your jaw."

Her first words were spoken barely above a snarl, carrying a generic sort of Americana accent that could place her roots anywhere from the Rust Belt to the Rockies.

I looked up. I smiled. "Wasn't my shin enough?"

Tanned cheeks flushed. Her gaze traveled through the windows and across the street. I didn't need to lift my head to know what she was looking at—it was an unmarked patrol car, parked in the lot of a burger joint across the street. Very surreptitious, easily missed by the average citizen.

But not by me. I picked it out like a horsefly in a banana split, because it was exactly the spot I would have picked for a stakeout back in my policing days.

"I see them," I said. "No need to threaten. Why don't you have a seat and we'll get down to business?"

A fuming glare. She spoke through her teeth. "I don't know who you think I am, but—"

"A fed, definitely," I said. "You could be a cop. Maybe you were at some point. That would explain your use of the ten-ninety-five code last night—*subject in custody*. But most cops don't carry Glock 19s. That's a fed's weapon, and pretty much all your behavior smacked of Quantico, anyway. So while you could be DEA or ATF, my money's on the good old *FBI*."

Silence. She didn't so much as blink. I shoveled collard greens into my mouth and savored the blend of buttery perfection with subtle bitterness. Rusty cooked his collards with rib bones, not ham bones. I appreciated the stylistic choice almost as much as the masterpiece of a result.

"You can deny it, of course," I said. "But it's a waste of time. The only reason you knew where to find me was because I called the SLMPD and reported my intention to be here. I'm guessing that they've got a special unit assigned to work with you." I jabbed my fork toward the unmarked sedan across the street. "Those will be the same guys you called last night, asking them to send squad cars to arrest me. The patrol officers who responded didn't draw their weapons when they exited their vehicles because they weren't aware they were walking into a violent situation— that information was withheld, because the special unit assigned to work with you is limiting all information concerning your identity and your mission. They have to... because you're under cover. *Deep* under cover. Is that about right?"

I smiled and sipped tea. A full ten seconds passed as those crystal eyes swirled with repressed rage.

At last she leaned down, one hand on the table, her free arm still cradling the helmet. She spoke slowly, menace dripping so heavily from her words I almost wanted to shield my meal.

"I'm going to say this once. You're a problem. For me, and a lot of other people. I need you to *leave*. Do it now, do it quietly, and that can be the end of it."

I considered, stabbing my tea with the straw to extricate flavor from a drowned lemon slice. I sipped. Swished. Shook my head.

"No."

"No?" Twin black eyebrows shot skyward.

"No." I repeated. "I reject your offer."

The crimson flush of her cheeks redoubled. She reached for the front pocket of her torn black jeans. A cell phone protruded there. I held up a hand.

"Before you call the cavalry—and blow your cover—I think we should talk."

She stopped, phone held motionless. She spoke through her teeth. "And why would I be blowing my—"

As soon as she said it, she knew it was a mistake. She broke off mid-sentence, but the cat was out of the bag. Confirmation had occurred.

I grinned, jabbing a fork full of potato salad her way.

"I knew you were a fed. But to answer your question, you'd be blowing your cover because the moment I reach lockup, I'll start singing like a canary. I have it on good authority that the halls of justice in beautiful St. Louis are populated by corrupt judges and prosecutors. It wouldn't be long before word reached the gang...a sad story of vicious betrayal. One sassy Harley girl with a nasty secret."

I shrugged. She still hadn't blinked. Her eyes looked ready to pop. I wiped my mouth.

"Alternatively, you could spare me ten minutes, and we could reach an understanding. One cop to another."

My smile faded at that last comment. I held her gaze. I didn't blink either. From the kitchen behind the counter Rusty stopped singing, and I had the distinct impression that he was watching us.

A slow ten seconds dragged by. Then she reached a decision. I knew it by the glint of resignation in her eyes, blended with just a trace of curiosity. She settled onto the bench opposite me. She set the helmet down with a slam and tapped one finger on the tabletop.

She looked something like a spring compressed to the point of molecular failure, just begging to be set free.

"You're a cop?" she said, at last.

I shook my head, biting into a rib. "Ex-cop. Detective, technically. Homicide division, Phoenix, Arizona. Before that, Army. And you?"

No answer. I wiped barbeque sauce from my face. She lifted my cup of tea without asking and drank half of it.

"If you're a cop," she said, "or *were* a cop, then you should respect the sovereignty of an investigation...and stay the hell away from it."

"Normally, I do. This time is an exception, for multiple reasons. I didn't pick this fight. It was shoveled into my lap. Some people I care about were caught in the crossfire. So I'm leveling the scales."

A soft snort. "You're a vigilante."

"If you like. I prefer the term *city-wrecker*, because that's exactly what I'm going to do if I don't achieve the results I want."

"The payout," she sneered.

I smiled. "So the boss talks to you. Very good. How long have you been under cover?"

No answer.

"Whatever you're doing," I said, "you clearly aren't getting very far. I pinned them on drugs, illegal gambling, and prostitution within twenty-four hours. That leads me to believe that you're investigating something else...something much more insidious. I'm not here to derail that. In fact, I could easily be persuaded to lend a hand. Call it a trade, if you like. Quid pro quo."

She leaned close, speaking through her teeth again. "I don't strike deals with *money-grabbing* vigilantes."

I cleaned my teeth with my tongue, weighing her words and measuring the sincerity in her gaze. It wasn't the term "vigilante" that draw her ire. No, that disgust was reserved for the other adjective in her statement—that bit about *money grabbing*.

She thought I was an opportunist. A greedy, exploitive criminal. It was what the boss had told her about my settlement demands. She didn't understand the context.

"It's not the way it looks," I said. "I'm not mining for gold, I'm recovering damages. Regardless, you either trust me or you don't. I honestly don't care either way. But I won't stop this campaign until damages are duly recovered, and if you try to have me arrested a second time, your cover is history. That's an ironclad guarantee."

No answer. I finished my meal in silence while she sat and stared. The woman had self-moisturizing eyes. I had never encountered somebody who could go without blinking for minutes on end.

But behind that empty stare, I saw the wheels turning.

The considerations, frustrations, desperations. She was a federal agent, all right. And she was way up the creek without a paddle. It was the only reasonable explanation for why she hadn't put a gun to my head and had me dragged downtown.

My threat of blowing her cover was out of her control. I could be prosecuted for obstruction of justice. Her bosses couldn't hold her responsible.

No, her concerns weren't about protocol and they weren't about job security. There was *need* in her brilliant gaze. The deep, personal, intrinsic kind. A consuming motivator I knew all too well and had some recent experience with down in Arkansas.

She couldn't walk away from this case, no matter how hairy I made things. She had to see it through. She was painted into a corner.

And that left my way as the only way.

I finished the last rib and wiped my lips, restraining a burp. I polished off the sweet tea. Pecan pie popped into my brain like the unwelcome cravings of an addict.

"You were a cop?" she asked.

I grunted.

"Details. Now."

Her voice was flat. I sighed and began with my name, recounting all the particulars of my military and law enforcement careers, sticking to the pertinent details and glossing right over the most colorful parts. The portions where "city wrecking" had occurred. I wasn't sure if she bought any of it, and I didn't much care. I had only enough respect for her predicament to offer the same information that I myself would have expected had the shoe been on the other foot.

I finished. She sat quietly. Her phone buzzed, and I looked out the window to the unmarked sedan. The cops were getting bored, maybe fed up.

Lifting the phone, she shot off a quick text message. A moment later the car pulled away. Then she stood.

"Wait here."

She was gone for the better part of an hour, stepping far enough out into the parking lot that I couldn't overhear the phone calls she was making, or look over her shoulder to see what web searches she was conducting. Sitting by myself at the table, slowly consuming another slice of pecan pie, I remained relaxed and gave her the time. I already knew what she was doing. I thought it was a good sign, even though what she would find when she looked up my name felt like an invasion of privacy.

At last she returned, phone in her pocket, helmet under one arm. When she stared at me something had changed in her eyes. They were still intently focused. But not quite angry or harsh.

Almost a little sympathetic.

"So you ride, huh?"

"Now and then."

A derisive grunt. "See if you can keep up."

22

Whatever her name was—she still hadn't said—she rode hard. Even harder than the night before, cranking the squat little Harley to max throttle almost directly out of the gate. I scrambled to follow, pushing the Fat Boy as we departed South St. Louis and raced across the Mississippi River. In seconds we were back in Illinois, rushing past the entrance of the Purple Crane Campground and turning north. We hopped up onto I-55 and she gave the Sportster S its head, leaning low over the handlebars as though it were a raw sport bike and hitting a hundred miles per hour with ease.

I swung in behind and worked the much heavier Fat Boy to its limits, unable to fully keep pace but at least keeping her within sight. After half an hour and nearly forty miles of hard riding, she took an exit in the middle of nowhere and swung onto a two-lane county road. Soon the riding transitioned from drag-strip speed to switch-backing technical turns surrounded by forest and low hills. She seemed familiar with each of them, frequently dragging her foot pegs as she stressed the Sportster S to its limits.

A real daredevil...or maybe a heavy heart with a death wish.

I gave her plenty of space and took the turns a little slower, dragging my own floorboards on occasion but not coming nearly so close to colliding with oncoming traffic. After another ten miles she finally slowed, the candy bar tail light glaring red as her righthand turn signal clicked on. I followed suit, and we departed the blacktop. She slowed to under twenty miles an hour as we rumbled across loose gravel, then rutted clay. There were no street signs and no mailboxes. Trees hung low over the washed-out road, their finger-like limbs occasionally brushing my shoulder as I swerved to navigate amidst them.

The drive terminated in a small clearing. I killed my motor beneath an oak tree and sat gazing around what had once been a hunting camp. All the signs were there—the fire pit, the basketball goal converted into a skinning truss, the pile of sun-bleached deer antlers gathered against the side of a woodshed.

At the center of the complex was a shabby little cabin with a slouching front porch. A metal roof laden with dry leaves. Windows covered over in dust and forest gunk. No visible power lines, and likely no running water. The outhouse constructed beyond the woodshed appeared authentic.

I glanced across the lot to where my host was swinging off her bike, gloves peeling away and modular helmet finding a resting place on the Harley's righthand grip. She cast a long glance at me, then approached through the leaves. They crunched beneath her riding boots, and I noticed that most of the yard appeared completely undisturbed by vehicle traffic. In fact, the only tire marks I could see anywhere were singular, and fat. The signature of the Sportster S.

Stopping alongside my bike, she put her hands on her hips, riding gloves wadded against her jeans. She stared me down another long minute. Then she sighed.

"I'm Riley," she said. "Riley Vaughn. And yes...I'm FBI."

I grunted, dismounting. I extended a hand. "Pleased to meet you. Just call me Mason."

She shook once. I liked the grip. It was plenty strong, but reflected more grace than a man's handshake.

"You're investigating the gang?" I said.

A grunt. "For seven months."

"What's the Bureau's interest?"

A pause. Riley tilted her head toward the cabin and I followed her. On the front porch she fumbled for keys to a simple padlock holding the door closed. Just before she opened it, she looked over her shoulder.

"All kidding aside, I'm only doing this for two reasons. First, your story checks out. Second, I'm seriously short on options and you've put me in a heck of a corner. Believe me when I tell you that if you jeopardize what I'm about to show you, I'll kill you."

She meant it. I could see it in her eyes, although I suspected there might be a third reason why she had elected to trust me...something else I'd seen in her eyes. I decided to leave that issue at rest and simply nodded. Riley opened the door. She led me inside.

The place consisted of only one room, with windows facing the front and back yards and a stone fireplace built against the lefthand wall. Hardwood floors scarred by age and use supported a card table, a couple of cabinets, two chairs, and a cot with a wadded-up sleeping bag piled on top of it. Butcher's paper covered the inside of the windows. A series of battery-powered LED lanterns hung from hooks screwed into the pitched ceiling. Riley flicked them on individually, shedding a bright white glow over the table, the dirty dishes, the open suitcase resting next to the cot...

And the murder board. Well, it probably wasn't a murder board. The FBI no doubt had their own name for the mess of photographs, notes, and connecting lines spread across the wood-paneled wall opposing the fireplace, but back in Phoenix we would have called it an MB—the strategic battle map where all the facts were arranged, the gaps highlighted, and the questions clarified.

I pocketed my hands and approached the display without permission, glancing over photographs of several characters and locations I was already familiar with. There was the boss—the dead-eyed guy from the fight club, whose legal name was apparently Jerome Withers. Displayed beneath him were his lieutenants, a half dozen of them. Then came the locations: the fight club, a pair of drug dens —including the one I had already handed off to the DEA— and at least one brothel that I had yet to discover.

There were dates and times. A plethora of notes inscribed with incredibly precise handwriting. Lines connecting people to places and places to events. Note cards and schedules. Phone numbers and questions catalogued by subject.

It was impressive. My old partner at the PPD would have salivated over the organization and attention to detail. Yet it was Greek to me, not because I didn't understand the machinations of investigatory work at the FBI level, but because I simply didn't care to.

You can fight to crack a case the slow, methodical—and legal—way...or you can simply toss the whole mess into a bonfire and stand by with a shotgun to obliterate whatever runs out. The further I drifted from my heritage in law enforcement, the fonder I became of the bonfire method.

"What are you looking for?" I said, cutting right to the chase.

Riley stood with arms folded, sharp eyes cutting over my head to survey her displayed investigation. She took her time answering.

"They call themselves the *Gateway Hounds*. They're a motorcycle club, technically. Not a gang."

"Six and half a dozen," I said. "All the worst gangs call themselves clubs. What are they up to?"

"Ostensibly? The usual street crime. There's the fight club, the prostitution, the drugs. They're also running a substantial fencing operation, moving everything from electronics to rare collectables. They have a network of pawn shops involved. It's quite a spiderweb."

"Sounds like enough to take them out," I said.

Riley shook her head. "Only the foot soldiers. The lower level." She advanced to the wall and plucked a single photograph from beneath a push pin. She handed it to me. "There's an entire echelon of leadership above the motorcycle gang. Half a dozen bad actors who pull the strings of the entire organization. We know their names, we know that they're involved—but we can't prove it. They're too thoroughly insulated."

I squinted at the photograph. The fat guy pictured in it was clean shaven and wore his hair down to his shoulders beneath a cowboy hat. White vest, gray pants. He looked like a mixture of Colonel Sanders and the villain from an old-school cowboy show.

"Carter Custer," Riley said. "The *real* boss."

"Who's that guy?" I pointed to the photograph of the dead-eyed man labeled Jerome Withers.

"Jerry's the go-between," Riley said. "Like a foreman. He runs things on the ground. Custer is the mastermind, not to mention the chief benefactor. He's raking in *millions*—off the books, of course. He works from the shadows, calling shots through Jerry and weaponizing the Gateway Hounds wherever necessary to smash competition and shield against legal repercussions. It's like—"

"A second government," I said. "A society within a society."

"Pretty much."

I folded my arms, chewing my tongue as I calculated the variables, identified the holes, and numbered my conclusions. It didn't take long. The hallmarks were as obvious to me as broken glass reflecting sunlight. Not a unified picture, but the implications were easy.

"Three things," I said, pivoting to Riley.

She waited, eyebrows cocked.

"One," I said, lifting a finger. "There's a business inside the business which generates the bulk of the profit. Something a heck of a lot more lucrative than drugs, prostitution, and fencing. You said this guy was raking in millions, but you don't make millions from petty street crime alone. I'm guessing the FBI is investigating a darker scheme and they're holding off on breaking up the street crime because they want the juicier slice."

No comment. I proceed, raising another finger.

"Two—that investigation is behind schedule and likely failing. You're the lead investigator and you're hitting a block wall, which is why you're willing to show your cards to a relative stranger. I know you checked into my background, but there's still no logical reason to bring me here. Not unless you're running out of answers and running out of time. I'm guessing that your bosses are getting impatient. They need a win. Maybe they're talking themselves into the merits of mopping up the street crime and calling it a day, which is an eventuality you can't accept. You *need* that juicier slice."

Still no answer. She had stopped blinking again. It might have tripped me out if I weren't so zeroed in. I lifted my third finger and pointed to the picture of Jerome Withers.

"Now we get to your method of cover. You told me you'd been on this job for seven months, which is a long time to be under cover, but not nearly long enough to build trust within an organization this savvy. That leads me to believe you have an edge, and given my knowledge of male weakness paired with your admittedly remarkable appearance, it's not a difficult riddle to solve."

She cocked an eyebrow. I tapped Withers's photo.

"You're sleeping with the street boss, which is a level of investment the FBI would neither condone nor allow if they knew about it, meaning they *don't* know about it. It was a choice you made on your own. A personal involvement both dangerous and highly violating..."

I lowered my finger. My voice softened. "All of which leads to the bonus round. Point number four."

Her lip twitched. Both eyes reddened, and she blinked hard. She knew what was coming. And I knew I was right.

"This is very, *very* personal for you. You're not just an

agent investigating a criminal enterprise. You're a woman at war, with her back against the wall. Running out of options. You brought me here because sacrificing your cover or surrendering your objective is simply not an option for you...and since you've already colored outside the lines, it's no big deal to do it again."

I stopped. Riley swallowed despite herself. She regained control of her emotions and her eyes cleared. She spoke in a flat monotone.

"Summary?" she said.

I folded my arms. "The summary is I can help. And I think I'd like to. But before I move a finger...I want to know *everything*."

23

Riley retreated across the room to an ice chest parked against the wall. Water sloshed as she withdrew a pair of dripping beer bottles. I took a seat across from her in a squeaking metal chair and gulped lukewarm Sam Adams.

Riley wiped froth from her lips and rotated the bottle on the tabletop, studying a scar on the wood floor. At last she inhaled a long breath, then looked up.

"You're right."

"About which part?"

"Pretty much all of it."

I nodded. Swigged from the bottle. Waited.

"There's a juicier slice," she said. "We just can't put our finger on it. The FBI first initiated this case on suspicion of human trafficking. Essentially, we thought Custer was running a sex trade operation. Migrant girls, mostly. Picked up off the street and funneled to big cities around the country...and likely outside the country. A much larger prostitution scheme."

"You can't find evidence?"

"We can. It's just...backwards. We have evidence of people going missing. Migrants, mostly. Undocumented migrants. But can't trace them to a point of sale. They just...disappear."

"Okay..."

"Then there are the numbers. We've cataloged half a dozen confirmed disappearances that we can link to Custer's operation, but that's not nearly enough to explain the level of cash flow he's reporting on his tax returns. Two and three million per year...and that's just what he admits to."

"What's his explanation for that income?"

"The usual. Liquor stores, gas stations. A crummy hotel. Nothing that should generate millions."

"He could be a middleman," I said. "A logistics pipeline. He might not necessarily kidnap the victims himself, except when a special opportunity presents itself."

"We've considered that. But..."

I cocked an eyebrow. Riley looked vaguely apologetic.

"Half the victims we've linked to Custer are men," she said.

"So?"

"So...if it's a sex trade..."

"Men are sex trafficked too, you know."

"Well, yeah. But these guys aren't...uhm..."

"Attractive?"

Riley flushed. She chugged beer. I knew what she was driving at.

"It just doesn't feel right," I said, offering her an escape.

"No. It doesn't."

I waited. Riley was fixated on the bottle, scraping at the

label with a manicured thumb nail. She was fighting back tears again. I knew we had reached the crux of the issue.

"I can leave," I said. "You don't have to explain. We can call it a day and go our separate ways."

"Will you lay off the gang?"

"Not a chance."

"You're jeopardizing my operation. This chaos is putting them on full alert. I can't get anywhere."

"And I'm sorry about that, but justice isn't cheap."

She clenched her teeth. I wasn't sure if she was angry at me or herself. She drained the bottle. I didn't push her.

At last Riley closed her eyes.

"Her name was Kaley. She was a singer in a St. Louis bar. Pretty good. Had plans to move to Nashville. She was my sister."

My stomach tightened. I could already guess where this story was headed. Another easy riddle to solve.

"They gang-raped and murdered her," she finished, facing me. "Some of Jerry's boys. The police ran an investigation, but the state offered plea deals and..."

She trailed off. I didn't need her to finish—I could already connect the dots.

Plea deals. Corrupt judges and prosecutors. My fingers tightened around the bottle.

"Kaley was eight years younger than me," Riley said, seeming to collect herself. "The baby of the family. Our parents died in a car accident when she was fifteen. Extended family took her in. I felt like...you know...I was responsible for her. We were close."

I learned in the Army—and relearned as a homicide detective—how much you can tell about a person's credibility by contrasting their body language against their professed motivations. A witness who's angling for immunity while avoiding your gaze is about as credible as kosher pork.

But a broken, hurting woman, professing guilt over the loss of her sister, and now dedicated to exacting justice on that sister's behalf? I bought it. Every word. Not just because the body language checked, and the story rang true, but because the look in Riley's eyes resonated with me on a personal level. I understood her pain—I had experienced it myself. Most days, I still experienced it. It was *real*.

And yet...I was still struggling with the logistics. With technical problems that the investigator in me couldn't ignore.

"So the gang murdered your sister... Now you're snuggled up next to them. How are they not connecting the dots?"

Riley didn't seem hurt by the question. She flicked her hand dismissively. "I was adopted. Kaley came after. She's... she *was* redheaded. We looked nothing alike."

"And the name?"

"Fake ID. The Hounds think my name is Riley Vancura. The FBI provided me with an alternate Missouri driver's license."

Logical. I'd seen the feds work this way before. Selecting a fake last name while keeping the agent's first name and initials minimized the opportunity for careless, cover-blowing mistakes. Riley was used to answering to Riley, she was used to signing her name with an R and a V. Simplicity is king when it comes to special operations.

But I still had questions.

"I've worked with the FBI before," I said. "I've never

known them to task an agent with personal connections to the case."

Riley met my gaze. She didn't blink.

"They don't know?" I asked.

"They didn't. Not at first. I was stationed in Newark when Kaley was killed. I took personal leave for the funeral, and as soon as I hit the ground I knew something was wrong. I was the one to discover the link between Kaley's murder and the Gateway Hounds—by which time the plea deal was in place and they were already skating to freedom. I knew I wanted to work the case personally, so I kept my mouth shut about what I knew. I asked for a transfer to St. Louis. I finagled my way into joining the human trafficking investigation. By the time my bosses drew the connection, I was already successfully under cover. What were they gonna do? Terminate a promising investigation? The FBI is practical, Mason. And hungry."

Fair enough.

"So how did you infiltrate the gang?"

I already knew the answer—or thought I did. I still had to ask.

To my surprise, Riley smirked at the question. It was a cold and humorless expression.

"Very, very carefully. I made a habit of encountering them at a bar. I hit on Jerry—off again, on again. Hot and cold. I played with him in front of his guys. I knew he was the boss, and I knew he had an image to uphold. Then I got lucky. I discovered that Jerry suffers from a particular medical issue. Something very personal. Very...difficult for a guy in his position."

I squinted, reviewing my memories of Jerry at the fight

club, and then again at the cop bar. His inhuman bulk. The overstated definition of his muscles.

Steroids. Lots and lots of them.

"He can't get it up," I said, suddenly understanding Riley's smirk.

"Not even a little bit. His junk is fried. One of the bartenders he knew told me—she said she spoke to a prostitute who had an awkward encounter with Jerry a couple years back. He's totally impotent."

"But in a testosterone-infused gang, he can't admit to that," I said, now connecting the dots. "He needs to look like an alpha dog... He needs a flashy woman."

"Enter Riley Vancura." She sighed, no longer looking smug so much as exhausted. "Once I knew his weakness, it was easy. I convinced him that I was content to be arm candy —that I didn't have any needs he was unable to fulfill. Also, I was happy to keep his secret. For a price, of course. I make him buy me all kinds of designer brand crap. I show up at gang events and make his underlings drool. I stroke his ego. It's been grueling work...but it got my foot in the door. Jerry is getting sloppier by the day. He takes phone calls in front of me, now. He brings me along to Custer's house. He lets me watch TV in the next room while he meets with his guys. It's only a matter of time before I bust this thing wide open."

I grunted, genuinely impressed by the artistry of her plan, to say nothing of her extreme patience and dedication. It was remarkable, truly.

It also made me want to run for cover as fast as humanly possible.

"This..." I started. Hesitated. "This is a powder keg. This whole thing. The way you're set up with the FBI, the way you're set up with the gang. You're playing Russian Roulette, here. There are a million things that could go wrong. It's only a matter of time before you blow your own brains out."

Riley ran her tongue over her lips. "I know."

"Is that why you brought me here?"

Riley didn't answer. She spun her bottle on the table. Then she stood and approached the murder board. She put her hands behind her back and studied the photographs for a long time.

At last she said, "My bosses are getting antsy. Bureaucratic pressure is building...to say nothing of growing risk every day I remain under cover. They're getting impatient. They gave me a week...four days ago. If I can't uncover the juicier slice by then, they're busting up the street crime and calling it a day. Jerry will go down. Most of the street soldiers will go down with him. Custer will walk, scot-free. We've got nothing on him."

"And that's not acceptable because..."

Molten iron returned to her gaze. She spoke through flashing white teeth.

"Because Custer paid off the prosecutors in my sister's case."

Right.

I sat back in my chair and considered the story from every possible angle, measuring the sincerity in Riley's body language against the realities she had outlined. I could feel the walls closing in around her with only a glimmer of hope left to keep her fighting. My experience as an investigator was mostly with homicide, which is altogether different from organized crime. But there's one thing all investigations have in common—they take time. Sometimes, a lot of it. If Riley had any prayer of busting this thing in the next three days, she was going to need more than access, intelligence, and assistance. She was going to need luck.

But despite my inclinations to distance myself before the powder keg blew, I knew I wasn't going anywhere. I believed her story. I resonated with her pain. And my vendetta with the gang was unsatisfied, anyway. Why not run this thing all the way to the top?

Make Custer himself pay for Lily's surgery.

"I'm in," I said. "Whatever you need. We can make it happen."

A glint of hope entered Riley's face. She saluted me with the bottle again. Wiped her lips.

"Honestly, the biggest thing you could do would be to stand down. Stop causing so much ruckus. Allow me some room to do my job."

"That might have worked a month ago," I said. "With three days left, you can't afford the indirect approach."

"Gee, thanks. That's so helpful."

I held up a hand. "I'm trying to clarify the problem. You say Custer is the heart of the operation?"

"Right."

"So it's logical that if there *is* a juicier slice, he would know about it."

She frowned. "Yes, but...you're not suggesting—"

"A kidnap and interrogation?" As soon as I said it out loud, flashbacks of Arkansas played across my mind. A pair of bloody bodies tied off to trees...a hefty baseball bat clenched in my hands.

No. Not that. Not again.

"Not an option," I said. "Any information we tortured out of him would be inadmissible in court. We need an indirect approach...something more covert. What about Custer's personal space? An office or something?"

"He doesn't have one. He rides out to the fight club now and then to meet with Jerry. They slink off together. Custer has a house in Missouri outside the city—big place. I've been a few times. He likes to throw fancy parties." Riley rolled her wrist, exposing a watch. She grimaced. "He's throwing one in about four hours, as a matter of fact."

"You ever poke around out there?" I asked.

"I've tried. Playing arm candy is a double-edged sword. There are always eyes on me. I haven't been able to slip away."

I grunted. "Well, there you have it. The intersection of your need and my ability. I'm a pro at slipping away."

I drained my beer and reached for my half-helmet. Riley's frown returned.

"What do you mean?"

"We keep it simple. Get me an address and I'll infiltrate after the party starts. You draw the eyes, I'll draw the truth."

I turned for the door. Riley rushed to follow. She cut me off on that slouching front porch, a strong hand on my shoulder.

"Sharpe. *Wait.*"

I turned back. There was desperation in her eyes— desperation and uncertainty. It reminded me again how far I had drifted from the structured world of a bona fide law enforcement officer. It was nothing for me to break into a rich crook's house and ransack his office for the truth.

Warrant? Who needed a warrant?

But I was a long, long way outside Riley's world.

"I still don't know you," Riley said.

Of all her complaints, it was the one I least expected. Yet

in truth, it was the most logical. It cut right to the heart of the problem.

"I'm just a guy," I said. "A guy who's been places, seen things, and lost more than he's won. I'm nobody special and I won't be here when the smoke clears. You can be sure of that. But..."

I put gentle hand on her arm. Riley flinched, but she didn't pull away.

"*Neither will they*," I finished.

I squeezed her arm, ever so softly. Then I pulled a Walmart receipt from my pocket and wrote my burner phone number on the back. I placed it in her hand.

"The choice is yours," I said. "Text me with the address if you want my help."

Then I got back on the Fat Boy and turned west.

24

I made it halfway back to the city before the phone in my pocket vibrated. Pulling off at a gas station to top off the thirsty Fat Boy, I flicked the phone open and scanned the message.

It was from Riley. It was curt and right to the point, just a county road address and a time—seven p.m.

Just as I finished reading, another message popped through almost like an afterthought. All caps. Two words.

NO FIREWORKS.

I smiled, tapping the address to cue up my GPS app. It opened automatically, loading a destination way out in the sticks northwest of St. Louis, just as Riley had described. It was a two-hour ride from my current position in central Illinois, giving me ninety minutes of breathing room before the party kicked off. Really though, I'd wait a little beyond then. Embrace the cloak of full darkness and the added benefit of flowing booze.

Slip out of the shadows...just the way the Army had trained me to do.

I mapped out a non-highway route to my destination—back roads are built for motorcycles—and then I hit the saddle.

I REACHED Carter Custer's rural estate just past eight p.m., my face darkened with fresh camo paint, a small backpack loaded with all the goodies I had purchased at the hardware store the day prior. Pulling the Fat Boy off the road a mile from my mark, I rolled it behind a cluster of underbrush and smeared additional camo paint on the head light, tail light, and turn signals to mute any reflection under passing high beams.

Then I was ready. I set off at an easy, swinging pace, abandoning the road and cutting straight through the trees. It was a hardwood forest, and with a half-moon hanging overhead, it was easy to see. I tracked Custer's house first with my phone's GPS, but soon I didn't even need that.

There was light. The distant thump of music. The occasional growl of Harleys with modified exhausts. A hundred yards from the next tree line I was confronted by a ten-foot chain-link fence topped with three strands of barbed wire. It ran in a straight line through the forest, streaking out to my right toward the county road and to my left deeper into the trees. A wire-tied yellow sign displayed a lightning bolt and a warning about an electric charge, but I wasn't fooled.

The fence was overgrown by ivy, so even if it had been electrified at some point—which I doubted—that current was thoroughly grounded out.

I dropped the backpack and retrieved my pair of compact bolt cutters, whistling softly as I worked. It was that Ray Charles tune Rusty had been singing—"Hit the Road, Jack". It was stuck in my head, and I was starting to think I might like to learn it on my violin.

It certainly sounded more fun than Vivaldi's Four Seasons.

I made it through the fence with no hint of electric shock. I stowed the bolt cutters and bent low amid the trees, taking my time as I neared the sound of drunken revelry. The ground sloped gradually downward, and as I reached the tree line I detected the first of several security lights mounted low to the ground to map out a length of asphalt driveway. It orbited the outskirts of a sprawling fish pond, complete with an illuminated fountain, before rising to a low hill where the house—or *mansion*—was built.

Riley and her FBI chums were certainly right about one thing: Custer wasn't making bank, he was breaking the bank. The house couldn't be smaller than six thousand square feet, constructed of dual levels with a section of flat-topped roof surrounded by a low fence to form an observation platform. The construction was new, but the architectural style was Antebellum. Columns guarded a wrap-around front porch, white-washed siding framing large windows. A detached garage was connected by a covered walkway. Additional security lights glowed over flower beds and a miniature golf course. There was even a tennis court built off to the left side, fully illuminated and looking totally unused.

I squatted at the base of a live oak tree and shuffled through my bag for the pair of cheap binoculars I had purchased at the hardware store. They focused over the sprawling asphalt terminus of the driveway where a flotilla of parked Harleys gleamed beneath the moonlight. I counted nineteen, including Riley's Sportster S. They were backed in with handlebars cocked to the left in true biker style. I didn't see any people.

A buzz from my pocket heralded a text message. I lowered the binos and checked it. Riley again.

> Pool party. People throughout house.
> Watch yourself.

I pocketed the phone and slung the backpack. My route took me down the hill just inside the tree line, orbiting the pond and circling the tennis court. The house appeared even bigger as I approached, its wide windows staring like black eyes over the estate. The front porch lights were on, but much of the noise seemed to come from behind the house.

As I completed my circle, I discovered why. It was a pool party, all right. And a heck of a party at that. The pool stretched the width of the house, complete with a giant semi-circular hot tub, a diving board, and a multi-tiered waterfall feature. Cabanas lined the back side of the pool deck, alongside a curved bar and a large outdoor kitchen.

There were lights. There was thumping music. And there were a *lot* of people. Hairy, shirtless biker guys lounged everywhere, some in the pool, some in the hot tub, some beneath the cabanas. They sucked from long-necked beer bottles, and a pair of them openly snorted lines of cocaine from a side table. Accompanying the men were blonde and brunette cocktail girls clad exclusively in skimpy swimsuits. More of the same manned the bar and delivered drinks on trays. I recognized several of their faces from the rave club.

Settling onto my stomach, I deployed the binoculars, zeroing in on the bikers. They were all men—all except

Riley. She appeared by herself, dressed in a black one-piece with a sheer swimsuit cover. Kicked back on a lounge chair, eyes hooded, a drink in one hand.

As though she was the only person on the planet.

Several of the guys were ogling her. I didn't see Jerry. What I *did* see was Carter Custer—he was impossible to miss. Dressed in a full white suit with gleaming black shoes and a cocked black cowboy hat, the circus master himself held court from behind a sprawling barbecue grill, cocktail girls close at hand, a cigar protruding from the corner of his mouth.

Custer laughed a lot. He shouted jokes at his men and swigged beer. He groped the girls whenever they passed within arm's reach—which was often. In short order he was flipping steaks off the grill onto china plates, and the cocktail girls went to work delivering dinner to the scattered members of the club.

Leaning low. Tolerating the leering looks and careless hands.

I lowered the binoculars, my stomach turning. There was something so vaguely grotesque about the entire scene that I couldn't quite put my finger on. It was like a redneck's fantasy of a Hollywood Hills pool party—all the ingredients were there, but none of them really mixed. It was sloppy. Dirty. Overboard, like bad barbeque drowned in over-sweetened sauce. I observed the girls tensing and trying not to recoil from the grubby fingers of the men who—*accidentally* —missed the proffered steak plates and grabbed something else instead.

The girls laughed, but when they turned away they looked dead inside. Whatever they were being paid, it wasn't enough.

I broke my attention away from the pool scene and swept the binoculars across the parking pad as three bikes arrived —more hairy guys in leather vests marked with what I now assumed to be the Gateway Hounds logo, that snarling dog inside the Gateway Arch. To my left, the hillside sloped down to another tree line, a shooting range complete with target steel constructed on a level patch just short of the forest.

But between the pool and the shooting range stood a metal building. Maybe sixty feet long and twenty feet deep, it featured a trio of rolling metal doors, all closed. The asphalt driveway split off and led to each of the doors, while bright lights glared down from the tops of tall poles. There was a man-sized door on the right side of the building. It was closed, but just as the binos settled over it, the door opened.

Jerome Withers stepped out. Unlike the men gathered around the pool, Jerry was neither drunk nor happy. His face was dark. His eyes as lifeless and cold as ever. He shot a suspicious look around him, then turned and stuck a key into the door's deadbolt. He locked it. He pocketed the key and started up the hill toward the pool deck as a slow grin crept across my face.

Target acquired.

Anything worth locking for Jerry was worth investigating for me.

25

I started back into the trees. Down the hill and across the shooting range where my boots crunched over a dozen different types of fallen brass. Handgun calibers ranging from .380 ACP to .45 ACP, and elongated rifle casings spat from the ejection ports of AK-47s, AK-74s, and AR-style rifles chambered in both 5.56 and .300 Blackout.

Noted.

Back up the hill through the shadows, I approached the metal building with the mansion about a hundred yards off my right shoulder. It wasn't enough distance to make me comfortable, but with the aid of the shadows and the free-flowing booze on that pool deck, I felt confident enough to dash across open ground.

Sliding to cover at the end of the building, I rocked my head out to survey the knot of sweaty thugs. None had observed me. They were still lost in the revelry, Riley now rising from her lounge chair to wrap her arms around Jerry and plant a kiss on his lips, for all the world as in love with him as Cinderella with her knight in shining armor.

One heck of an actress.

I looked briefly to the man-sized door at the far end of the building, but quickly dismissed it. There was a lock, which I could pick, but that would take time and leave me fully exposed to the security lights overhead. I had a better idea.

Circling to the backside of the building, I drew my faithful Streamlight MacroStream flashlight from my pocket and clicked it into moonlight mode. I placed it between my teeth and felt along the metal ribs of the building's exterior skin.

There were screws holding the sheet metal to the steel bones of the pole barn-style construction. They were Phillips head with little rubber gaskets to keep the moisture out. Each sheet metal panel was ten feet tall, reaching all the way to the roofline and overlapping the one next to it. A corner-cap at one end buttoned the entire shell together.

But really, what are a bunch of screws?

I dug the Victorinox Locksmith out of my pocket and deployed the Phillips-head screwdriver. It protruded from the middle of the knife like a corkscrew. I fit the head into the first screw and leaned against the wall before rotating counter-clockwise. The screw was tight, but came loose with a predictable application of torque. In short order it fell to the dirt and I moved to the next, working one string of screws at a time, peeling back the corner cap and loosening a man-sized section of the shell before finally squatting to bend the metal back.

It popped and rattled a little. Still held in place by dozens of screws above my reach, it bent at the point of attachment, allowing a two-foot gap that exposed a wall of fiberglass insulation.

There was no drywall on the far side of that insulation. The razor blade of my Victorinox sliced through a binding layer of plastic. I kicked away the fiberglass, and then at last...I was through.

The first room was a bathroom. I ducked through the gap between a toilet and a shower stall, still clutching the knife as a weapon while the Streamlight illuminated my path.

Blank concrete. Unfinished interior walls built of two-by-fours and plywood. A shabby door. I eased forward and tried the knob. It was unlocked. I stepped out, switching the flashlight to my left hand and bumping it into full power mode.

The rest of the building was one giant room. It stretched to my left, spreading out in front of the three roll-up doors. Paved in smooth concrete, pitch black save for the illumination of the MacroStream. The section of the building directly in front of the bathroom was a mechanic's shop, and a pretty good one at that.

Multiple workbenches. A motorcycle lift with a disassembled Harley Lowrider strapped to its top, tools and parts scattered everywhere. Banks of powerless florescent lights overhead. An oil drum with a few dozen gallons of pitch-black engine fluids swimming in it, dead flies sprinkling the surface. A mini fridge plastered with biker-themed bumper stickers.

Four wheels move the body...two wheels move the soul.

I scanned the light beyond the motorhead paraphernalia and moved left. Beyond the mechanic's shop, at the core of the building, the space was more open. A giant Confederate flag stretched across the building's back wall, several couches parked beneath it. There was an office space mirroring the mechanic's shop on the opposite end of the building.

And in between were motorcycles—not a *lot* of motorcycles. Not like I expected. But a very specific collection of motorcycles. There were four, and they were identical. Classic black in color with gloss black trim and red lettering, they were Harley's brand-new CVO Road Glide ST model, each featuring the gargantuan 121-cubic-inch engine. Pillion seats and tour packs, Missouri license plates and tinted windshields. As I approached the nearest bike and surveyed the tires and floorboards, I noted plenty of road grime. There were scratches and swirl marks in the paint. Splattered bugs on the windshield.

The bike had seen some use—both recent and heavy— as had the other three. They were all forty, maybe forty-five-thousand-dollar motorcycles without any hint of customization. It struck me as odd the moment I realized it. For bikers, especially those in a biker gang, modification and personalization is everything. It's self-expression. It's identity. It's a calling card.

Yet here I was surveying the better part of *two hundred grand's* worth of elite touring hardware, heavily used...but nothing.

No stickers. No fancy lights. No modified handlebars or leather tassels. Not even a gremlin bell. I circled to the back of my subject, ready to memorize the license plate. An old cop habit.

As I did, the glow of the Streamlight glinted against a color that contrasted with the smooth black and sharp red of the Harley's theme. It was a sort of dull orangish brown. Copper colored?

I kneeled, examining a narrow gap between the top of the righthand saddlebag and the bottom of the tour pack. Sure enough, it was copper—literally so. A half-inch copper pipe traversed the three-inch gap between the two storage compartments, mostly shrouded by black insulation, but revealing its core where a chunk of that insulation had torn away. I rocked my head and followed the pipe through a tiny hole in the tour pack. I frowned.

Then I was back on my feet, unlatching the brake-side saddlebag and spilling light inside.

It was full—packed to the brim not with riding gear, but with some kind of mechanical mechanism. There were copper pipes, a radiator-style grill, a metal bottle, and a few valve controls. It was a custom job, no doubt about it. Designed to fit precisely inside the unique confines of the saddlebag. I traced the mechanism with one finger, placing the flashlight back in my mouth as I orbited the side of the bag and cocked my head to read the label on the bottle.

R-134a — REFRIGERANT.

What?

I closed the saddlebag around the copper pipe and circled to the back of the bike. I unsnapped the tour-pack's lid and rocked it open. LED illumination spilled inside, and my confusion redoubled.

The interior of the tour-pack was empty—or, at least, it wasn't loaded with any luggage. It wasn't stock, either. Both the bottom and the top half of the clamshell design had been coated with a thick layer of spray foam insulation, cutting the tour-pack's storage capacity by half. Imbedded in the insulation at the bottom of the pack was a standard baking sheet, like something a person might bake cookies on. The tip of the copper pipe protruded through the hole in the bottom of the tour-pack, pumping in cold air...

I dropped the lid in disgust, drawing the flashlight from my mouth. It was a *beer fridge*. Custom-built, no doubt with a battery pack in the clutch-side saddlebag to power it. Or maybe it ran off the bike's alternator. Who cared? It was the product of redneck engineering coupled with too much money.

And yet...

I stepped back and swept the light, noting a similar apparatus on one of the other Road Glides. The final two appeared to be stock. Still no customizations or personalization of any sort. Just road grime.

That lack of style somehow bothered me more than the bizarre tour pack fridge assembly. It felt...blunt. Utilitarian.

Cold.

I departed the garage section of the building and headed for the office. There was one desk—a large L-shaped metal thing with locking file cabinet drawers and a laptop. I couldn't find any keys to the drawers. The computer was passcode protected. I sifted through a waste basket but found only beer cans and potato chip bags.

The only item of note was literally a note—or a notepad, rather. The top sheet was blank, but as I angled the flashlight across its surface, I thought I detected vague indentations. Pencil marks? Maybe a pen.

Whatever was written there had since been ripped away, but the trace marks remained. I searched for a pencil but couldn't find one. Stepping to the nearest Road Glide, I stuck an index finger into the tailpipe and orbited the interior, coating my fingertip with a thin layer of black soot.

Back at the paper pad, I held the pad of my finger over the surface and brushed it gently. Soot transferred onto the paper like charcoal, and letters took shape as white outlines. Sloppy handwriting hastily scratched. But legible.

R KUMAR NEW, it read, followed by ten digits. I couldn't be certain whether one of those digits was a four or a nine, but I recorded the number both ways in the notes app on my phone before tearing off the grease-smeared sheet and crumpling it into my pocket.

Outside the building the sounds of revelry were louder than ever. A girl shrieked, followed by the explosive crash of somebody falling into the pool. Men laughed. Music thumped. I scanned the interior of the pole barn once more, then headed for the bathroom to exit through the wall. There was nothing more to see in this place. I had failed to uncover anything that exposed details of Riley's "juicier slice".

But still...

I stopped next to the Road Glides one last time and passed my light over them. I chewed the inside of one cheek and juxtaposed two polar opposite truths in my mind.

Expensive, elite bikes...and zero personalization.

It was wrong. I simply didn't know why.

26

I exfiltrated the property the same way I infiltrated it, returning to my Fat Boy and turning back toward the city. Riley and I had agreed on a rendezvous point, but I knew she would be engaged at the party for a few hours longer, so I took my time. I stopped for a late-night dinner at a Waffle House—an old standby of mine during my years on the Phoenix Police Force. I ordered the *All Star Special* with eggs scrambled with cheese, three strips of bacon, hash browns smothered and covered, and chocolate chips on my waffle.

The food hit the spot. I knocked back three cups of coffee with the waffle, then I was back on the bike, right shin throbbing. I retreated to the Purple Crane Campground and showered in the Airstream.

No motorcycle thugs were around. According to my neighbors, nobody with so much as a motorcycle bumper sticker had been admitted to the park all day. "Security measures" had been implemented, they said, ducking their heads in the conspiratorial way civilians do when they're making innuendos about firearms.

I strapped my violin to the Fat Boy's luggage rack and headed out again, north of the campground along the river, all the way to Malcom W Martin Memorial Park. Across the train tracks, straight to the river's edge.

I abandoned Vivaldi and devoted myself to Ray Charles. It was a bouncier tune than I was feeling, so after fifteen minutes I swung instead into my old standby. One of my late fiancée's favorite tunes—the soundtrack of my life, it felt.

"Hallelujah", by Leonard Cohen.

Riley arrived at a quarter past midnight. The snarl of her Sportster S rumbled from behind me, followed momentarily by the crunch of motorcycle boots. I was still playing, drifting from hymns to folk classics, sad country melodies to classic rock, each tune drawn out with slow passion.

Riley stopped behind me as I finished a rendition of "Be Thou My Vision", an Irish hymn that Mia loved. I was still confused by what it meant, but I couldn't deny its power.

"You're just full of surprises," Riley said.

I lowered the violin into my lap, not looking up from the spotlight-illuminated elegance of the Gateway Arch. It was somehow even more beautiful at night. Simple, strong...promising.

"Eighty percent of a soldier's life is sitting around waiting to be shot at," I said. "Some guys played video games. Some watched movies. The smartest Ranger NCO I ever knew played the violin. He said it kept him human."

"So he got you into it?" Riley took a seat next to me in the damp river sand. I turned away from the Arch.

"He died," I said. "Taliban IED blew him in half. Took us a while to get his things back to his family. I guess it felt like keeping him alive, at first. Then...it was just part of me. It kept me human."

Our gazes locked, and for just a moment the brick wall constructed behind Riley's iron gaze faltered. I saw behind it into a world of pain, confusion, guilt. Self-hatred. Loneliness.

"That's beautiful," Riley said.

I simply grunted, twisting the screw on my bow to loosen the hair. I'd played enough for one evening.

"There's a bruise on your arm," I said.

Riley shook her head, looking across the river to St. Louis.

"I got into a tiff with Jerry. I embarrassed him in front of the guys...didn't mean to. I swear, male ego is just a mountain of eggshells."

I smirked, unable to argue.

"You find anything?" Riley said, her tone back to business.

I dug into my pocket, producing the cell phone. I passed it to her with the notes app open.

"Does that name mean anything to you?" I asked.

"R. Kumar..." Riley squinted. "Never heard of him."

"Can your FBI people run a trace on the number?"

"Sure. Where did you get this?"

"Metal building."

"You got inside?" Both eyebrows arched.

"Sure."

"I've *never* been let inside. Only Custer and Jerry go in there. A couple of the others. What is it?"

I shrugged. "Just a garage, really. A mechanic's shop. A desk. That's where I found the number."

Riley retrieved her own phone and tapped out an

email, both thumbs jabbing like the legs of a tapdancing spider. She input the name and the number, then thumped *send*.

"Shouldn't be long. What else?"

I cocked my head. "You ever see Jerry ride a CVO Road Glide?"

"Road Glide? Never. Jerry's not a fairing guy. He rides a Road King Special, usually. No windshield."

"What about Custer?"

Hesitation. A shake of her head. "Not that I can recall. Maybe a couple of the street guys ride Road Glides, but they aren't CVOs. They don't make that kind of money."

"There's four of them in that garage," I said. "All brand new. All well used. Two of them have refrigerators built into their tour packs. Custom coolant generation in the brake-side saddlebag."

"What? Why?"

"A great question. The weirdest part is the appearance. Other than the refrigerators, the bikes appear bone stock. No customization at all."

"That doesn't sound like Jerry..."

"It doesn't sound like any hardcore biker. Those bikes are nearly fifty grand a pop and they're not even washing them. Road grime all over them."

"What does that mean?"

"I'm not sure. They've got money—that's obvious. More evidence of your juicier slice theory. But I don't think we're any closer to identifying it."

Riley chewed her lip, staring at the Arch but not really seeing it. She looked...consumed.

I knew the feeling.

I pulled myself to my feet, dusting sand off my jeans.

"We'll figure it out," I said. "Bank on it. We just gotta be patient."

"Where are you going?"

"To check on a friend," I said. "And get some shuteye. You should also—put some muscle cream on that bruise. It'll be nasty in the morning."

The mark on her arm bore the clear imprints of a heavy hand. Someplace deep in my gut the visual unleashed a stream of outrage. I imagined Jerry's face crashing through a block wall.

It was an artistically perfect mental image.

Riley stood and her lips parted. She hesitated. Closed her mouth. I wasn't sure what she was thinking, but I knew what I was thinking.

"Be careful with Jerry," I said. "I've met a lot of cold men. This guy's as frozen as they come."

Riley's jaw clenched. Her eyes flashed. "I know what I'm doing, Sharpe."

"I never said otherwise." I turned and started back through the brush, headed for the railroad tracks. "Text me when you have something on Kumar. Unless and until we get something better, he's our next step."

I RODE BACK into North St. Louis and found Spencer Meyers alone in his hospital room. He wasn't asleep. The TV played a news broadcast, which I thought was odd for a kid to be watching. Then I zeroed in on the scrolling headline beneath the talking head of an Asian-American man, and I understood.

Senator Park Campaigns for Healthcare Reform Bill.

The volume was low. The senator's words were barely audible. I turned to find Spencer slumped back on his pillows, his eyes heavy with medication, hands limp in his lap.

There was no sign of his mother or Lily.

"What's up, killer?" I rapped softly on the open door. Spencer flinched and looked my way. A dull smile stretched across his face.

"Hey, dude."

I welcomed myself in and dragged a chair toward the bed. Next to Spencer, a plastic bag dripped medication into his arm. He was still bandaged. Still immobilized by casts.

He looked terrible, but it was the defeat in his lone good eye that struck hardest.

"You gonna live?" I asked. It was a joke. The joke didn't land. Spencer simply grunted, still fixated on the TV. I settled back into my chair, rubbing my hands over worn jeans.

My shin ached, and my right eye socket stung with swelling. My mind was numb.

Most of all, though, the weight of the room bore down on me. It was more than Spencer's physical condition—those afflictions would heal and fade with time. It was that brokenness of his soul that landed hardest.

"Watching a little news?" I said, tilting my head toward the TV. Spencer snorted. He lay a while before answering.

"It's all just talk," he mumbled. "They get up there in Washington and they talk about change...but the bills just pile up. Consume everything."

Consume everything.

I knew Spencer was talking about a lot more than just a broken healthcare system. The weariness in his voice reflected battle scars worse than any kid should ever experience.

"How long with the cancer?" I asked.

Spencer shrugged. "Two years...maybe three."

"Was it always this bad?"

"No. Lily got better at first. The chemo helped. Then the cancer came back hard."

I wasn't surprised. I'd seen this same sad story before... but maybe not with a kid so young.

"You make any progress with those thugs?" Spencer asked. There wasn't much hope in his voice.

"Who says I'm trying?" I asked.

Spencer's grin was weak, but sly. "You got that look, man. That kinda guy who keeps getting up." His eye rimmed suddenly red. He looked away.

"Was your father that way?" I asked.

Spencer nodded..

"Military?" I asked.

Spencer forced a laugh. "He drove a garbage truck, man. Not much of a hero, I guess."

"Never say that. Hero is a trait, not a job title. If he was a good man, he was a good man."

Spencer looked up. He tried to smile again but couldn't make it work. "He was a good man. Absolutely. Did everything he could to help Mom with her addiction. None of it stuck, but that wasn't his fault. He got hit by some drunk on his way home from work. Off duty, so the city never paid Mom nothing. She's been in and out of using ever since."

Story as old as time.

I put a hand on Spencer's arm. He looked away.

"I'm...I'm really sorry about the money, man. Dad woulda whipped my ass."

"I guess those biker guys did it for him."

Spencer shrugged. Didn't laugh.

"Look at me, kid."

Spencer did. He was still crying. His face was black and blue. Stitches crisscrossed it like the decorations of a horror mask. I looked past all of that—I looked deep.

I liked what I saw.

"You know what you are?" I asked.

"What's that?"

I squeezed his arm. "A guy who keeps getting up."

That was almost more than he could take. His arm quivered. I stood.

"Hang in there, Spencer Meyers. You've got friends in dark places."

27

I awoke in another grimy, nondescript motel to the ding of my burner phone. It was Riley. She had a full report back from her FBI people. I sat up in bed and scrubbed sleep from my eyes, checking the clock.

It was seven-oh-three. Riley was up and swinging.

The text was short and sweet. The phone number I'd found in Custer's metal building had included a four, not a nine. It linked to a guy named Ravi Kumar, an Indian expatriate living and working in St. Louis. He owned a restaurant services company providing kitchen essentials, cleaning supplies, and basic equipment to restaurants across the region. There was an address for his office, and nothing more.

Just as I was finishing the text, another message shot through from Riley.

Cannot investigate. They may recognize me.

I knew what she was asking. I also knew that at this stage

any associate of the Gateway Hounds gang was just as likely to recognize me. But then, I wasn't worried about blowing deep cover.

I texted back.

> I got it. Will reconnoiter shortly. Standby for sitrep.

I tossed the phone onto my bed and ran my hands over a rough face, tracing tender flesh and a razor stubble that was creeping gradually closer to early beard status. Glancing into the mirror I regarded my bruised face, uncombed hair reaching down to my ears. I couldn't be blamed for the sloppy appearance—not fully—but I also couldn't deny that it bothered me. The Gateway Hounds had declared war, and I was the soldier standing squarely in their path. It was time to look the part.

Showering, I dressed in my mostly clean Walmart clothes and grabbed a stale bagel from the "continental breakfast buffet" on my way out. The Fat Boy grumbled to life with its usual carbureted complaints. I allowed it time to warm while I used my phone to locate a barbershop. I ordered a high and tight haircut and a full shave. When the guy passed a hand mirror in front of my face for inspection, I nodded with satisfaction.

A lot of years—and even more mileage—had transpired since I last wore a military uniform. But all things considered, I didn't look too bad. I was ready to meet Mr. Ravi Kumar.

Kumar Food Services sat north of town on the outskirts of the industrial district, and only about three miles from the Gateway Hounds's rave club. I kept my eyes open for other motorcycles as I rumbled down a busted two-lane street lined mostly by houses. Kumar's building sat off to my right between the street and the river. It was constructed of block, with a gravel lot and an eight-foot chain-link fence surrounding it. That fence was overgrown with ivy, and the gate stood open.

Only two vehicles sat in the lot. The first was a delivery truck—like a small moving truck, maybe thirty feet long, sun-bleached blue in color. Kumar's logo was printed on the side of the cargo box, but that paint was also faded and peeling. One of the truck's headlights was busted. The bumper hung loose on one side.

It didn't look safe for the road, but judging by the tall grass growing beneath its sagging frame, it hadn't seen the road in some time.

Standing in sharp contrast to the unkempt delivery truck was the second vehicle in the lot. Parked near a set of concrete steps that led to a glass-door entrance, this vehicle was anything save unkempt. A year old at most, and gleaming with wax beneath the midmorning sun, the Mercedes SUV was a GLS model, jet black, not a scratch on it. And it *wasn't* a customer's vehicle. That much was assured by the vanity Missouri license plate, which proudly read: KUMAR.

Well, then. Life was good in the restaurant services business.

I stopped the Fat Boy alongside the GLS, heedless of the gravel dust I was casting over that brilliant black paint. I tossed my half helmet over the sissy bar and cast another look around the property as I dismounted.

The place was...quiet. Strangely so. It wasn't just the lack of other vehicles; it was the lack of any *indicator* of other vehicles. There were no ruts. No worn places in the grass that encroached along the parking lot's edge. In fact, the only disturbance in the gravel at all formed a single distinct highway—leading right to the GLS.

And everything was strikingly still, almost as though Kumar's business was *out* of business.

I mounted the steps and reached a dusty glass door printed with the same logo as I'd seen on the truck. No hours of business. No posted phone number. Pushing inside, I was greeted by an almost overwhelming wash of icy air. It was mid-sixties outside and comfortable, but this guy had his office ramped down as though it was mid-August.

The floor was worn linoleum. A single counter ran the length of the wall facing me, with a telephone and computer planted on top. Two chairs faced that counter, forming a sort of half-hearted waiting room. An old water cooler stood empty and now covered in dust.

Nobody was around.

I advanced to the counter and looked left through an open door into a dark hallway. A blade of light cut out from a doorway someplace out of sight. Only the tail end of it was visible.

But I could hear things. Things I certainly shouldn't have heard at a place of traditional business. Sounds of...adult behavior.

I smacked the bell on the counter, hard enough to send the little thing hopping. The noises of ecstasy halted almost immediately, and unintelligible whispers carried from around the door. I waited. Half a minute passed.

Then a girl appeared. Not a woman—she was college-aged at best. Skinny, South-Asian, and a little disheveled. She hurried to run fingers through her hair as she approached, flushing a little.

She was cute, I supposed, but in the context of what I'd just heard it was difficult for me to consider her that way without feeling filthy.

"Can I help you, sir?"

I cocked an eyebrow. Waited a long beat. "I'd like to see Mr. Kumar."

"He's...uhm..."

"Missing his pants?"

That brought a darker flush. I almost felt bad.

The harsh clearing of a throat arrested my attention as a short man with perfectly black hair and undersized eyes appeared around the corner. He wore pants—hallelujah—but also appeared disheveled. He was middle-aged. He was overweight.

He did not look happy to see me.

The man addressed the girl first. Not in English, but in what I thought was Hindi. She ducked her head and disappeared back into the hallway. Then Kumar approached the counter, placing two small hands on its top and forcing a smile.

"How can I help you?"

He spoke with a heavy accent. Clear English, but certainly a second language. I squinted and didn't answer, just taking a measure of him. Waiting for him to break first.

It didn't take long. He shifted on his feet, lips twitching. A trickle of sweat ran down from his scalp. Maybe not from my sudden arrival, but from whatever physical activity had preceded it.

An exhausting day at the office.

"Are you Ravi Kumar?" I said.

"Who's asking?"

"Whose lips are moving?"

He took a half-step back from the counter. "Look, I don't know what you want—"

"I want to purchase spaghetti sauce," I said. "That's what you do here, right? Sell stuff for restaurants."

"We don't sell food. Just food service supplies. Kitchen equipment. Plastic wear. Cleaners."

"Fine. Then I want to buy some oven cleaner. Say, a truckload of it. Can you deliver?"

His mouth opened but he didn't speak. He looked thoroughly confused. I leaned against the counter, deciding to push my advantage. There was little value in bothering with a subtle angle at this point.

"The truck doesn't run, does it?" I asked. "You can't deliver."

"I'll have it fixed next week," Kumar said. "Maybe you should call to place an order?" He reached for a card. I ignored it.

"That's a heck of a nice car you've got, Mr. Kumar. What's a thing like that cost, anyway? Sixty grand? Maybe eighty?"

His gaze switched impulsively toward the GLS. Then his face hardened.

"I think I'd like you to leave."

"I will," I said. "Just as soon as you explain your association with a Mr. Jerome Withers."

Kumar blanched at the name. The reaction was instant and impulsive. No chance for him to suppress it. He finished his half-step backward, lips parting.

Then he made a sudden—and very bad—decision. He dipped his hand beneath the counter and went for the shotgun hidden there. I saw it coming as a black flash and threw myself instinctively forward. The weapon wasn't chambered—it wasn't "cruiser ready", as we would have said at the Phoenix PD. He had to pump it to bring it into action, and he didn't have nearly enough time.

I grabbed the weapon by the shortened barrel even as he grasped at the pump. A quick wrench of my swimmer's muscles tore it straight out of his sweaty hands. He fell back against the wall as I returned to my feet in front of the counter, the shotgun now in hand. I spun it, working the action. With a sharp *schlick-schlick* a shell entered the chamber. Kumar's face drained of blood and he hurtled toward the hallway, shouting in Hindi. He reached the door and slammed it shut just as I pivoted around the end of the counter.

A metallic click signaled the deployment of a thumb lock. I placed the muzzle of what turned out to be a Mossberg Maverick 88 against the door frame directly adjacent to the knob, and pressed the trigger. Shards of wood exploded through a fist-sized hole, carrying the entire door knob along with them. I drove my boot into the door and sent it crashing open. I entered the hallway, pumping in a fresh shell and clearing the first room.

Supply closet, nothing. The room after that was an office packed with clutter, but no Kumar and no girl. From further down the hallway, a voice shouted. It was female, raised in a shriek.

I reached the next door and pivoted inside, muzzle first. It was a break room with a kitchenette. The girl sat on the floor, back against the wall, both palms held up.

"Please—"

"Where is he?" I said.

"Warehouse!" She pointed. I departed the breakroom and reentered the hall. The final door was a steel one, complete with security glass. It was locked from the other side.

I blew a grapefruit-sized hole through the security glass and reached through to disengage the latch. Then I was pumping the shotgun and passing across worn linoleum onto equally worn concrete. A warehouse opened ahead of me, just the way the girl had described. Tall shelves laden with dusty boxes. Overhead lights that flickered, half of them burned out. A forklift in one corner covered in cobwebs. Rolling doors that faced the loading dock, all of which were closed.

And then Kumar, sprinting down an aisle between shelves stacked high with bottles of cleaner. He was headed toward the end of the building, toward another door. I raised the shotgun.

"Stop!"

He didn't stop. I fired, aiming a yard above his head. Buckshot struck the concrete wall, unleashing a shower of gray. He sprinted right through it. The door slammed. I took a half-step down the aisle.

Then I stopped. A sound reached my brain through ringing ears. The auditory calling card of incoming trouble. Not police sirens. No, this sound was worse.

It was motorcycle engines—a lot of them.

28

I hesitated only a moment, rolling the shotgun in my hands to inspect it. The Maverick was a shortened model—a home-defense setup with an eighteen-point-five-inch barrel. The correspondingly short magazine tube likely only held five rounds, and I'd already fired three.

Two rounds of buckshot, twelve gauge or otherwise, wouldn't be nearly enough to hold off a horde of motorcycle thugs thirsty for blood. I had underestimated just how quickly Kumar's business associates could—or would —respond.

It was time to beat a tactical retreat.

I made it back to the parking lot just as the first motor-cycle appeared at the entrance of Kumar's fenced lot. It was jet black with a single giant headlight that flashed as the bike crossed onto gravel. A brand-new Road King Special, and astride its saddle rode the one and only Jerome Withers.

Terrific.

I sprinted for the Fat Boy, throwing my leg over and holding the shotgun beneath my right arm. The engine rumbled to life, I dumped the clutch and laid on the throttle. The rear tire spun, hurling gravel broadside across Kumar's GSL a second before I gained traction. My feet were snatched off the ground as the bike bounded, then hurtled for the bottleneck of men now gathered at the facility's entrance. There were three bikes there, with a fourth rumbling in. Forty yards shrank to twenty, and I released the left grip. I snatched the shotgun from beneath my right arm. I jammed it into my shoulder and swung the muzzle forward.

Jerry saw the gaping mouth and blanched. He gunned his Road King, yanking the handlebars and hurtling out of the way as I opened fire on the guy directly behind—or rather, on his bike. It was an Indian Super Chief with tassels hanging from the grips.

A full load of buckshot tore through the bike's front tire and zipped into the rider's shins. The fat guy astride the Indian howled like a scalded dog and tumbled forward. His bike went down. His friends scrambled to get out of the way.

I tossed the Mossberg into the gravel and cranked on the throttle, roaring for the gap. As I blazed past the wrecked Indian I counter-steered hard to the right. The Fat Boy dipped toward the pavement, floorboard hanging hard beneath my brake foot and scraping against raw asphalt. I almost went down.

I pulled out of the slide just in time, and a split second later I was howling away from the compound, looking back over my shoulder to check for pursuers.

My half helmet was gone, bounced from the sissy bar during my escape. The pileup of bikers at the gate had descended into a tangle of chrome and leather. Not all shiny sides were up, but two of the guys who hadn't yet entered the lot when I burst through were now directly on my tail. A hundred yards, and thundering after me.

LED headlights glared. Meaty faces were disguised behind oversized sunglasses.

And *guns*—I saw guns.

I blew through the stop sign at the end of the street and took a left on impulse. The river was someplace to my right and I didn't want to run out of road. I would get up on the highway and test the limits of the Fat Boy's modified engine. Give these brutes a run for their money.

The next street was residential. Houses packed close together with postage-stamp yards. It was technically a two-lane but reduced to a single lane by the stacks of cars parked along both curbs. I took the middle and leaned close to the handlebars as the first gunshot cracked behind me. The bullet whizzed directly past my ear. It struck the headlight of a Volkswagen and I swerved left around a manhole cover. The Fat Boy ran at sixty miles per hour, blasting through the subdivision and clearing a four-way stop. I could see my pursuers in my mirrors. They were closing the gap. A hundred yards was down to fifty. Left hands lifted semi-auto handguns, and muzzle flash blinked. A bullet pinged off the Fat Boy's frame and another blew away my left mirror. I looked ahead to a traffic light as it turned red and a bread truck crept into the intersection. He was blocking my path. I couldn't see to the left to measure oncoming traffic.

I took the turn anyway, laying on the rear brake until the back tire broke traction and slid to my right. I arced around the curve just as the front bumper of a pickup truck appeared in my lane, also racing into the intersection. He laid on his horn, tires squealing. I rolled on the throttle and missed his front bumper by inches, pulling out of the slide and goosing the bike up the next street.

It was a divided two-lane with a turn median running down the middle. Houses lined the streets, but sprinkled among them were small shops, gas stations, chiropractors, and dentists. Traffic thickened enough so that I could no longer blast along at full speed. I looked into my one remaining mirror and saw my two pursuers pulling onto the street three cars behind me. Their guns were out of sight, but they were still coming, and despite the vehicles between us, they had a clear enough view of my tail to know if I turned back onto a residential street.

No. That wouldn't work. I needed distance.

I downshifted and lurched ahead, swerving into the turn median to blaze around a mail truck. My tails followed suit, and now I could hear the thunder of additional bikes roaring toward me. Jerry and his friends, collected from their logjam and now catching up. There must be some kind of communications system at play—my tails had marked my location and were calling up reinforcements for an ambush.

Screw that.

Swerving back into my lane, I reached an intersection just as the light flicked from yellow to red. The car ahead of me slowed near the white line. I swung right, flashing up the gap between the car and the curb and flicking my right turn signal on.

But I didn't turn right. At the last moment I leaned left and rolled on the throttle, cutting across the front bumper of the car and entering the intersection. Oncoming traffic was just crossing off their respective white lines. I blazed around the front bumper of a school bus and slid into position just ahead of a minivan. The minivan honked. A grocery store flashed by on my right. I was headed down a hill and gaining speed, weaving between traffic and looking to my mirror.

They were *still* on me. The stunt at the intersection had gained me a few dozen yards, but my nearest pursuers were unimpressed by the oncoming traffic. They slowed for only a moment before rushing to follow. Horns blared. A set of tires squealed.

And then they were behind me, headed down the hill as a shopping district swarmed around us. Multiple cars were now entering and exiting the street, some half-hanging out of parking lots as they waited for an opening. I was forced to swerve back into the turn lane to clip past a rusty old sedan, then jerk immediately out of the turn lane to avoid a head-on collision with a pickup truck. Heart hammering, vision narrowing with adrenaline, the mental risk meter programmed into my mind through a thousand close calls and mortal situations warned me that I was slipping danger-ously close to redline.

This wasn't workable. I wasn't gaining any distance. No matter how hard I pushed my bike, they pushed just as hard, and the faster I rode, the greater my risk of t-boning the next minivan pulling out of a daycare.

Highway. Where is the highway?

Before I could answer, the potential deathtrap I had feared appeared as an old lady behind the wheel of a faded Buick. She must not have seen me as I reached the bottom of the hill. The nose of her land yacht edged out of a doctor's office parking lot, and I knew by instinct that she wasn't stop-ping. She was turning left. Before she cleared the lane, I would broadside her.

I clamped on the front brake, right foot crushing down on the rear. The Fat Boy's tires howled and the back end fishtailed. The old lady finally saw me and did the worst possible thing—she froze up, wide and terrified eyes staring through her window. My brain computed the math and I knew I would never stop in time. Never swerve. There was no room.

So I did the thing no motorcyclist should ever have to do —I laid the Fat Boy down, rolling to the left and shooting out my leg to keep it from being pinned beneath the engine block. The crash bar struck the asphalt and sparks flew. The left highway peg blew off and hurtled past my head. I struck pavement and tumbled. The bike rocked sideways and smacked the Buick in its front wheel. I rolled over the asphalt with arms curled around my unprotected skull.

Tumbling. Tumbling. Stopping with a slam.

I landed on my back, staring up at a bright blue midwestern sky. My head spun and my ears rang. I could no longer hear the throb of the Fat Boy. I choked on gasoline fumes and gasped for air.

Then I heard another rumble. The choke of V-twins engine braking down a long hill. I twisted my head and saw their headlights.

A hundred yards, and closing fast.

29

I rolled to my busted knees and tried not to puke. Vertigo almost overcame me. I staggered to my feet even as the leading Gateway Hounds slowed. They approached the bottom of the hill, left hands reaching for pistols while right hands clamped down on front brakes. No cars stood between us. The old lady in the Buick remained at my back. At the top of the hill, Jerry's jet-black Road King Special appeared in a flash, flanked by four of his thug friends.

Move.

It was the only play. I scrambled for the Fat Boy. I grabbed the handlebars and heaved the six-hundred-fifty-pound bike off the ground, already grabbing the clutch as the motorcycle reached its balancing point. Throwing a leg over. Mashing the starter. The engine choked and turned over. I looked back up the road in time to see the nearest Hounds reach a screaming stop. Black muzzles rose over handlebars, gaping at me from twenty yards—and at the innocent old lady behind me.

The Fat Boy roared to life just as the gunfire began. I dropped into first and dumped the clutch, leaning forward and hurtling down the length of the Buick. Bullets zipped into the big car's fenders. One skimmed over the top of the Fat Boy's fuel tank and whistled past my arm. The next grazed my shoulder blades.

The last struck my upper left thigh, about six inches down from the hip. I felt it like the impact of a freight train slamming into a block wall—or, rather, a wall of swimming muscles. Hot pain exploded up my leg and into my spine. I bit back a scream as I raced across an oncoming lane of traffic. Narrowly missing a Jeep, I hurtled onto a residential street. The Fat Boy gained speed as I released the left handlebar and clutched at the wound.

I touched blood. My pants leg was already sticky with it. My vision blurred, but I didn't stop. Behind me the street was clogged with traffic and a siren wailed. I could no longer hear the thunder of oncoming V-twins. I assumed they had been stalled by the choke of cars, but I was having so much difficulty keeping my bike balanced that I couldn't find them in my mirror. I topped a low hill and clipped through a four-way stop. I turned right and released my wound, forced to clutch through another gear. I reached fifty miles per hour and stabilized, too focused on not falling off the bike to risk a higher speed.

A right turn. A left turn. I gasped and clutched the wound again. It was still wet, but not spurting. That likely meant the bullet had missed my femoral artery.

Small wins.

I wrestled the bike another two miles through the neighborhood before bursting out at an intersection with another split-lane city thoroughfare. A grocery store stood to my

right, and I turned automatically into the parking lot. I
circled behind the building and finally ground to a stop next
to a dumpster. I cut the motor, one hand clamped over my
gun-shot thigh, looking over my shoulder for signs of my
pursuers.

Trees blocked my view of the street I'd run down. I
checked the pavement behind me, but there was no clear
blood trail. No doubt drips had fallen from the end of my
pants leg, which was predictably saturated.

I sagged against the handlebars, panting through the
pain. It wasn't the first time I had been shot, but I couldn't
recall any bullet wound hurting as much. It was searing,
throbbing through my hip and exploding in my brain.
Inspecting my pants leg, I couldn't be sure how much blood I
had lost, but the dizziness clouding my head was a certain
enough indicator that I had lost too much.

What to do?

I peeled my hand back and looked beneath my arm to
gain a view of the wound. I couldn't quite see it. It was on the
lower side of my thigh, so high up it could almost count as
my hip.

Medical. I needed battlefield bandaging at the least. I
could still flex my left ankle enough to shift gears. I wasn't
disabled, but I also didn't have an exit wound. The bullet
was still lodged in my muscle mass.

A hospital?

No. That wasn't an option for several reasons, not least of
which was my existing level of medical debt. This problem
could be solved the old-fashioned way.

I started the bike and rumbled out from behind the
grocery store. Turning in the direction of a sign that
promised a highway, I rode one-handed, only releasing my

bullet wound long enough to shift gears. I was looking for a motel. A cheap, pay-by-the-hour place where I could pay cash and escape without too many questions.

I found my target next to the highway. The Motorway Inn had seen better days, with a patched shingle roof and potholes big enough to swallow full-sized dogs in the parking lot. I stopped the bike behind the building, sheltering my bloody vehicle from view of the street. Then I jammed my left hand into my jeans pocket and used it to block the wound.

The bleeding had subsided, confirming my hopes that no artery had been damaged. It still hurt like hell to stagger to the motel office. Thankfully, there was no door. Just a security window with a grate through which to speak to the attendant.

The guy was high as a kite. He never noticed the left hand jammed into my pocket as I passed him forty bucks for a downstairs room. Then I stumbled down the breezeway, reaching my door and fumbling with the lock. My head went light again. I leaned against the wall to keep myself from collapsing. The pain was so constant I barely noticed it anymore. I pushed through the door and kicked it closed behind me. I fumbled for the lamp switch. I reached the bed and collapsed onto my side, teeth gritted.

The bed covers smelled of cigarette smoke. The floral wallpaper I faced was faded, and seemed to dance in front of my very eyes. I blinked but couldn't regain focus.

I clawed the burner phone from my pocket and thumbed through the passcode, smearing the screen with blood. I reached a text message window. I dictated a message via the voice-to-text function.

I couldn't see clearly enough to determine whether the

message was accurate or even intelligible. I simply hit send, then closed my eyes to embrace the darkness.

30

Knuckles thumped against my motel room door exactly sixty-four minutes later. I had lain on the bed that entire time, measuring my breaths and blocking out the pain. The loss of blood left me dizzy and disoriented, but I couldn't quite pass out.

I wasn't *that* lucky.

Returning to my feet, I stumbled across the room and unlatched the door. Riley exploded in with eyes wide, one hand resting on the Glock 19 holstered beneath her leather jacket.

"Mason? What the—"

She broke off as I nearly toppled. Slender arms encircled me, propping me up long enough to get me back onto the bed. I collapsed over it. Riley hurried to shut the door, looking both ways down the breezeway. Then she spun back.

"What did you do?" Her voice crackled with anger. I forced a laugh.

"You think I did this?"

She approached, prying my left hand away from my hip.

The blood flow had stopped, my pants leg now crackling with dry crimson. Riley breathed a curse.

"How long?"

"Just before I texted you." I spoke through my teeth.

"Exit wound?"

"Negative."

"Come on," she said. "We'll get you to a hospital."

I shook my head. "No good."

"Why in the world not?"

"Two reasons. First...no insurance. Second, they know I'm shot. They'll be watching hospitals."

A snort. "They can't storm a hospital, Mason."

"Yeah? Well they shouldn't be able to pop off shots in the middle of a busy St. Louis thoroughfare, either. Yet here we are."

Long pause.

"If we go to a hospital this whole thing's gonna unravel." I spoke quietly, managing the pain. "The police will get involved. The gang will go to ground. Your cover will likely be compromised. The FBI will pull the plug on your investigation, guaranteed."

Riley chewed her bottom lip, her gaze fixated on my leg.

At last she said, "You have an alternative?"

"I'll give you a list," I said. "There's got to be a drugstore nearby. It's not rocket science."

"I'm not medically trained."

"The FBI trains all their people."

"In *CPR*," Riley snapped. "In blood loss management. Not in bullet removal!"

I closed my eyes, starting to sweat. Riley's tone of voice was giving me a headache.

"I've done it before," I said. "I'll guide you through it.

The bullet isn't deep. I can feel it maybe two inches beneath the skin. Distance shot—it lost velocity before it struck."

No answer. Riley didn't move. I opened my eyes to find her still standing over me, arms crossed, lips pinched together.

"Hey!" Now it was my term to snap. "You wanna catch these pricks or not?"

Riley held up a hand. "Okay, okay. What do you need?"

I narrated the list and Riley left. She was gone for twenty minutes. When she returned, she seemed to have obtained everything I requested.

"I had to find a Walmart," Riley said, producing a plastic package with a scissor-style pair of forceps held within. "These are for *fishing*."

"They'll work," I said. "Alcohol?"

She twisted the cap off a bottle of rubbing alcohol and doused the tip of the hook-removing pliers. They were long and skinny, similar to medical forceps, although maybe not as refined. Properly sterilized by the alcohol, I hoped their crudeness wouldn't matter.

"Stitching?" I asked. "Disinfectant?"

"All in the bag. Drop your pants."

Under normal circumstances I would have made a joke with a request like that. I'd lost a little too much blood to think of anything on the fly, and "won't you buy me dinner first" felt lazy. I tore my nylon belt out of my jeans and dropped them. Boxer briefs were plastered to my thigh with dry blood. I started to drop those also, then changed tactics and simply pulled the leg up above the wound.

"Can't give all away," I muttered.

Riley didn't laugh. She looked a little pale as I lay on my

stomach across the bed. I folded the belt into a wad and prepared to insert it into my mouth.

"You gotta rip it out," I said. "Don't probe too long or you'll roll it sideways and make things worse."

"What if it mushroomed?" Riley asked.

I hesitated. "Then rip fast," I said. I placed the sweaty belt between my teeth and clamped down. I planted my face into the bedcovers and breathed deep. I braced myself.

But there was no bracing for Riley's intrusion. She was right—the FBI hadn't trained her. Nobody had. She was about as subtle as a dump truck crashing through an undersized tunnel. The fish hook pliers descended into my thigh and rammed against the base of the bullet. I howled a scream into the comforter and clamped down on the belt. It was all I could do not to backhand Riley across the face.

"Hold still," she growled. "I think I feel it."

Think?

I was reevaluating my aversion to medical debt as she expanded the pliers and rotated them inside the wound channel. It felt like she was scraping my raw flesh with a shovel. The pain came so fast and steady I no longer differentiated the more precise movements.

"I think I got it," Riley said. "It mushroomed a little. Hold tight."

She yanked. She lost it. I clamped down on the belt so hard I thought I might chomp right through it. Riley swore and went back in.

On the second tug, the bullet tore free. My leg throbbed and Riley whooped. I opened my eyes and looked over one shoulder. She held the slug in the lamplight, a gleaming chunk of copper-clad lead slick with blood. The visual wavered and faded as I continued to quake, so racked by pain it was difficult to focus.

"Nine millimeter," Riley pronounced. "It only partially expanded. Lucky duck."

Nothing about my current predicament felt lucky. I was going lightheaded again. I spat the belt out of my mouth.

"Clean and stitch," I hissed.

Riley dropped the bullet on the bedside table and went to work from her Walmart bag. Hydrogen peroxide flushed the wound out, burning like fire. A squirt of antibiotic ointment entered the wound channel. Then came the needle—a regular sewing needle with regular cotton thread, just like I'd used on Spencer. Riley pinched the tip of her tongue between her teeth and went to work.

I was so numb I couldn't feel the bite of the needle, only vague pressure. Five minutes later, Riley wrapped my thigh in a compression bandage, encasing my entire leg. She tested the clips holding the bandage together, then grunted her satisfaction.

"That's about as good as I can do."

I gritted my teeth and rolled onto my back, panting as though I'd just run a marathon. The ceiling overhead danced before my eyes. Riley whistled.

"You're white as a sheet. Drink something."

She passed me a bottle of lukewarm water. I drained it and extended a palm.

"Pain killer."

"Extra strength Tylenol is the best I could find," she said. "Should help."

I swallowed twice the recommended dose and breathed a little more evenly. I still felt miserable, but the fire burning in my leg dulled a little with each passing minute.

"Thank you," I said.

Riley used wet wipes from the Walmart bag to clean her hands. She was a little sweaty, and kept looking at my leg. I wasn't sure if she was morbidly fascinated or about to puke.

I rested my head against stained pillows and again closed my eyes. I tasted my own sweat and it was salty. Riley passed me another bottle of water before I could ask. I sipped it this time.

At last she said: "So...Kumar."

Right, I thought. *Sitrep.*

"It's a sham," I said. "The restaurant services business doesn't exist. Kumar is making plenty of money, though—he drives a new Mercedes."

"You spoke with him?" Riley asked.

"Something like that. It wasn't a very detailed conversation."

"And Jerry?"

I opened my eyes, cocking my head. Riley remained in the chair alongside the bed, hands knotted around a wadded-up wet wipe.

"Kumar must have had them on speed dial," I said. "His warehouse is only a little ways from the fight club. They responded in record time."

Riley simply nodded and looked at her hands. I breathed through another wash of pain and returned my focus to the ceiling.

"Any further word from your FBI friends?" I asked.

"Not yet. I've got somebody digging into Kumar. It'll take a minute."

"What, no magical overnight results?"

It was a joke. Riley didn't laugh.

"It's probably drugs," she said. "Some kind of heroin or coke operation. Something highly lucrative."

I shook my head. "No. If Custer was moving enough drugs to build mansions and throw pool parties, you would have found the network by now. He'd be moving a *lot* of product. That's not the kind of operation only a few select insiders would be aware of."

"So what, then?"

I closed my eyes, focusing on my breathing for a while. "It's likely still a product, but a small one. Something subtle but extremely valuable."

We lapsed into silence. I chewed my lip, backtracking the puzzle. I was exhausted. I was lightheaded. I was losing mental focus as the Tylenol slowly kicked in.

Four premium motorcycles, two with built-in refrigerators. A multi-million-dollar operation. An Indian expatriate businessman who wasn't in business at all.

What did it all mean?

"It could still be human trafficking," Riley said. "There's money in the sex trade. Plenty of it."

I made no comment. Riley was correct, but once more I was perplexed by the lack of an apparent logistical framework. Moving anything illicit—let alone human beings—takes strategy. Preparation. A system.

And often, a network of people. So where were those people? Why did so many of the Gateway Hounds appear to be operating on the fringes, so far from Riley's juicier slice?

"It's something small," I said again. "Only a few key people are directly involved. Custer, Jerry, maybe Kumar. They generate the millions and then pump those millions through a pyramid of sequentially less and less illicit enterprising. Call it progressive money laundering—cleaning the cash in stages instead of leaps. The core business feeds the drug operation, which then feeds the casino, which then feeds the rave club...which finally pays the operators. If the cops ever investigate, they'll only penetrate the first or maybe the second layer. They'll hit pay dirt. Make arrests. Walk away without ever realizing that they only scratched the surface."

I turned to Riley. "Custer's smart. He's concealed his core business inside a fog of lesser evils, which he then pays off judges and prosecutors to protect. The payments are generous, and those judges and prosecutors have no idea what they're actually turning a blind eye to."

"The core business?" Riley asked.

I nodded. "The real moneymaker. The machine that pays for two hundred thousand dollars' worth of motorcycles to sit dirty in a barn."

Riley tossed the bloody wet wipe into the empty Walmart bag. She pondered, chewing her lip again.

"So...what's the core business?" she asked.

I leaned back into my pillow, suddenly so exhausted I wanted nothing except to drift into oblivion. Maybe the Tylenol Riley had purchased was a sleep-inducing formula. Maybe I was just exhausted.

"Something ugly," I said. "Something worth killing for."

31

I didn't notice Riley leaving. Blackness consumed me like a blanket, and I slept hard without dreaming. When I finally awoke, the alarm clock on the bedside table read five thirty in the afternoon, and I tried to sit up.

Throbbing aches exploded out of my left leg and ripped through my entire body, hurtling me back to the bed. I bit back a scream and cursed every sweaty redneck thug who ever swung a leg over a motorcycle.

Jerry, his buddies, Kumar and his shady factory. Custer and his stupid white cowboy vest. I wanted to dump them all into a meat grinder and see what kind of Hounds they really were—listen to them howl.

Serves me right for getting involved.

I forced myself upright, panting and looking to the nightstand. There was a motel notepad there with two lines of text scratched in ballpoint pen.

Gang obligation. Do not text.

Food in the bag. Try not to die.

The last comment almost brought on a smile—almost. I dipped my hand into a Dollar General bag to find two additional liters of water, a box of breakfast pastries, two cans of sausages, and a bag of jerky. Reasonable sustenance, under the circumstances. I found the bottle of Tylenol next to the bedside lamp and rotated it to read the label.

Yep. It was a nighttime formula. *Terrific.*

I drained one bottle of water, then I started with the breakfast pastries and worked my way through the sausages to the jerky. I ate everything. I was suddenly famished, and focusing on the concentrated flavors helped to distract from the pain.

I'm gonna wreck them all—one bone at a time.

I made myself the promise, but it did little to assuage my misery. I checked my phone for messages from Riley, but there were none. Just a voicemail from Arty with an update on my truck. The painting was almost finished. The job would be complete in another week.

Then Arty would want his final five-thousand-dollar payment...which would pretty much exhaust my savings, thanks to Spencer.

Problems for a later date.

I planted both feet on the floor with a grimace, flexing my left leg to test mobility. It was limited but not inhibited. If I could stand, I thought I could walk. The damage was concentrated in my left thigh, where layers of additional muscle remained. Lifting the leg, I straightened my knee and gripped the bedclothes until my leg jutted out parallel to the floor.

It was all I could do not to scream. The stiffness was overwhelming, a product of the hours that had transpired while I slept. Hot fire pulsated out from the bullet wound and consumed that entire half of my body. My head throbbed, and I blinked to clear my vision.

But I didn't drop my leg. I held it out, slowly lowering it under my own volition. By the time my foot rested again on gunky carpet I was breathing in controlled gasps, but already the pain had numbed. Some flexibility returned.

I was regaining control.

Mopping sweat from my face, I reached for the second bottle of water resting on the bedside table. My hand was halfway there when the electronic lock on the door buzzed, and the handle twisted. I tensed, ready to lunge off the bed and launch myself at the intruder—for whatever good that would do. Then Riley appeared in the doorframe, rushing in with a half helmet under one arm, her leather jacket smelling warm from the sun.

"Good," she said. "You're awake. Time to move."

I exhaled and slumped a little. Rocking up the water bottle, I chugged half of it. Riley kicked the door closed and scooped my boots off the floor. She placed them next to my feet.

"Can you ride?"

I wiped water from my lips and held up a hand. "Take a breath, sister. What's happening?"

"*Jerry freaking Withers* is happening, along with a full mobilization of the gang. They're looking for you—everybody is looking for you. Technically, *I'm* looking for you."

"Joy," I muttered.

"Yeah, joy. And a lot more coming if they find you. Jerry is *pissed*."

I faced the floor, thinking slowly. My mind was fully

awake, but my options were limited. If I could walk, I could ride. That wouldn't make either task easy.

"I need an anti-inflammatory," I said. "*Not* the nighttime formula. I also need some hard caffeine. Like an energy drink."

"Excuse me?" Riley squinted. "I don't think you heard me. *They're coming.* Right now. That bike of yours is sitting outside. They're checking hotels."

"So you better hurry," I snapped.

Riley hesitated only a moment longer. Then she swore and slammed the door on her way out. I worked on my boots while she was gone, only just managing to lace them up before she returned. A Red Bull and dual packs of extra strength Advil—not the sleepy version—hit the bed next to me. I tore both packets with my teeth and swallowed the pills. Then I chugged the Red Bull.

Caffeine is a doubled-edged sword with an injury. Increased blood flow increases blood pressure, which intensifies pain. But that same increase of blood flow also jarred my system and gave me energy to move, to focus, and to manage that pain.

I would take the tradeoff and trust my resolve to land me on top.

"Okay," I said. "Help me up."

Riley yanked on my arm as though she were trying to dislocate my shoulder. I bit back a cry and made it to my feet, stumbling but not falling. The pain was fierce, pulsating with each thump of my heart.

But it was also just pain. Just a sensation. All in my head. An illusion. A pathetic nuisance.

I told myself every lie that had carried me through Ranger School, through Afghanistan and a half-dozen crummy missions in all the worst corners of the planet, and I reached the door.

"Helmet," Riley said, tossing me the half shell she'd brought with her. I caught it and stumbled down the breezeway. My bike rested right where I'd left it. Riley was parked nearby. She half-jogged her way to the Sportster S. I mounted my iron horse from the clutch side, temporarily resting my bodyweight on the injured leg. The pain redoubled. I blocked it out and got on the bike. The engine started up with a snarl. I looked at Riley and nodded once.

"Follow me," she mouthed.

I gritted my teeth and disengaged the side stand. I rolled out of the parking space and found first gear.

I could walk. I could ride. *This is nothing.*

We rumbled away from the hotel, Riley cutting through a neighborhood and behind a shopping mall before she raced onto the highway. There was no particular rhyme or reason to her route—she switch-backed often, headed first north and then southwest before eventually turning east. I trusted her instincts, or perhaps her knowledge of the gang's search pattern, and did my best to keep up. The Sportster S was so fast off the line, and Riley being such an aggressive rider, that it was difficult for the heavier Fat Boy to push the same sudden turns at the same speed. Especially with an injured rider.

Once we reached I-270 things became easier. We settled into the fast lane and ripped east across the Mississippi River. Within ten minutes of crossing into Illinois, I had a pretty good idea of our destination. Another half-dozen miles and my suspicion was confirmed as we rolled off the blacktop and onto a loose gravel road.

Every rut and bump was pure misery, radiating agony up

my leg. I wrestled the bike along, trailing Riley through the
trees and up a hill. Past a gate. Into a small clearing.

And then to the little cabin alone in the woods. Riley
parked behind it. I followed suit. I made a point of keeping a
straight face as I dismounted, dropping the half helmet over
my sissy bar and enjoying the empty calm of the forest.

Riley removed her full-face and tossed her hair to clear
the tangles. She sat astride her bike, staring off into space for
a moment, her features constrained in frustrated concen-
tration.

And uncertainty. Some fear. A lot of angst.

Then she seemed to slump, and she dismounted the
bike.

"Come on," she said. "I'll make you some dinner."

32

While Riley heated canned soup I sat at the dusty table and reviewed FBI investigation files concerning the Gateway Hounds "motorcycle club". They weren't the first FBI files I had reviewed. I was familiar with the format, and the content helped to distract from the continued throbbing in my left leg.

The investigation began just as Riley said—not long after the murder of her sister, Kaley. The initial trigger came as a tip from the Missouri State Highway Patrol. Tasked—among other things—with the identification and detainment of illegal aliens encountered on Missouri's highways, the MHP had a problem.

The aforementioned illegal aliens were frequently disappearing. Not from state penitentiaries, of course. As with many states, Missouri lacked the infrastructure to house the tens of thousands of migrants streaming through a porous southern border and eventually finding their way to the Show Me State. More often, the subjects were simply cataloged, their current addresses recorded, and that information was then passed off to Immigration and Customs Enforcement.

But when ICE arrived to collect the cataloged parties, they couldn't be found, and that wasn't because they were hiding. Their friends and relatives were often panicked to report that the individuals had vanished. Usually wary of any involvement with the feds, expatriates from south of the border were now begging for law enforcement assistance with the recovery of their loved ones.

After all, deportation was better than kidnap...or simply never knowing.

"ICE dismissed it at first," Riley spoke from the stove, answering my questions before I had to ask. "Obviously, when you know you're going to be deported, you have an interest in disappearing. But then two of the vanished immigrants were found on security camera footage at convenience stores near their homes just before they disappeared. In both cases, Gateway Hounds were also present."

"Heck of a coincidence," I said. "Women?"

"One was. The other was a teenage male."

Riley carted steaming bowls of clam chowder to the table. She plunked down spoons and bottles of water without ceremony. I allowed the soup to cool while I continued my study of the files.

"Nine confirmed missing cases over six months," Riley said. "All of those names have been placed on national registries, and none of them have resurfaced. Not anywhere in the country."

I nodded, knowing it was unusual. As a beat cop in Phoenix, I knew more than most about the undocumented thousands infiltrating the Land of the Free. Some were criminals, certainly. Some were gangsters. Some were running from their own governments as much as the American government.

Most were just normal people, desperate to put food on the table and give their children a brighter future. That dedication to establishing stability in America made them vulnerable to re-arrest if they were once detained and then slipped away. Getting another job, renting another apartment, being stopped for a blown taillight...all of those things could put them back on the radar of law enforcement anywhere in the nation. With their identities recorded on a national registry, they would then be arrested and detained. ICE would be called.

And yet that hadn't happened. Not for these nine names. Not even once.

"They might have gone home," I said. "It happens, sometimes. They slip back across the border and cool off. Generate a new identity. Then try again."

"It's a long way to the southern border," Riley said.

Yes. A long way.

I didn't really believe my explanation even as I said it. Northern Mexico was a brutal place, rife with drug cartels and corrupted government officials. What rational human would roll the dice on a lengthy journey back into an effective war zone when they could simply slip into the shadows and hope to dodge American cops?

"Soup's getting cold," Riley muttered.

I shut the folder and dumped black pepper on my chowder. It wasn't great—it wasn't bad. It was exactly the sort of mediocre fare I had become so accustomed to during my wanderings in the back of a pickup truck. I ate in silence and drank the water. The Advil had kicked in, and the inflammation in my left thigh had relaxed a little. Likewise, the pain.

I could think more clearly. I watched the sun sink through the cabin's kitchen window. I surveyed the murder board spread across the wall and sifted through each X and Y in the equation. The unidentified variables. The question marks.

What was I missing?

"Kumar is the key," I said. "He's not a member of the gang. He's an outsider they're paying as a contractor. That can only mean he has some unique resource or expertise— something integral to their operation. We bust Kumar, and we split this thing wide open."

Riley made no comment. She was staring into her empty soup bowl. I turned back.

"Did your FBI people get back to you about his history?"

A grunt. A shake of her head.

The slow gears of federal bureaucracy.

"I'll go back in the morning," I said. "Give me a night to rest up and some more Advil. I want another look at his facility. You'll need to run interference."

No answer. I faced her. "Riley?"

She looked up slowly, and it was only then that I noticed the tears bubbling at the bottom of her eyes. Her lips parted. She swallowed.

"I'm failing her," she whispered.

I didn't have to ask whom she was talking about. The pain in her gaze was as familiar to me as my own right hand. That gut-wrenching desperation, the recycling stages of grief. Of failure. Of irreversible loss.

"I've given this everything," Riley said, voice dry. "I'm freaking dating a monster...and getting nowhere. It feels just out of reach, like I could touch it if I could only lean a little farther..."

She trailed off. My own stomach tightened. I leaned close, placing a hand atop hers.

"Look at me," I said.

She did. I squeezed her hand once.

"You can't bring Kaley back. No matter what happens next, you will carry her memory with you for the rest of your life. The pain will remain...but you will learn to live with it. It just takes time."

One tear slipped down her cheek. She didn't fight it.

"You sound so sure," she whispered.

"I'm about two years ahead of you on this road."

Something passed across Riley's face, and I knew she already knew. She'd Googled me, after all. She'd found that article from The Arizona Republic—that story about the school shooting that had followed me like a ghost.

"I didn't mean..." Riley trailed off. I didn't push her. "Does it ever get easier?" she finally finished.

I considered. I withdrew my hand and folded my arms, retracing those thousands of literal miles from Arizona to North Carolina. Through Georgia. Alabama. Florida. Louisiana. Arkansas.

"No," I said. "Not really. But you get stronger. And you learn, in time...that you have to accept what happened."

They were hard words—I almost didn't say them. I wasn't sure if Riley was ready. She simply nodded her head.

"You're a good sister," I said. "And you need to know that you are *not* failing Kaley...because these guys are *not* getting away."

33

Riley had only one cot, but plenty of blankets. I layered a couple of them into a pseudo mattress that was only a little better than stretching out straight across the hardwood floor. I would be sore in the morning, but what did that matter?

I was already sore. With the gun-shot leg, I would be doing well to sleep at all. Luckily, Riley had thought to grab the nighttime Tylenol on her way out of my mangy motel room, and I knocked back well more than the recommended dosage.

"Wake me if there's a world war," I said. Riley turned out the lights. I lay back on the pallet and listened to the creak of her cot as she wiggled down beneath her blankets.

The last thing I remembered before darkness swallowed me was the subdued cadence of constrained sobs. That cyclical grief digging in again.

I understood.

I AWOKE to a different sort of sound—and a much happier one. A crackling sizzle of bacon, perfumed with the greasy smell of the same, rose from the kitchen. My eyelids fluttered open, and I hesitated a moment before stretching my legs.

When I moved, the persisting throb of constricting muscles and the magnificent burning agony of that half-inch hole in my left thigh were nothing short of cataclysmic. I gritted my teeth and held back a shout, enduring it. Embracing it. Accepting it as part of myself.

I felt a lot stiffer than I had the night before. My thigh was swollen again, tense to the touch. But a quick visual inspection confirmed that it wasn't inflamed, which meant it wasn't infected.

Riley had done her work well.

Rolling to my feet, I found Riley busy in the kitchen, hair held back in a ponytail, her lips puckered in a soft whistle. She didn't look like she'd slept well. Dark circles ran beneath her eyes. Collateral damage of the pain swarming in her stomach, I knew. Only time would quell the squall.

Time...and justice.

I bit back a grunt as I steadied myself against the edge of the table. Riley looked up from the kitchen, a semi-amused smirk breaking her whistle pucker.

"Having trouble, old man?"

"Not at all," I managed. "Ready for a triathlon."

That brought on a derisive shake of her head. I pulled back a seat. It hurt even worse sitting down than it had when I stood up, but for all the discomfort, I enjoyed plenty of control over my left leg. I could flex each toe individually, rolling my ankle with ease and locking my knee out without resistance.

That meant I could walk. I could ride. I could still kick ass straight through the pain.

"Cream or sugar?"

"Black," I said.

Riley placed a hot cup of coffee on the table alongside the bottle of daytime Advil. I grunted my thanks but held off on the medication until I'd put something in my stomach. Alongside the bacon, I noted eggs frying in a skillet...and were those pancakes?

Riley served up a piping-hot plate. She dropped a bottle of maple syrup on the table and I proceeded to stack the bacon atop the pancakes before dousing them both with warm, sticky syrup.

"Kaley used to do that," Riley said, setting her own plate down. "She could clean two plates at every meal and fit into the same jeans she wore in high school. So unfair."

I wasn't sure how to answer. I sipped black coffee, and Riley noted the awkwardness. She reached for the syrup.

"You have any siblings?"

I shook my head. "Orphan."

"I'm sorry."

I shrugged. "There are benefits."

She cocked an eyebrow, waiting. I chewed pancakes. Then I forced a grin.

"I mean, I haven't thought of any just yet."

That brought on a laugh. It was a good laugh—not harsh, but boisterous. Very sincere, starting in her belly and rumbling out like a tidal wave.

"I grew up in Phoenix," I said, deciding that my own biography was a safer subject than Riley's. "I joined the Army after I got busted boosting motorcycles."

"So you've always been a piece of work?"

"Oh, absolutely. With pride."

"You stay long?"

"In the Army?"

"Right."

I hesitated. Shrugged. "Long enough. Made it through Ranger School and scored a slot in the seventy-fifth Ranger Regiment. Lots of time in Afghanistan...a little time elsewhere."

"Why'd you get out?"

It was a simple question. I stalled with the fork halfway to my mouth, maple syrup dripping from the underside of a fluffy chunk of pancake.

"I'm sorry," Riley said. "Didn't mean to pry."

"No." I set the fork down. "It's nothing like that. The Army treated me well. I was a good solider. I guess...I just needed a change."

"I get that." Riley speared more bacon and pancake, speaking through her food.

"I became a cop. Worked my way up to detective. Met my fiancée. All that was back in Phoenix. After I lost her...well. It was time for a change again."

"And now?" She asked.

"What do you mean?"

"What do you do now?"

I hesitate. Then grinned. "This."

It was a vague answer, but Riley accepted it. I reached for more syrup.

"What about you? How long with the Bureau?"

"Eleven years."

"Eleven years? How old are you?"

"Thirty-one. Why?"

Her tone edged with defensiveness. I held up an apologetic hand.

"You just don't look old enough to have served that long."

A pause. A grunt. "Thanks."

She returned to her plate, and I decided to forgo the remainder of my inquiries into her résumé. It clearly wasn't a popular subject. I could certainly appreciate the value of privacy.

Plates cleaned and coffee almost exhausted, I swallowed my Advil and looked out the kitchen window toward a bright fall sunrise. The sky was clear. Song birds flitted amongst the trees.

And we had work to do.

As though she'd read my thoughts, Riley broke the silence. "So what's next?"

The sleep I'd enjoyed the night prior, as uncomfortable as it may have been, had at least cleared my brain and reset my thinking about the problems at hand. In fact, I had deliberately not engaged with the subject of my present war with the Gateway Hounds, content to enjoy my meal and let my subconscious percolate on the problem.

It was a good strategy. As I brought the subject to the forefront of my mind, I found it easy to process, and the solution I had defaulted to the previous night seemed more logical than ever.

"I'm circling back to Kumar," I said. "I've burned buildings and broken bones, and they never pulled a trigger. But the minute I turn up at Kumar's place, these fools were ready to gun me down in broad daylight. I want to know why."

"Maybe they're just cumulatively pissed off," Riley said. "These aren't the sharpest knives in the drawer."

"No, they're not. But Custer clearly is. I assume Jerry's pretty bright, also. And they're the ones calling the shots.

You don't make millions on a criminal enterprise this well concealed without being smarter than the average Joe—no offence."

Riley shrugged. She finished her coffee.

"So again I ask. What's next?"

"I'll infiltrate the Kumar facility," I said. "Subtly, this time. And while I'm at it, I need to know that an army of iron-horse thugs aren't going to pop out of the woodwork."

"So you want me to cover you."

I suppressed a grin. "Unless you think Jerry might be into limping white guys."

Riley flicked a crumb of pancake at me. I set my cup down, growing serious.

"I know what it feels like when I'm close to the truth," I said. "Right now, we're right on the edge. One good push, and we break through."

"But?" Riley could hear the subtext of my statement. She was a good investigator. She could feel the undercurrent.

"But the closer we get, the more desperate they'll become. Whatever I find in that warehouse, you've got to be ready. When the cards hit the table, the last man to draw never walks away."

Our gazes locked. Riley's eyes grew hard.

"They're not walking away."

"No, they're not," I said. "So let's roll."

34

The Advil hadn't quite kicked in when I returned to my bike. Riley and I rode together out of the woods, every subtle vibration of the Fat Boy shooting red-hot fire through my thigh and deep into my hip. When we reached the highway, I shot her a two-finger wave, and then we split.

We were both headed west, but with the Gateway Hounds spread across the city and thirsting for my blood, it wasn't worth the risk of us being observed together. Riley would head west of town, where she planned to rendezvous with Jerry at his apartment. They had "making up" to do, she said. A produced resolution to the lover's quarrel that had left bruises on her arm. Riley would bury her anger and find a way to keep Jerry and his army of trigger-happy thugs corralled.

Meanwhile, I would pay another visit to the distinguished Ravi Kumar. It was time to dig deep, to keep pushing until I found the truth. To determine just exactly how a restaurant services entrepreneur with no business was able to afford a brand-new Mercedes GLS.

But first I had a stop to make, because I wasn't returning to the lion's den unarmed.

The Purple Crane Campground was alive with activity as I slipped past the camp office and routed toward Slot 12. The dually trucks that had temporarily blocked the entrance had moved, and a work crew was on site to replace the automatic gate. While kids played at the playground and adults fished off the riverbank, Christine and another group of workers were busy cleaning up the site of the old camp store, prepping the ground for the arrival of a new mobile building.

Recovery was underway. The healing was taking hold. Just watching it gave strength to my battered body.

Waving to Christine, I pulled into my slot and killed the bike. Inside the cramped confines of the Airstream I stripped out of my bloody clothes and scrubbed myself in the stainless steel shower stall. I toweled off and brushed my teeth. I dug clothes out of the wardrobe and pulled on fresh jeans and a black t-shirt, gritting my teeth against the pain erupting in my hip.

The Springfield Garrison rested right where I'd left it in a kitchenette cabinet. I quickly unloaded and broke the pistol down, inspecting each component before I reassembled it, placed one round in the pipe, then tucked the weapon cocked-and-locked into an interior pocket of my leather motorcycle jacket. I'm hot natured, and I had yet to wear the jacket that year, but without a holster it was the best way to conceal the pistol.

Lacing up my boots, I was at last ready to depart. I stepped out of the Airstream and locked the door behind me. I was halfway to the Fat Boy when Ms. Dottie appeared from her rebuilt maze of truck-tire flower beds, her face glowing as bright as the noonday sun when she saw me.

"Oh, Toddy! You're back!"

She extended both arms and rushed across the blacktop, meeting me next to the Harley. Face buried in my chest, she sobbed and clutched me close, not raising her face until I gently pushed her back, concerned she would suffocate herself. Ms. Dottie's eyes were an aged blur of tears, the absolute joy in her face so overwhelming it cut me. I didn't begrudge her the fantasy. I'd indulged it for months, always half-convinced that she herself was only half-convinced.

But today something was different. There was a belief in her gaze that transcended the illusions of dementia.

Christine appeared behind her mother, tugging work gloves off and gently taking Ms. Dottie's hand. I shot her a look, raising both eyebrows. Christine's sad eyes settled on me, and she mouthed a single word.

"Haircut."

Of course. I felt like a moron. I'd already forgotten the high and tight I'd ordered at the barbershop. Now I saw the connection, and I felt like a fraud. A deliberate puppet master, toying with an old lady's heart strings.

I remembered what I'd said to Riley back at the hunting camp—all that encouragement about growing stronger and moving forward. About acceptance, the final cycle of grief. I couldn't push Riley to that stage—I couldn't push Ms. Dottie, either.

But nobody who truly cared for either one of them would stand in their way.

I settled slowly on one knee, cupping Ms. Dottie's hands in mine. I looked into her longing face and gave her fingers a gentle squeeze. Tears ran down her cheeks, and I blinked as I felt tears bubbling up in my own eyes.

"What's wrong, Toddy?" Ms. Dottie said. "Are you hungry? Did they feed you? I love your jacket!"

I looked to Christine. Her gaze dropped. From across the blacktop, half a dozen other campers were observing us. I felt like I was under a microscope. It wasn't the situation I would have selected for this particular conversation...but I couldn't string her along any longer. I shouldn't have strung her along this long. What began as thoughtful indulgence had become something far less kind.

"Ms. Dottie...I'm not your son."

Her eyebrows wrinkled in confusion. "What?"

"Your son died in the first Gulf War, Ms. Dottie. He died thirty years ago...he died a hero."

Confusion washed into aching pain. Hesitation. Denial. Dottie looked to Christine, who was also crying. Then the old lady looked back at me and slowly raised a hand. Trembling old fingers extended toward my face. She touched my cheek, still not accepting.

Then the harsh reality set in. Ms. Dottie flinched. She withdrew her hand, staring a moment longer. Then her mouth closed. She ducked her head and turned away. Christine guided her toward her fifth wheel, and I straightened. I could still feel the eyes on me from all around the campground. I was no longer concerned about them.

I watched the old lady helped by her daughter into the camper, and my jaw tightened. I thought about heartbreak and the power of senseless death. It had eaten Ms. Dottie alive just the way it ate Riley alive. Just the way it had eaten *me* alive for so many years.

But this time, it didn't have to continue. It wouldn't extend from one sister to the next.

Custer's little empire was going down in flames.

35

I reached the cracked streets of North St. Louis without event and parked the Fat Boy behind a Dollar General, three blocks removed from Kumar's place. I didn't want him to hear the pipes as I approached. I had to assume he would be on site.

I couldn't help limping as I crossed the street. The Advil was working overtime, but the stiffness and throbbing pain were still there, exploding from my left thigh and radiating all the way into my skull. I bottled the pain. I buried it. I taunted it and sneered at it.

Each tactic lasted a few minutes, and then I rotated to the next. It wasn't the first time I'd battled through serious war wounds. With chagrin, I admitted it probably wouldn't be the last, either. The mission kept me pressing ahead, through a battered neighborhood and at last to the edge of the fenced lot surrounding Kumar's building.

In the early morning glow, the building appeared dusty yellow. The truck was still there. I couldn't see through the fence to determine whether the GLS was present. The gate was now closed—dragged across the entrance and secured with a chain.

No sign of the Gateway Hounds. No sign of anyone at all. The place was oddly still, and something about that sent red flags spiking in my mind like fireworks. I approached the facility from the sheltered side of the abandoned lot next door and kneeled in the tall grass. Peering through a gap in the plastic fence slats, I found the parking lot empty. No Mercedes GLS, no armada of dusty Harleys.

Yet still, my instincts warned me that all was not as harmless as it seemed. I worked my way down the length of the empty lot, wading through grass and briars and swallowing the leg pain. At the back side of Kumar's fence line I squatted again, sliding the fence slats apart to gaze through the chain link.

Behind the concrete block complex ran a narrow alley, about eight feet wide, with the fence bordering it. The space was littered with all the usual trash that clogs alleys. Rotting shipping pallets, stacks of cardboard boxes...and metal cylinders. Tall, silver ones, labeled with yellow stickers.

I squinted. I couldn't read the labels from fifty yards away, but something about their general appearance rang familiar. My mind worked a little slower, mired by Advil. I backtracked through the previous few days.

I stopped cold at the pool party—at Custer's place. The four Road Glides.

And the *Freon*.

Sweeping across the lot once more, I checked the gate. Still no sign of any flesh-eating motorcyclists. I drew my phone and checked for messages. Riley had texted eight minutes prior.

Jerry under wraps. You're clear.

Pocketing the phone, I wrapped my fingers around the chain link and gritted my teeth. Then I started up. It was a brutal, eight-foot climb. The privacy slats interfered with the toes of my boots, and the wire bit into my hands. The three strands of barbed wire running the top of the fence line provided an additional obstacle. I clung in place on the fence and peeled my jacket off, tossing it over the wire and pinning it down. Then I was rolling over the top, slinging my leg with no regard for its fiery protests. I made it to the other side and dropped.

The jacket remained in place, pinned by the wire. I reached up and tried to tug it free, but it was caught fast and beginning to tear. I muttered a curse and dug out the Springfield, resigning myself to add the expense of the garment to Custer's tab.

It was becoming a heck of a bill.

Back on the gravel, I kept the 1911 clasped in both hands as I turned for the compound. An awkward sprint brought me to the alley, where a quick inspection confirmed my initial suspicion. They were Freon cylinders—large ones. Industrial refrigerant used for chilling a large space. That might be logical for a restaurant services business, except Kumar had claimed that his company didn't deal in actual food items. Only dry goods.

So was he lying? Or was the Freon used for chilling something other than food?

I reached the front entrance and checked the door. It was locked, but the only visible security was a simple key lock holding the glass door against its steel frame. I squatted and went to work with my lock picks, tongue clenched between my teeth, hip burning.

Within two minutes the bolt rotated out of the frame with a *thunk*. I glanced over my shoulder to check the gate, but still saw no sign of Kumar or the gang. The door swung open with ease and I listened for the chirp of an alarm system.

All was silent. The dusty receptionist's desk just inside stood dark and empty. I slipped inside and locked the door behind me, disengaging the Springfield's safety with a flick of my thumb. For thirty long seconds, I remained motionless, just listening.

The building was still, but it wasn't quiet. Someplace in the distance a dull humming emanated toward me. I circled into the hall, lifting the gun to eye level inside a two-handed grip. I passed Kumar's office and the break room, clearing each. They were both empty. No sign of the South-Asian girl. There was a refrigerator in the break room, but it wasn't the source of the humming. I reached the metal door at the end of the hallway and looked out through the shotgun-blasted security glass into the warehouse beyond.

Tall, dirty racks. Faded cardboard boxes. Random stacks of metal soup cans and plastic chemical bottles. The rusted, broken-down forklift.

No Kumar. No gang.

As I proceeded through the door the humming grew louder. Still distant, but impossible to mistake for a product of my weary imagination. I kept both eyes open as I cleared each aisle, my trigger finger only a flick away from unleashing forty-five-caliber death. Each shelf was laden with exactly the sorts of products a restaurant services company should have supplied—plasticware, cleaning supplies, industrial oven parts, fryer oil.

Only none of it was being sold. That was evident by the thick layers of dust coating each item. I reached the back of the room, tracking the intensifying hum. I stopped at a tall silver wall sheathed in a skin of aluminum. It rose to just shy of the warehouse's roof, and as I placed my hand against the aluminum and pressed, it gave a little against a backstop of spongy insulation. I looked left and found the door. Tall and broad, with a heavy-duty latch. It was like the entrance to a cooler at a large restaurant. A green light gleamed next to it, alongside a temperature readout—forty-five degrees Fahrenheit. A thick padlock held it closed.

It was the door Kumar himself had fled into just before the Gateway Hounds arrived, and resting on the floor next to it was a white jumpsuit. Rubber, not cloth. Complete with boots and rubber gloves.

All three sprinkled with crimson dots.

My stomach tightened, instinctive dread closing over my gut in a wash. The inkling of an idea for what lay behind that door kindled in the back of my mind, but I didn't want to accept it. It was too gruesome. Too ugly.

Too absolutely unbelievable.

I drew the picks and went to work on the padlock. It surrendered inside of twenty seconds. I tore it free and dropped it onto the piled jumpsuit. I placed my left hand on the latch and held the Springfield close to my chest, ready for a thrust.

Then I entered, dragging the door open as the hum of a heavy-duty refrigeration mechanism intensified. Lights clicked on automatically, a rush of bitter cold air filtering between heavy rubber flaps. It stung my lungs and misted in front of my face. I thrust the flaps aside and entered the room, a twenty-foot square, insulated chamber with counters running along every wall. Banks of razor-sharp steel implements were held by magnets against the walls. A dozen lunch-box-sized ice chests packed a metal rack to my right, each labeled with dates and times.

And in the middle of the room, resting on an elevated table beneath a powerful LED light, covered in a white sheet —a human-sized form.

My stomach clenched into a knot. And I knew.

36

My burner phone rang as I approached the elevated platform. I ignored it, swallowing back the nausea already coursing through my gut. I placed my free hand on the edge of the sheet and breathed deep. Then I drew it back to expose the face.

She was young. Early twenties, perhaps. A little chubby. Hispanic, although death and chill had long ago drained the caramel from her face, leaving her skin a sickly, chalky white. Her eyes were closed. Her left temple was bruised purple, dried blood caking her hair. And beneath the sheet... she was nude.

And carved open.

I dropped the sheet, bile bubbling up in my gut and threatening to erupt through my esophagus. My phone continued to ring as I caught myself against the rack of ice chests, heaving. Surveying their labels.

And knowing—I'd been an idiot. It was right in front of me the entire time. Those insulated tour packs, complete with custom refrigeration mechanisms. Beer coolers?

Hardly. Not even close. Their application was far more sinister, but just as simple. I should have *known,* not only because it was so simple, but because Jerome Withers himself had practically told me what the Gateway Hounds were up to the very first night we met.

"I'll carve out your organs and dump your rotting corpse in the river."

His voice echoed in my mind as my phone finally stopped buzzing, the call going to voicemail. Then it rang again, somehow feeling more insistent this time. I jammed the Springfield into my waistband and clawed the phone from my pocket. It was Riley.

"Mason! I just heard from my people at the FBI. You're not going to believe this. Back in India, Kumar—"

"Was a medical doctor," I finished, gaze switching back to the elevated table. "A *surgeon.*"

Dead silence. "How did you know that?"

I never had the chance to answer. The cooler door swung open with a soft groan of metal hinges, followed by a tentative footfall. I looked to the left just as Kumar himself stepped into the operating room, dark eyes wide with shock and outrage. He saw the phone pressed to my ear. His jaw tightened.

Then he reached beneath his jacket.

I slung myself to the right, falling beneath the end of the covered operating table as the gunshots rained in. The phone flew out of my hands and skittered across concrete. I scrambled for cover at the base of the operating table, right hand clawing for the Springfield still tucked into my pants. Kumar continued to fire, dumping hot lead into the room at random, bullets pinging off metal cabinets and ricocheting off the floor. Breath fogged in front of my face and I huddled behind the imperfect cover, finally retrieving the Springfield from my pants. My finger found the trigger, but I couldn't move. The ceaseless gunfire had me pinned down.

Not only that, but Kumar was moving. I felt him coming, battlefield instincts warning me that his point of aim was shifting. He was orbiting the table. My cover would be compromised.

I did the first and only thing that came to mind. I braced my feet against the wall-mounted metal cabinets, and shoved my spine into the base of the operating table. It was like a giant leg press—enough sudden energy to send the bunched muscles in my left thigh erupting in volcanic pain. I screamed. My knees locked.

The operating table toppled backward, toward Kumar. I felt the body of the dead Hispanic girl shifting just as the base of the table departed my spine. Kumar shouted. His next shot zipped over my head. I rolled to my knees just as the table struck the concrete with a cataclysmic crash of steel. The corpse toppled off, tangled in the sheet. She struck Kumar's shins, and he danced backwards. He was eight feet removed from me, a tangle of medical implements and the fallen table standing between us. His pistol was brandished in one hand. He yanked his feet from beneath the corpse and redirected his aim.

I shot him in the shoulder. The Springfield cracked, its heavy steel slide ratcheting back, a single brass casing gleaming in the overhead lights as it arced through the air. The heavy report of the gun echoed off the walls, exploding in my ears. The round tore Kumar and sent him hurtling backwards into another wall of cabinets. Blood spurted in regular geysers, and he slumped to the floor, clawing at his shoulder and screaming.

I circled toward him, the Springfield held at the ready. Kumar's handgun—its slide now locked back over an empty magazine—toppled from his grip. I stepped over the girl's body and closed the distance, a steady finger resting over the trigger, ready to blast his face into oblivion even as I closed in.

Kumar was dying. It may have simply been a shoulder shot, but with so much blood saturating his shirt, his time was limited. The bullet had cut his subclavian artery. Per my battlefield wound training, I knew Kumar was now losing blood at the rate of roughly one liter per minute— and he could only lose two or three before his body shut down.

Yes, he was short on time. He needed a doctor—a legitimate doctor—immediately. But that wasn't my emergency.

Kicking past the tangled bloody sheet that had covered Kumar's victim, I put the Springfield on safe and kneeled next to Kumar. He wriggled backwards, gasping and crying out. I grabbed his shoulder, left thumb finding the open GSW and clamping down hard. The end of my thumb entered the wound channel, stemming some of the blood loss. Kumar screeched and retched. He tried to jerk free.

I smacked him across the side of the head with the barrel of the Springfield. His skull slammed into the metal cabinets. I shook him.

"Shut up!"

Kumar quaked. I spat bile across the floor next to him.

"Shut up and listen to me. I don't have to tell you what your situation is. You've got minutes, at most. If I take my thumb away, you might have seconds. Do you understand?"

A moan. A jerking nod.

I kept the Springfield's safety on as I jammed the muzzle

into his left eye. He screamed and jerked again. I clamped down on the wound.

"Who are you selling to?"

No answer. Kumar choked, murmuring what sounded like a plea. It might have been Hindi. I gritted my teeth.

"Nobody is coming, you swine. I know what you've done. You carved them all up, didn't you? All those missing migrants. You carved out their vital organs and buried their bodies. *Didn't you?*"

I shoved with the Springfield. Kumar shouted. He held up two bloody hands.

"Please! Please call an ambulance!"

I belted his skull with the handgun a second time. "I'm not calling anybody. Now you listen to me. I know Custer's paying you. He must be selling the organs. Who's the buyer?"

Another choking sob. I rammed with both my thumb and the pistol. He shrieked.

"Who's buying them, Kumar?"

"I don't know! I swear I don't know! I'm just a doctor!"

The sincerity of his voice was difficult to deny. I withdrew the handgun, shoving him into the wall before I retracted my thumb. The spurt of blood returned, draining down his shirt. Kumar's face faded to white. He gasped and clawed to block the hemorrhage, slumping sideways.

"Please...a doctor...please..."

"Aren't you a doctor?" I said, rising to my feet. "Heal yourself."

I remained motionless as Kumur grew to look more like the corpse lying next to him—the girl he had murdered, then carved apart like in a high school biology experiment.

No. I wasn't going to help him. I wouldn't have executed

him if he wasn't already shot, but now what had happened had happened. An ambulance would never arrive in time, anyway.

"You have seconds," I said, voice icy cold. "This is your last chance to make it right."

Kumar pressed his left hand against the wound. It wasn't enough to stop the blood flow. A couple liters of sticky crimson were now spreading across the concrete. A little more, and his heart would short-cycle. His brain would blink.

Death would envelope him just the way it had enveloped his victims.

"I don't know..." Kumar whispered. His dark eyes blinked slowly. I squatted again, pistol lowered, not reaching for his bullet wound.

"You know *something*, Kumar."

His gaze flitted across the room. His chin sagged. I thought he was fading. Then our gazes locked one last time, and dull anger consumed him. I saw it as a flash of crimson. Just enough to bring a little color back to his cheeks.

"I know..." he started, "what I came here for. I wanted a... be-better...life."

I leaned close, my breath hot on my own lips. I spoke in a growl, right through my teeth.

"*So did she.*"

I didn't have to point to the body. Kumar knew whom I meant, and there wasn't enough strength left in him to argue. His left arm fell limp. It slid south of the bullet wound and a final surge of blood splashed across my knee as his heart pumped once more...then he slumped. The breath left his lungs. His eyes misted over.

And just like that, Ravi Kumar was gone.

I straightened again, wiping sweat from my face. For a long moment I simply stared at the twin bodies, the Springfield held at my side. Then I surveyed the room, gaze passing over the toppled operating table. The cabinets. The steel racks laden with lunch cooler-style ice chests, each labeled with dates and times...

All containing, at one point or another, human organs. Millions of dollars' worth, carved straight from the helpless bodies of undocumented nobodies.

I spat Kumar's blood from my lips and staggered away from the table. I kicked through the mess, searching for my phone. I found it beneath the Hispanic girl's body, and I took a minute to cover her face with the sheet.

Then I dialed Riley, placing the phone on speaker. It connected with a click, and I was already speaking.

"It's organs," I snapped. "A trafficking scheme. Kumar was harvesting them, Custer's boys are delivering them. Those modified bikes are used for rapid transport. They must have a regular buyer with deep pockets."

No answer. Dead silence. I squinted, wiping my face with the back of my hand.

"Are you hearing me?" I said. "Riley!"

"Try again."

The voice was icy cold and harsh. Not Riley's.

It was Jerry Withers.

37

A brutal long second dragged by. Maybe a few of them. I looked down to the blood-smeared phone as the call log counted. The voice didn't return, but Jerry hadn't hung up.

He was waiting.

"Where's Riley?" I said, already knowing there was no way to wriggle out of the corner I'd put myself in. I'd said too much—*much* too much. But even if I hadn't, the fact that Jerry answered Riley's phone and heard my voice was testament enough. She was screwed.

"In a dark, cold place," Jerry snarled. "Right where she belongs."

Move.

It was my first tactical instinct. I searched the floor for Kumar's fallen handgun and found it against the wall. It was a SIG, one of their new compact-carry models. The gun was empty, and a quick check of Kumar's pockets failed to produce a second magazine, but I kept the weapon anyway, tucking it into my left pocket.

Then I was headed out of the cooler, back into the warehouse. Listening for the thunder of incoming motorcycles. There was nothing, only Jerry's continued snarl.

"You've made quite a mess, Sharpe. More damage in three days than an army of cops in three years."

"I offered a settlement," I said. "You turned it down. This is what punitive damages feel like."

"Yeah? Well, how about I damage *you*? I'm gonna carve this whore apart, one six-figure organ at a time. Before you know what's happened, she'll be in two dozen pieces."

That stopped me cold—not because of the horror of what Jerry promised, but because of the subtext of his statement. The fact that he was threatening me at all, and not promising my immediate death.

He doesn't know where I am.

"I'll call you back," I snapped. Then I hung up and ran back into the operation room. The burner phone buzzed like a crazed dog toy as I switched on my Streamlight Macro-Stream, casting a bright LED glow over the interior of the surgery room.

Kumar lay with his mouth hanging open, dead eyes pointed at the ceiling. The custom-built operating room surrounding him now stank of cooling blood, the smell of the battlefield. Looking at the man, I couldn't help but wonder if I'd ever shot a nastier enemy.

He was a monster. A fiend. A disgusting animal.

But before all of those things, Ravi Kumar had been a legitimate surgeon. A properly trained medical doctor.

And what do all doctors do?

They keep notes.

I held the flashlight in my teeth and tore through the medical lockers as the phone in my pocket continued to vibrate. I found spare surgical gowns, rubber booties, a box of condoms—what a freak—and stacks of medical reference books. One cabinet contained a dedicated freezer, packed to the brim with cakes of dry ice.

But no notebooks. No voice recorders.

It must be digital.

I rushed out of the room, down the hall to Kumar's office. I found his laptop resting open on the table, plugged in with a full charge. It was locked. The machine demanded a passcode...or a thumbprint.

I snapped my knife open and returned to the cooler. Kumar's body wasn't yet stiff. He flopped onto the floor as I completed my grisly work, snatching a plastic baggie from a wall dispenser before I returned to the office.

Kumar's detached thumb rested on the computer's print reader. The machine unlocked without hesitation, opening to a main screen populated by all the usual business suite software—email, a spreadsheet application...and a video player.

I hit the jackpot with the video player, but it didn't feel like a win. I was correct about the notes, but had guessed wrong as to their format. Kumar hadn't written things down. He hadn't even recorded them using a digital recorder.

He had *filmed* himself conducting surgery, narrating each step of the process with sadistic clinical detachment that sent a chill down my spine.

"November 18th, five thirty-four a.m. Female subject, Hispanic heritage, believed to be Mexican. Five foot four, one hundred twenty-four pounds. Believed to be in her late twenties. Organs for direct target—heart and liver. Consideration of kidneys. This should be a good one."

Kumar pivoted the camera away from his face. I closed my eyes, wincing as my stomach tightened.

It was the girl lying stiff in the cooler behind me. The Hispanic girl. She lay nude on the table, her head rolled to one side, mouth open. No visible wounds, but the kiss of death had been recent. I could tell just by looking into her wide eyes, which Kumar had left open.

Animal.

I smacked the laptop closed and ripped the charger from the wall. I returned to the cooler once more and found an empty lunchbox ice chest, dropping Kumar's bagged thumb inside along with a brick of dry ice. I removed his car keys from his pocket.

Then I was headed to the front of the building, ignoring the buzz of my insistent burner phone as I reached the parking lot. The Mercedes GLS fired up with the press of a remote button. I placed the ice chest and the laptop on the passenger's floorboard, then I rolled the driver's seat back to accommodate my extended frame.

There was still no sound of incoming motorcycles, but I wasn't taking any chances. The repeat phone calls were declaration enough—Jerry was desperate. Even if he didn't know where to find me, he would cover his bases soon enough. I hit the street and smashed my foot into the accelerator, racing away from the warehouse. The GLS ran like a mix between a Porsche sports car and a Bentley luxury sedan, smooth but quick as lightning. In seconds I was blocks removed from the site of Kumar's butchery, and at last I answered the phone.

"Are you out of your mind?" Jerry screamed. I switched to speaker mode and held the phone away from my face. "You think this is a game? I'll kill her!"

"No, you won't," I said flatly. "You're keeping her alive because you don't know how much I know, and Riley is your only leverage to find out. So why don't you cut the crap and let's get down to business?"

Momentary silence. A door slammed. Jerry spoke through clenched teeth.

"We looked you up, Sharpe. We know all about you. Seventy-fifth Ranger Regiment, multiple deployments. You think you're a real badass, don't you?"

"You tell me, Jerry. I've already disassembled half your little club of brainless morons, and I'm well on my way to the other half. You're about three days too late to be wondering who I am."

"What do you *want?*" Jerry snarled.

"What I wanted from the beginning—a settlement. Fair compensation. Only, the damages keep ballooning. You've got a heck of a lot more to answer for than a broken kid and a wrecked campground. Now we're talking serial *murder.*"

"What are you, a priest? I didn't call to play games, I called—"

"To set me up," I finished. "To pin me in a corner, find what I know and who I've told, and then to kill me. Am I right?"

Dead silence.

"Let me make it easy for you," I said. "I know *everything.* I've got a laptop full of Kumar's video notes for every surgery he's ever conducted. The faces of his victims. The organs he provided you. The final customers they were sold to. We're talking about enough evidence to stick a needle in the arm of everyone who ever *sneezed* near this operation, and that's assuming I don't get to you first."

Some of my claims were exaggerated. I didn't know for

certain what all the laptop contained—but I could guess. If Kumar had documented the previous night's surgery, he'd documented plenty of other things.

The hitch in Jerry's breathing told me I was correct.

"What do you want?" Jerry repeated. I glided to a stop at a traffic light and glanced quickly around. I didn't see any motorcycles. That hardly made me feel any better.

I breathed deep and considered my options. The situation felt more like stalemate than checkmate, but it was much more complicated than that. My next steps could very easily seal Riley's fate—one way or the other.

"I want Riley," I said. "Alive and unharmed. I want half a million dollars in small bills placed in a bag. You bring me both, and I'll give you the laptop. We call it a day."

It was a flimsy arrangement at best. Jerry would be a raging idiot if he let me walk away alive after what I'd already discovered. Handing over the laptop could never prove that I hadn't made copies of the files.

They wanted me dead, certainly. But the only way I could hope to arrange a meeting and attempt a rescue was for Jerry to fully believe that I wasn't working with the police —that I truly wanted the money and expected to get it. That was why I demanded the cash. With luck, it would be convincing enough a demand for Jerry to arrange a meeting. To set a trap.

And maybe his trap would work—maybe I would die. But I'd outsmarted them before, and I liked my odds of doing so again a heck of a lot better than the odds of Riley's survival if the FBI stormed in. Jerry would blow her brains out before the choppers even landed.

I just needed the meeting.

"How do I know you haven't made copies of the files?" Jerry demanded.

"You don't. Just like I don't know you won't kill her the moment I raise my head. But this is your offer. Take it or leave it. I want Riley, and I want the cash."

Long pause. Then it was Jerry's turn to stall.

"I'll call you back."

38

J erry kept me waiting for exactly eleven minutes, and I drove the entire time. Heading straight out of North St. Louis, I picked northwest by default—it was the general direction of Custer's mansion. I couldn't be sure that the Gateway Hounds had taken Riley there, but it was as good a guess as any. With my foot jammed into the gas, I kept one eye on my rearview mirror, the other checking the phone.

This wasn't my first experience with a hostage situation —far from it. I had participated in several as a beat cop back in Phoenix, one even as a homicide detective when my murder suspect got wind of a closing noose and turned his landscaper into a human bargaining chip.

Then there were the hostage situations overseas as an Army Ranger. Usually short-lived, usually resulting in mass carnage on every side. One time in particular, the Taliban had kidnapped a senior US diplomatic official and barricaded themselves inside a hotel. While awaiting a detachment of Delta Force operators—the Army's premier hostage rescue professionals—my Ranger unit had been tasked with the simple objective of securing the perimeter and maintaining the status quo.

That hadn't worked out. While Delta was still hours away, the Taliban got wind of a trap, and opened fire on our position outside the hotel. Trained for combat, not hostage negotiation, my Rangers had done exactly what I would have expected them to do—they shot back. A cease-fire order was given, but by then the Taliban fighters inside that hotel weren't the least bit interested in negotiation.

The situation went haywire. We charged in. A lot of people died—including the diplomat.

What that experience had taught me were the fundamentals of a hostage scenario. First, the kidnapper needed a *reason* to keep their hostage alive. The moment Jerry lost logical motivation for holding Riley, he was very likely to execute her, which was another reason for me to demand the cash. If Jerry believed I was corrupt, he might believe I would retain my evidence in exchange for the money. There was hope, however slim, that he could wriggle his way out of this mess unscathed. Therefore, there was hope for Riley.

Second, escalation is the enemy. Once I had established suitable leverage against the gang, it was a top priority to push them no further. A misunderstanding or a heated moment of broken communication could easily result in Riley's death. Certainly, involvement of the FBI would be a massive escalation. There was no win for Jerry and his thugs in attempting to negotiate with the US Justice Department. If the FBI was directly involved, they were all going to jail. Period. I couldn't afford to call Riley's bosses.

And that brought me to the third and final fundamental. The lesson that dry night in Afghanistan taught me so well.

Time itself can be an escalation. Every dripping second added risk to the equation. Jerry could get suspicious. Maybe Riley's bosses would miss her and come looking for her.

The sooner this thing was resolved, the better.

I mashed the answer button with my phone connected to the GLS's stereo system, allowing a hands-free call.

"What's the story, Jerry? You got my money or not?"

The voice that burbled over the phone wasn't Jerry's. I had never actually heard Carter Custer talk, but I knew it was him based simply on my mental image of his syrupy slow, fried-chicken drawl.

"Son, you've made quite the mess. Quiet the mess!"

"Is this Custer?" I demanded.

A snort. "You really expect me to answer that?"

"I don't care either way. I just want to know that the person I'm talking to is stacking half a million dollars into a duffel bag with my name on it."

Pause. A click of his lips. Custer sounded like he was eating.

What?

"A half mil seems a touch steep, what with the girl and all. That's a fine piece of ass. She ought to be worth a few hundred by herself."

"Are you *negotiating?*" I added an undertone of disbelief. "Maybe Jerry didn't properly communicate your predicament. I'm holding a computer—"

"Full of video recordings, I know," Custer said. "Would have kilt that fool myself if I'd known he was recording himself."

"He was a sick puppy," I said. "And now he's a *dead* puppy. So what's it going to be?"

Pause.

"Seventy-fifth, huh?"

I didn't answer. Custer's tone fell just short of relaxed, but far too close to calm for my own comfort. I wasn't getting under his skin. He was maintaining the initiative.

"I was in the Army," Custer continued. "Well, National Guard, anyway. Fourteen years. Never deployed no place, but I reckon I understand the brotherhood."

A wet chuckle. I gritted my teeth. I wasn't sure if he was pushing my buttons or simply insane.

"Here's the thing, son. You and I are both smart men. You gots to understand there's no way I can let you walk out of this. Not as long as there's even a *chance* you can come back to bite me."

"What's your proposal?"

A sucking sound. I got the image of Custer licking his fingers. He burped.

"Well. The digital world is a sticky one, ain't it? I can't be sure you haven't copied the files."

"I already said I haven't."

"Sure, sure. But what's honor amongst thieves?" A grunt. "I tell you what. I think we're gonna need some counter-leverage. A dynamic of mutually assured destruction, like JFK and Khrushchev. Just so we all know what happens if anybody gets frisky."

My gut tightened. I wasn't exactly sure what Custer was up to, but my instincts warned me that I wouldn't like it.

"What did you have in mind?"

"Well, you don't leave a guy a lot to work with." Custer said. "A loner like you, just drifting around. Departed from the Army, lost a beautiful young fiancée in Phoenix...what a shame."

Now I *knew* he was pushing my buttons. The ghost of that news story had struck again.

I remained quiet, and Custer continued.

"You do your best to appear unattached. But of course, Mia tells a different story. You're really quite sentimental, aren't you?"

"*Get to the point.*" My voice snapped with emotion. I knew it was a mistake, but I couldn't help myself.

"The point is this. I know about that kid in the hospital, the one my boys roughed up. I know about his mama, and the cripple girl in the wheelchair. Then there's the old crow at the campground. The fat ass at the barbecue joint...what's his name? Rusty?"

How in the world?

"Anyway, the point is this. I'll get you the money. You can even have the girl. After that you're going to disappear— vanish right off the face of the planet, never to return. Because if I *ever* hear from you, or her, or any of your kind again...I'll *kill them all.* You hear me? I'll carve them up into little, tiny giblets. I don't need no fool surgeon for that. I got a knife."

The GLS speakers fell silent as I flicked the cruise control on. I was well outside the city on an open highway. Nothing but trucks and light traffic. My heart thumped with restrained anger.

And I understood. It was a ploy, just the way my demand for cash was a ploy. There was no chance Custer would let me walk away. Not with what I had seen. No chance he would let Riley walk away, either. She was a federal agent.

But in order to lure me out of hiding, he had to give me the illusion of a way out. Just the way I'd offered him an illusion. A premise that made rational sense.

Give me the cash, and I'll split.

Sure, boy. And if you don't, I'll kill these randoms.

Custer wasn't striking a deal. He fully intended to kill me. And yet, no matter how clearly I saw it, I had no choice but to charge straight ahead.

"I understand," I said.

"Do you, now?"

"Perfectly."

Custer's voice brightened with produced southern charm. "Whall heck, then. I guess we got ourselves a deal! Half a milly and one fine piece of tush for you, business as usual for me."

"We all walk into the sunset," I said.

"Just like Kennedy and Khrushchev." A dry laugh. I clenched my jaw.

"Where do we meet, Custer?" It was the question at the crux of the issue. The first clue as to what sort of trap Custer was planning.

"I'm gonna have to pass you off to my associate for the details, Mr. Sharpe," Custer said. "Be sure to pay attention, now."

Jerry's angry snarl returned. "Where are you?"

"Someplace with a laptop full of evidence."

Pause. The line went so perfectly quiet that I knew Jerry had muted it. He was consulting. Making a plan.

Then he was back. "You got a pen?"

"I've got a smart phone."

"I'm gonna text you a time and a place. You be there—alone and unarmed. The first sign of funny business, and we'll waste the girl. Understand?"

"I understand," I said. "And just to be sure *you* understand, if she turns up with so much as a paper cut, I go public with everything. Am I clear?"

"And here I thought you were all about the money."

"I'm a complicated man, Jerry."

"Aren't we all?"

"No," I said. "Men like you are pathetically simple. Text me the address."

Then I hung up.

39

I pulled the GLS off the highway at a truck stop and rammed a fuel nozzle into the tank while I waited for the text. Kumar's premium SUV held a quarter tank of fuel, but I had absolutely no idea where I would be headed, and I wanted to be ready for anything.

While the pump ran, I sifted through the front floorboard of the SUV to inspect Kumar's captured SIG. It was a P365XL model and looked almost new. Fully loaded, the weapon would hold twelve-plus-one rounds of 9mm, which wasn't bad. The Springfield, meanwhile, held eight-plus-one rounds of forty-five, but the Gateway Hound I'd captured the weapon from hadn't topped off the magazine after chambering a round, and I'd fired once into Kumar's shoulder. Seven rounds now remained—I needed to make a stop at a sporting goods store to buy ammo.

The pump clicked off. I was just settling back into the driver's seat when my phone vibrated, signaling an incoming message. It was Riley's number, and I noted the time.

It was two twenty in the afternoon. Sunset was still

three hours away, and somehow that felt like a bad thing. I would so much rather deal with Custer and his V-twin thugs under cover of darkness, my ideal operating scenario.

Jerry's message came in the form of a question.

You in Missouri?

I texted back a blunt:

I can be.

Drive to Monroe City.

I squinted. The directions were vague, and that unsettled me. I couldn't predict what Jerry might be thinking. Punching the name of the town into the phone's GPS, I found that it lay two hours northwest of St. Louis, about fifty minutes from my current position. Mark Twain lake—which was actually a man-made reservoir—stretched out in an irregular splatter pattern beneath the town. Custer's mansion lay thirty or forty miles south of the lake, nearer to St. Louis.

So what was in Monroe City? A lake house? Was the gang keeping Riley off site? Or was this some kind of obscure trap?

Alarm bells chimed in my head. Nothing about this made sense, and it certainly wasn't the location I had expected. My default reaction was to stall—but I reminded myself that time was an escalation. Every passing minute lessened Riley's chances of survival.

Before I could make up my mind, the next text shot in. Four short words.

Be there at 5:30.

I blinked, caught off guard. I checked the GLS's clock again, my mind spinning. It wasn't a logical move for Jerry to name the time. Why should he? He had no idea where I was, and if he left time on the table, he left time for me to scheme. He should be adding pressure, not relaxing it. Commanding me to hurry. Keeping me on my toes.

Instead he'd listed a place and a time...and cut me loose?

The phone buzzed a third time. Another text from Jerry.

Confirm.

I made a quick decision and tapped out a response.

I'll be there.

Then I slapped the GLS's gear selector into drive and mashed the gas.

It didn't matter what Jerry was up to. His plans could change on a dime anyway, so there was no benefit in trying to outsmart him ahead of time. The best I could do was load up, arrive early, and think on my feet.

Riley's very life depended on it.

40

I found a sporting goods store and reloaded both the SIG and the Springfield. My next stop was a fast-food joint where I ordered the largest burger on the menu, along with a box of fries and a soda. I parked in the back of the lot with a clear view of the adjoining streets, barely tasting the food as I packed it in.

I hadn't eaten since breakfast, and I vaguely considered that this might be my last meal, ever. If I'd thought about that sooner, I would have opted for a filet mignon or at least have added bacon to the burger. None of that really mattered. My mind was already grinding to the showdown ahead, processing the situational calculus and solving for an answer that kept both Riley and me alive.

I didn't see many such options. Jerry's choice to name a rendezvous time so far in advance could only mean that time was no factor...or maybe time worked in his favor. Maybe he was scraping together the remnants of his little two-wheel army and preparing an ambush.

He could gun Riley and me down. That would be the

obvious plan—put a sniper in the trees to blow my brains out the moment Jerry took possession of the laptop. Somehow, I felt that Jerry's strategy was more complex than that. After all, sniping is an advanced skill, and gunshots draw attention. If he was planning to gun us down, why had he drawn me closer to a public place?

I let the clock wind down to three thirty before I hit the highway again, my GPS locked on Monroe City. The fifty-minute drive left me just a little time to survey the landscape before signaling my arrival. I might have arrived sooner, but Kumar's SUV wasn't exactly subtle, and by now Jerry's crew would certainly know that it was missing. They would be looking for it.

Even in the plush leather seats, the ride was brutally uncomfortable. My left thigh burned, muscles swelling as the final effects of the Advil faded. I was exhausted from a poor night's sleep on the floor of Riley's cabin. My head throbbed. My eyes stung.

But mostly I pictured Riley, tied up, with much worse than paper cuts to add to her misery. Jerry was a rough customer. I already knew that. Riley had done worse than jeopardize his operation. She had compromised his ego. Such behavior wouldn't go unpunished, not with a brute like Jerry.

I had to get her out. Alive and safely removed from the inferno, we could then arrange for the complete destruction of the Gateway Hounds.

One step at a time.

I reached Monroe City just as the sun faded toward Kansas. The term *city* was generous. It was more of a dot on the map, hours removed from any significant metropolis. I scanned the usual accouterments of small-town life—a local library, a couple of grocery stores, a gas station and a high school—but I didn't see any motorcycles. At least, none of the sort I was most concerned about. A kid blazed past me on a crotch rocket, but the high-pitched whine of his engine wasn't the throaty rumble I was looking for.

Fifteen minutes of surveying brought the sun deeper into the western horizon. I pulled off at a grocery store and parked with easy access to the exit. I kept the doors locked, both handguns tucked next to my leg, ready for action.

Then I texted Jerry.

> I'm here.

Seconds passed. I scanned the parking lot again, checking for more than motorcycles. Any random loiterers. Tough guys in pickups. Redneck ninjas hiding behind light poles.

My phone buzzed.

> Are you alone?

> Yes.

> Unarmed?

> Of course.

I doubted Jerry believed the lie, but at this point the board was set, regardless. He could either come for the laptop or run for the border.

Wait.

The next message wasn't what I expected. I thumped the Mercedes back into drive, keeping my foot on the brake. I surveyed the lot, ready to spring into action at a moment's notice.

> Did they have a tracker on Kumar's SUV?
> Do they know where I am?

It was a paranoid thought, but it still consumed my attention for the five seconds required to dismiss the concern as the nonsense it was. If they knew where I was all along, they wouldn't have arranged a meeting, or even wasted time with the initial phone calls. They would have jumped me long ago.

Minutes dripped by. It was fully dark. I checked my watch and almost texted back. I forced myself to wait a little longer.

Don't rattle him.

At last, at five forty-one, Jerry texted again. Only this time, it wasn't a message. It was an address that automatically populated into my GPS with a simple tap of my thumb.

The location was another dot on the map, this one thirteen miles southeast of Monroe City, quite literally in the middle of nowhere. No other towns, communities, or even a crossroads.

It wasn't until I switched to satellite mode on the GPS that I understood. The spot Jerry had marked lay in the middle of a two-lane road, but it was the location of the road itself that bore significance—it ran straight across the top of a dam. Specifically, the Clarence Cannon Dam that bottled up the Salt River, creating the Mark Twain Reservoir.

What?

I puzzled over the new development for only a moment before Jerry's next text blipped through.

You've got ten minutes.

I dropped my foot off the brake and mashed the gas. The Mercedes lunged ahead and I clipped through downtown, turning south on Main Street. The GLS's dash-mounted display mapped out my path down arrow-straight farm roads toward the north shore of the lake. The dam itself stood in the lake's eastern corner, and even though the rest of the countryside was drenched in darkness, I marked the concrete structure by its powerful overhead streetlights long before I reached it.

I slowed the Mercedes, squinting through the windshield. A part of me expected a hail of bullets to rain out of the trees at any second, but no barrage of gunfire came. The road was split by double-yellow lines. It curved a little, but remained relatively flat. I passed a brown sign on my left advertising North Spillway Park. I rounded the gentle turn.

Then I stepped on the brakes. There was no gate ahead. No security whatsoever. The road itself ran right across the top of the dam, carried by a bridge with guard rails on either side. The lake spread out to my right, the spillway a hundred feet below me to my left. Even sheltered inside the GLS, a hundred yards away from the bridge, I could hear the thunder of water exploding out of multiple hydro-electric turbines.

But it wasn't the noise of the dam that drew my attention, it was the quartet of beefy guys gathered around a parked Cadillac Escalade situated halfway down the length of the bridge. I recognized the vehicle from the drug house I had scoped out, and I recognized Jerry also. He stood amid three of his leather-clad, ugly-as-sin counterparts. Custer wasn't there.

But Riley was. Gagged and bound, she stood sandwiched between the Escalade and the righthand guard rail—the one protecting her from the black depths of the Mark Twain Reservoir. The guard rail rose to her thighs, and one of the thugs pressed her against it, a black metallic mass rammed into her gut.

A gun.

Jerry spat and advanced a step away from the bumper of the Escalade. He lifted a phone to his ear. My phone buzzed. I kept my foot on the brake and answered, switching the phone to speaker mode so that I could keep my hands near my firearms.

"What is this?"

"You bring the computer?" Jerry demanded.

I looked into my rearview mirror. I looked ahead. There was nobody on the road. No other cars, no other lights. Just the illuminated bridge with that expanse of dark water pressed against it.

"I brought it," I said. "Where's my money?"

Jerry moved the phone and muttered something to one of his guys. The Escalade's tail gate rose, exposing a cargo compartment with only one item resting inside—a black duffel bag.

The guy hauled it out and tossed it onto the blacktop. It landed heavily. Jerry returned the phone to his ear.

"Bring me the computer, you prick."

I bumped the Mercedes into park. Flexing in the driver's seat, I opted for the SIG over the Springfield—it would be easy to conceal. I slipped the weapon into the small of my back. Then I lifted the laptop off the floorboard, tucked it beneath my left arm, and stepped out of the Mercedes.

At a hundred yards the taillights of the Escalade glared

into my eyes. I approached slowly, right hand free. Jerry and his two Hounds stood facing me at the bumper, the bag between us. The last guy kept the gun rammed into Riley's stomach, pushing her against the guardrail.

As I approached, the roar of the dam grew louder. I glanced left and observed white water exploding across the spillway—a gravity-induced tsunami of it. To my right, the lake appeared perfectly calm, but I knew better. Only feet beneath that unbroken black surface, wicked undercurrents dragged thousands of gallons into the mouths of multiple spinning turbines.

I pictured it. And then I understood.

Stopping with thirty feet between us, I looked to Riley. Gagged and jammed against the rail, she gazed at me in a blend of fear, pleading, and rage. I made eye contact and nodded once, calm and collected. I noted the bruises on her face. The dried blood staining the gag.

Then I turned to Jerry.

"What did I tell you about paper cuts?"

Jerry sneered. "Time's up, hotshot. Bring me the computer."

"Get it yourself," I said, stooping to set the computer on the asphalt.

It wasn't the answer Jerry wanted. His teeth gritted.

"Five *million* gallons per hour," Jerry said. "That's how much water passes through those turbines. Unbelievable water pressure. Blades spinning at five hundred RPM." He took a half-step forward. His ugly lips lifted in a sneer, greasy beard tugged by a breath of wind. "You know what that adds up to, Sharpe? *Fish bait.*"

The guy with the gun jabbed Riley again. She cried out behind the gag. Jerry snapped his fingers.

"Bring me the laptop!"

I didn't budge. I looked back to Riley, observing the bonds holding her feet. Not zip ties, not duct tape. Simple cotton rope, a quarter inch in diameter. The kind that would be chopped to fragments by the spinning turbines, just like her gag.

No evidence. A heartbreaking accident.

"You didn't bring any money," I said, turning back to Jerry.

His smile lifted into a broader smirk. "It's simple math, Sharpe. As long as you're alive, there are no guarantees."

"So you're gonna kill me?" I said. "What if I made copies?"

Jerry cocked his head. Pretended to consider. Then he shrugged.

"I guess I'll have to find them."

With that, his left hand flicked. I saw what was happening even as it unfolded in slow motion directly before my eyes. The two men gathered behind Jerry fanned out, guns flashing from beneath leather jackets. Jerry himself lunged past the duffel bag, headed for the laptop.

But it was neither the guns nor Jerry that drew my attention. It was the fourth man, the one guarding Riley. As Jerry moved the gunman twisted, grabbing Riley by the arm. With a jerk he hauled her body up and over the rail. Riley thrashed. The guy shoved and released.

My hand flew for the grip of the SIG as Riley fell over the side of the bridge and plummeted into the black water beyond.

41

There was no time to think. There was barely any time to shoot. Jerry knew what I would do the moment Riley plummeted into the lake—he was counting on it.

And he wasn't wrong.

I opened fire even as I hurtled across the road and toward the guardrail. The SIG snapped off a hail of shots and all three men scrambled for cover. At least one of my bullets struck home, marked by an agonized shriek. I reached the guardrail and placed my left hand over the cold steel. Handguns cracked behind me like popcorn in a microwave. Bullets zipped past my ears. My feet cleared the rail.

Then I was crashing into the darkened water, just like Riley.

Within a split second of dropping beneath the surface, the light simply vanished. It was like being in a house at night when the power fails. One instant I could see, the next I simply couldn't. Then came a bone-chilling rush of icy cold. The November water had long ago lost its summer warmth, and the air vacated my lungs even as the SIG flew out of my hand and I flailed to tread water.

I returned to the surface with a heave and gasped down fresh air. Voices shouted from the bridge—not friendly ones. An engine roared. Then I was going under again, in control this time. Kicking to the midsection of the dam where Riley had gone down and diving head-first myself.

I was only a few feet beneath the surface when I first felt the undertow. It was little more than a vague suction, at first. A brush against my arms that marked the passage of lake water toward the mouths of open turbine shafts far below. Another kick downward and the suction grew by an order of magnitude. It tugged on me. I barely had to kick at all. I couldn't see a thing. I tumbled downward and my arm brushed against slimy concrete.

It was the dam. I bounced off it as the sub-surface rip current snatched me sideways. Lungs burning, head throbbing, it felt as though I was swimming through gelatin. I pictured the curvature of the dam wall in my mind, stretching farther and farther toward that muddy base where the turbines whirred like the blades of giant blenders.

Five *hundred* rotations per minute. Enough force to chop a full human body into a flesh puree. Even if there was a grate that blocked Riley's body from entering the turbine shaft, the suction would be enough to hold her against the dam.

And then she would drown.

I counted the passing seconds to calm my racing my mind. Fifteen had evaporated since I dove for the second time. I figured I could last sixty to ninety seconds beneath the surface before my lungs gave out and my body shut down. That was an optimistic measure. With the physical exertion, I was burning oxygen at far greater than the average rate, and this wasn't anything like my lap swims in the muddy Mississippi. This was a blind war in a void of darkness and cold, with raw fear as my only companion.

The wall. Find the wall.

I kicked left. My hand brushed the invisible surface of the dam wall, thick with algae and gunk. I used it as a guide to proceed farther downward, deeper into the water. I had no idea how far I had progressed from the surface, but the suction was growing stronger. I was sinking. I released the last of the air from my lungs as the timer in my head reached forty seconds.

Then my leg landed on something much too hard and flat to be the bottom of the lake. I leaned against the wall and the suction dissipated. Both feet rested on the hard surface and I staggered, my own buoyancy counteracted by what undertow remained.

I felt something new. A sound—the roaring thunder of machines deep inside the dam—the turbines. It pounded in my head along with the blood flow surging through my heart. My eyes opened, but I couldn't see a thing.

I didn't need to see to know where I was standing— directly on top of an open turbine shaft. Which one? There was no way to be sure. There might be two, there might be six. I was already out of air and didn't have time to think. In another twenty seconds, I would be out of time altogether. Then there would be two bodies rotting at bottom of the lake.

Where's Riley?

It was the only thought that mattered, ringing through the fog in my brain and bringing my mind back to the present. I dropped by instinct onto my knees, my body tugged down by what felt like the weight of magnified gravity. I turned instinctively away from the dam wall and crawled to the opening of the turbine.

I still couldn't see. The last of the precious air in my lungs was gone and biological alarms sounded in my head with every slowing heartbeat. My hand touched the edge of the turbine shaft and I dropped onto my chest, sweeping my arm down.

An immediate increase in suction slammed my arm against a rough metal grate. I choked, mouth opening. Water rushed in. I swallowed it before I knew what I was doing. I wanted to choke again. My head was going light, my heart thundering ever slower.

I *couldn't* find Riley. If she was pinned against the grate, her body was out of reach. How large was the opening? Ten feet across? Twenty?

And there were other turbines. I was out of time. I couldn't explore them all. I was about to drown. I could feel death closing around me like a shroud. The icy water felt like a tomb itself, crushing down on me. Consuming me.

Was this the end?

Maddened panic took over. I rolled left. I swept my arm once more and touched nothing but a metal grate and a thrashing catfish caught against the steel. I choked again. I was *done*.

Talk to him, child.

The voice came out of nowhere, a vague whisper in my mind. For a split second, the roar of the turbines faded, and I was alone in the water. Total stillness consumed me. I blinked and was swallowed by the darkness. The desperation in my mind redoubled.

But the biological panic, that physiological reaction of impending death, subsided. Just for a second. One last flash of a thought passed across my mind—*Help me.*

Then I rolled left, one last time. I swung my arm.

I touched flesh—pinned against the grate, cloth saturated by water, a body held frozen by the suction. I felt an arm. I wrapped my fingers around it. I tugged.

It was useless. I wasn't nearly strong enough. The suction was too much.

Help me!

The thought repeated like a gunshot. I pressed my knee against the concrete and pushed. It wasn't enough. I was giving out. I started to collapse.

Then the water pulsated with a sudden *thunk*. A strange stillness washed over me, the current exploding over my shoulders so hard I almost lost my grip on the invisible arm. My legs floated up. The suction faded along with the noise.

The turbines had cut off. My body was rising. I sank my fingers into the arm and tugged once more, the last of my energy exploding through sore muscles.

Then the body broke free of the grate. Buoyancy took over. I thrashed my legs in a weak kick. We headed for the surface. The body wanted to sink again. I kicked harder, reaching up with my free arm.

I'd stopped counting. Ninety seconds or ninety minutes may have passed. I bent my head back and longed for a fresh gasp of air. I imagined the surface dragging slowly closer, one agonizing moment at a time. The body was sinking again. I kicked harder. The darkness closed around my legs and reached in long, sadistic fingers up my spine. It was coming for my chest. Coming for my soul. I was inches away from permanent darkness.

And then I reached the surface. I exploded out of the water with a desperate heave, gasping in the sudden glare of streetlights. I went under again, dragged by the body. I wouldn't let it go. I kicked, lungs fueled by precious oxygen. I resurfaced with a heave and choked. I thrashed with my free arm.

And this time, I didn't go down.

"Grab the rope!"

The voice called from someplace to my left. I twisted my head in that direction—not toward the lights, but away from them. A dull green glow lit the night, and a splash of water marked the drop of a line into the lake. I kicked toward it, flailing with my right arm. My hand closed around the line and lost it. I flailed again. I went under. I choked on water, still dragging that limp body.

Then I caught the line and held it. I jerked. The line jerked back. In another moment I was tumbling across the surface, dragged by the rope. Gasping for air and clinging to the arm. I rocked my face toward a blackened sky and heaved, still choking. My arm struck something metal and a voice heavy with a Missouri accent shouted, *"Grab 'em!"*

Hands closed around my forearm. They pulled me upward. I slammed against the metal curvature of a pontoon.

"Gimme yer other hand!" the voice called.

I sank my fingers deeper into the arm beneath me and shouted, "Just pull!"

The hands did pull. I rose out of the water and my chest struck the deck of the pontoon boat. A moment later a gasp was followed by, "There's another!"

A splash heralded somebody diving into the water. The arm was wrenched from my hand. I was pulled onto the deck and lay gasping and choking up water, my head so light I felt as though I was spinning through outer space. The voices continued as I rolled onto my back, looking upward. Another splash of the line hitting the water. More heaving and cursing.

Then a second body struck the deck next to me. My head rolled to the left. I blinked the water away. I recognized the face.

It was Riley—chalk white and motionless, mouth hanging open. Eyes closed.

As cold as ice.

42

"Have mercy, have mercy. She's drowned!"

The Missouri accent returned, the speaker stumbling around on the boat behind me. I coughed up more water and rolled onto my chest, forcing myself to my knees. I nearly fell, the dizziness washing over me in waves. A heavy hand landed on my shoulder and held me back.

"Easy, fella! I'll call an ambulance."

It'll never come in time.

I pushed him aside and reached for Riley. She lay motionless on her back, wrists and ankles still bound with saturated cotton rope. I clawed the Victorinox from my pocket and snapped the blade open. I needed her arms out of the way. The two men behind me bustled and swore, one of them shouting into a cell phone. I blocked the noise out and cut Riley's wrists free. I threw her arms to either side of her body and dropped the knife. I rested the heels of both palms over her sternum and pumped.

I didn't shout. I didn't frantically call her name the way

they do in the movies. I'd done this before, more times than I'd care to admit. I knew how the biological clock works as organs shut down. If I couldn't get her lungs and heart going again within the next few seconds, she was a goner.

I pumped. I leaned over her face and pinched her nose closed, forcing air into her lungs. I pumped again, harder but still with perfect rhythm. Behind me, the two Missourians had fallen silent, simply standing and watching as the routine continued.

Twenty seconds. Thirty. I kept going, conscious of a sloshing sound inside Riley's torso. She had water in her stomach or her lungs—maybe both.

Help me. The thought coursed through my mind one more time. I pressed. I forced air down her windpipe. I pumped again.

Riley's eyelids fluttered. Her lungs sucked. I pumped again, shaking her a little.

Then Riley Vaughn returned from the dead, hands clutching at the plastic carpeting of the boat's deck as her eyes snapped open. She gasped. Water and bile exploded from her throat. I held her up, lifting her shoulders off the deck to keep her from choking.

"Lift her arms!" I called.

The two men bumbled forward. They lifted Riley's arms above her head, helping to keep her airway open. She gasped, quaking from head to foot. She vomited again, straight into her lap. It was mostly river water, with a little unidentifiable food.

"Praise Jesus!" one of the men proclaimed. "She's alive!"

I patted Riley's back, holding her close as she shivered. Wide eyes darted from one unfamiliar face to the next, then finally to me. She blinked in confusion, seeming not to recognize me. Or maybe it was her environment.

Then, suddenly, she sobbed. She threw herself into my arms, and I held her close.

———

COLD WIND BLEW off the lake, sending racking shivers off my spine as Riley finally withdrew. Her face was still chalky blue, but a little color crept up her neck. She stared into my eyes, unmatched gratitude streaked with residual tears of horror.

I knew the feeling. I also understood Riley's thought process as those crystal eyes turned icy cold.

"Where are they?" she spat.

I looked over Riley's shoulder, back toward the dam. Street lamps poured yellow glow over the two-lane, but there was nothing to see. No Cadillac Escalade, no Mercedes GLS. No bag of money—or random magazines—and no laptop. The Gateway Hounds were gone, clearing out while I was beneath the surface.

"Which way?" I addressed the question to the nearest Missourian. He was tall, bulky, and sported a bulging beer gut. He scratched his head, looking a little dazed. A quick sweep of the pontoon boat's deck revealed the source of his confusion—empty beer cans lay everywhere.

"We weren't really lookin'," the other man said. He was rail skinny and shirtless despite the chill. "Soon as we heard the gunfire, we turned this way. Then we saw you go under... didn't even know there was somebody else! George called the dam people."

The skinny guy pointed to a metal post protruding from

the water near the dam. Beneath the glow of nearby street-lights, I made out the reflective red letters of a phone number—an emergency line to the dam operators.

A miracle.

Riley withdrew from my arms and struggled to her feet. She staggered as she reached the edge of the pontoon deck, shielding her eyes to survey the dam. She swore. I remained on my knees, wiping water from my face, still struggling to catch my breath.

But also thinking as fast as I could. Scrambling for a next move. Because these guys were *not* getting away.

"What did you find?" Riley said, head snatching back toward me. "Right after they caught me, Jerry took my phone. You called. He panicked."

She doesn't know.

I pulled myself to my feet and turned my attention to the skinny guy—he seemed the most sober.

"You got a truck?"

The guy scratched his bearded chin. "Uh...yeah."

"We need a ride. It's important."

Another hesitation. The two inebriated Missourians exchanged a look.

"She's FBI!" I said, pointing. "Those guys you saw are human organ traffickers. Murderers. We need a ride!"

Skinny came awake about halfway through my plea, someplace around the word "murderers". He blinked and looked back at Riley.

"You FBI?"

"Right."

"You...got a badge?"

That was too much. Riley took over. "*No,* I don't have a

badge. I was under cover, and now they're getting away. Can you help us or not?"

The plea was enough. Skinny nodded, shoving past a tangle of fishing rods and fumbling for the boat's ignition.

"Right, right! I'll get you to the ramp. Ain't far."

"Organs?" Riley said. I turned to face her dripping form, her face now flushing red. As soon as our gazes locked, I knew I didn't need to explain. She already understood. She had already connected the dots. She dropped another curse and rushed to the boat's console, slapping Skinny on the back.

"*Move!*"

The pontoon was designed for stability, not speed, but the forty-horse outboard did an admirable job of pushing the big craft across the reservoir. Skinny—real name, Jimmy—turned the boat south, nervously chugging beer as he navigated between buoys and raced into a no-wake zone.

I detected the outline of a pier alongside a boat ramp from three hundred yards away. Trees leaned close to the water, thick shadows blocking out the parking lot beyond. I dug my dripping Streamlight out of my pocket. The beam reflected off a single pair of tail lights—a nineties model Dodge pickup, regular cab, hitched to a pontoon boat trailer.

"That your truck?" I asked.

Jimmy nodded, dropping his beer can. "We'll drive you!"

I shot Riley a look, knowing we were both thinking the same thing.

"What if we borrow it?" I asked.

Jimmy hesitated. "It's my favorite truck..."

He pulled back on the throttle and the motor died. The pontoon boat glided up to the pier. George fumbled with a line, pulling us against a piling. Water sloshed against the pontoons.

Then Riley put a hand on Jimmy's arm. "They killed my sister," she whispered.

Jimmy's drunken eyes flashed with pain. His lips parted. He looked at me, then George.

Then he dug a pair of truck keys out of his pocket. "The tank's almost full... Don't forget about us!"

Riley took the keys, pulling Jimmy close and kissing him on the cheek. He flushed crimson. Then she and I were bounding out of the boat and onto the pier, racing toward the truck as George slurred to Jimmy, "You think she's really FBI?"

We reached the truck and Riley circled automatically to the driver's side. I skidded to a stop at the rear bumper and pulled the latch on the trailer's hitch. I spun the jack and lifted it off the pickup's ball. Then I was scrambling to the passenger side door. Riley unlocked it. I hopped in as soda bottles and empty chewing tobacco canisters rained out. The cab smelled like cigarette smoke. The back glass was obscured by a large American flag sticker, peeling at the edges. Dirty t-shirts littered the dash. Dog tags hung dangling from the rearview mirror.

It was an *American's* truck. Just climbing inside it already made me feel better.

Riley twisted the key and the V-8 fired up with a chugging cough. She ratcheted the column shifter into drive and mashed the gas. Worn tires spun. We rocketed toward the parking lot's exit as I dropped the glove box open.

A pocket knife. A screwdriver. A cheap flashlight. Dirty work gloves.

And a Smith and Wesson 5906 chambered in 9mm, fully

loaded, with a handful of spare cartridges rattling around in the bottom of the box.

God bless American trucks.

I drew out the weapon and chambered a round. Then I smacked the box closed as Riley stepped on the brakes.

We had reached the terminus of the road. A stop sign reflected the pickup's headlights. A wide two-lane stretched into the trees on either side.

There were no other cars. No street signs. No houses or people.

Riley looked to me, and I breathed deep. For a long moment, neither of us spoke. My mind wound back to the confrontation at the dam, then back again to the phone call with Custer and Jerry...the text messages.

The rendezvous time.

"What was Jerry waiting for?" I said, pivoting to Riley.

She frowned. "Waiting?"

"He gave me too much time to reach the dam. He was waiting for something."

Riley shook her head. "I was in a closet... They had me gagged and blindfolded." Her knuckles turned white around the steering wheel. "Where are they, Sharpe? Where did they go?"

I held up a hand. I closed my eyes. I focused.

Time...time...

Then my eyes opened. Not because I'd seen anything, but because I'd remembered something Kumar had said in that sick surgical video. *Five thirty-two a.m., November eighteenth.*

I glanced quickly to my watch—it was November eighteenth.

"They were making a final delivery," I said, wheeling

back to Riley. "I found a body at Kumar's place. He removed her heart. Custer and Jerry must have had a buyer. A big payout. They were killing time until the delivery was complete."

"And now?" Riley said.

And now they're splitting, I thought. *Cutting bait. Destroying evidence. Headed for Mexico.*

"The mansion," I said. "Custers's place. Let's go!"

Riley's foot dropped off the brake. She punched the gas and pulled us into a hard right. The digital compass built into the truck's aftermarket rearview mirror read southeast... toward St. Louis.

Toward Carter Custer's blood money compound.

43

Navigation was a problem. My phone was ruined by my dive into the lake, and of course Jerry had taken Riley's phone. The truck featured no GPS. We used the rearview mirror's compass to chart a course in the general direction of Custer's place until we found a Dollar General sitting alongside the road in the middle of nowhere. I ran in and bought a pre-paid burner phone using soggy cash from my wallet. Almost all prepaids are smart phones these days. This was a cheap model, not quick or powerful, but it made calls and it featured a GPS. That was all we needed.

During the fifteen minutes it took us to find the DG, I caught Riley up on everything that had transpired since our last phone call. She answered the question I hadn't asked but had wondered about—how she had been busted.

"It was my own fault. I was at the rave club, waiting for Jerry to show up. I heard from the FBI. I called you—I turned my back to the door. He heard everything."

Just like Kumar had snuck up on me.

It was an ugly pair of mistakes on both of our parts, but after seven months of grueling undercover work, at least Riley could be forgiven. I was without an excuse.

"Call the FBI." I'd already programmed Custer's address into the new burner phone. We were forty-eight minutes out —the way Riley was driving, it might be a flat forty. She took the phone and dialed a number from memory. She placed the phone on speaker so that she could monitor the navigation. The route was all rural county roads, bereft of traffic but fraught with curves and stop signs.

"This is Special Agent Riley Vaughn." Riley rattled off a serial number and an authentication password when requested. The tension in her voice demanded speed, but whoever had answered the phone on the other end was in no hurry.

"What can I do for you, Special Agent?"

"I need an immediate detachment of HRT dispatched to Montgomery County, Missouri—I'll send you the address. We've got multiple heavily armed suspects attempting to flee the country. Expect heavy resistance."

Pause. "Say what?"

Riley looked ready to explode. I double-checked the Smith and Wesson as she repeated her commands. The weapon was a little rusty. It looked like it hadn't been fired in a long time. The copper jacketed bullets themselves were darkened with age.

They might not work. The gun might jam.

Whatever the case, those fifteen rounds of nine-millimeter, plus whatever raw ingenuity Riley and myself could pull out of thin air, were all that stood between Carter Custer and a scot-free escape. I could already tell that even after the FBI took Riley seriously, even after her requests filtered far enough up the chain for somebody with authority to take action...it would still be hours before boots hit the ground.

This wasn't the Army's Regimental Reconnaissance Company, a detachment of the 75th Ranger Regiment on perpetual standby at Fort Moore, capable of deploying anywhere in the world inside of forty-eight hours. No— these were bureaucrats. A three-letter agency at its best.

Riley ended her call and slammed the phone into the bench seat next to her.

"How long?" I said.

"Three hours," she snapped. "*If* they get the order. They're still making phone calls."

We're on our own.

I thought it. I didn't say it. What was the point? I looked to the GPS. We were still twenty-nine minutes out. I figured that Jerry and the goons in the Escalade had a fifteen-minute head start...maybe twenty. Of course, Carter Custer could have already split. He could be halfway to Mexico by then.

But I didn't think so. My money was on Custer waiting for his bodyguards. His entourage. Waiting for the payment to arrive from the final sale of that Hispanic girl's heart, not to mention the all-clear from Jerry. It would take time to cover all their tracks.

And besides—Custer was arrogant. He wouldn't leave until he was good and ready.

"We can't expect to arrest them all with a single hand-gun," I said. "The best we can hope for is to pin them down... stall for time. There's a good chance Custer has already departed his mansion."

Even as I said it, I was developing another plan in my mind—a more logical one that I couldn't share with a bona fide agent of the US government. Alone with the Smith, I could close on the compound the same way I'd infiltrated during the pool party. I could slip up behind one of Custer's bodyguards, preferably a heavily armed one, and slit his throat with my knife.

Then I could take his weapons. Fade back into the darkness. Take the Gateway Hounds apart one at a time, leaving nothing but a field of rotting corpses in my wake. It wouldn't be easy, but it was doable.

I just had to get rid of Riley, and the moment I felt her crystal eyes on me, I knew that was never happening.

"Are you trying to ditch me?"

"There's only one gun," I said. "And only one of us is a combat Ranger. Park the truck on the street and watch the exit. You'll have Custer in the end."

"*Alive?*"

I didn't answer. Riley began swearing again—not a single curse, but a whole hailstorm of them. A deluge of angry profanity as she slammed her hand open-palmed into the dash of Jimmy's truck. We reached a stop sign and Riley mashed the brakes. The tires squealed. She turned on me, red faced and red eyed. Gasping a little. Starting to cry.

"I did *not* endure seven months of snuggling up to that mangy pig just so you can systematically murder these people! This was my case long before you turned up. *My job.* Do you hear me? Nobody is taking it away from me. *Nobody.* If you can't agree to that, get the hell out!"

The wretched agony in her face was absolute. I couldn't make myself look away. I saw a mirror in Riley's eyes—the reflection of two long, brutal years. Almost to the day.

It began with the gunfire in Phoenix. It spilled into broken bones and dead bodies all over the American Southeast.

A war? Maybe not with anyone as much as myself. It was a rutted road up a volcanic mountain, nothing but sulfur to breathe and rocks for a pillow. A brutal path. An unforgiving journey. A meat grinder I wouldn't wish on my worst enemy.

But that was the thing—tickets to this ride were nontransferable, nonrefundable. If your name was called, it was called. Nobody could climb the mountain for you.

And nobody could pull you from that journey once you began. The best anyone could do was walk beside you.

Riley extended a hand, tears bubbling into her eyes.

"Give me the gun," she said, voice hoarse.

I laid the Smith into her outstretched palm. She rotated it muzzle downward, checked the safety, then rammed it beneath her right thigh. The truck took off again, and we both faced forward. Riley kept her foot jammed into the gas, eating up asphalt as the burner phone vibrated against the steering wheel. The mileage counted down, now descended to single digits. The ETA read eight minutes. Riley blew through a stop sign without so much as blinking and I drew the Victorinox from my pocket, keeping the blade closed as I clenched the knife against my side.

I knew we were closing on Custer's property long before I actually saw it. Not because I recognized any landmarks, but because I smelled the smoke.

And looking out the filthy windshield, south toward the horizon...I saw a column of fire piercing the sky.

44

Riley laid on the brakes at the end of Custer's driveway. An iron gate stood there, blocking the mouth of an asphalt road winding down the hill toward the sprawling fish pond I'd seen before. The surface of that pond was perfectly still, as smooth as glass.

But it wasn't dark. It reflected the blazing orange glow of the absolute inferno that engulfed Carter Custer's mansion. Rising well over a hundred feet off the ground, the fire seemed to touch the sky as the building burned from every side, windows rushing with flame, doors standing open. The detached garage next door was also on fire, casting a daytime glow over the parking pad where Riley had left her Sportster S during the pool party.

That parking lot was not empty. A black Cadillac Escalade sat there, its windows reflecting the hellish blaze only yards away.

"That's them," I said, my right hand instinctively tightening around my only weapon. The Victorinox felt even more pitiful than the Smith, but I wasn't about to ask for the gun. I reached for my door handle instead.

"Wait," Riley snapped. She ratcheted the truck into reverse and hit the gas. We spun backward away from the entrance. She cut the wheel and sent us arcing toward the ditch. The back tires dropped off the blacktop and Riley hit the brakes. She switched back into drive. She wrapped both hands around the wheel. My gaze flicked ahead, and I knew what was coming—I knew, and I didn't like it.

"Riley..."

"Hang tight!"

Then she smashed the accelerator. The back tires spun. Dirt exploded against the underside of the pickup's bed. The Dodge ran like a rocket across the double yellow lines, off the road into the mouth of Custer's driveway.

Straight for the double iron gates.

I grabbed the A-pillar-mounted handle and rammed my feet against the floor, deliberately avoiding the dash just in case the air bag deployed. By the time the old pickup reached the double iron gates, Riley had it running at thirty miles per hour. The engine surged under full throttle, the middle of the front bumper aimed straight for the crack where the two gates joined.

Then we struck. The truck hit with a colossal screech of metal on metal, one gate exploding backwards as the hydraulic cylinder operating it failed altogether. The second gate was stronger, and the back end of the truck fishtailed to the right as I clung to the handle and plowed into my door. Riley wrestled the wheel.

Then the lefthand gate exploded backwards in a shower of sparks. Steam erupted from the nose of the Dodge and the hood buckled upward, but the engine continued to run.

Riley wrenched the wheel to pull us out of the fishtail, then we were hurtling forward again. Down the hill, orbiting the fish pond. Headed up another hill with trees lining us on either side, the glare of the burning house just a hundred yards to our left. I could already feel the heat of it.

And then I heard something else—a shout. A rattling pop.

"Down! Down!"

I grabbed Riley by the shoulder and wrenched her toward the dash as a storm of gunfire burst through the windshield. She kept her foot planted into the accelerator and we hurtled to the top of the hill, leaving the asphalt and leaping a shallow ditch. All the while the gunfire persisted, bullets zipping through the cab and pinging against the truck's bodywork. I risked a glance through the shattered windshield just in time to see a towering oak tree, not fifty yards ahead of us. We were headed straight for it.

"Brake! Brake!"

Riley's foot found the brake. The truck fishtailed again, but not enough to bring us off course. We hurtled toward the tree in a flickering glow of firelight, tires locking and sliding over sandy soil. Fifty yards shrank to ten. The speedometer dropped, but the truck was still moving.

Then we hit. The airbags hadn't deployed when we struck the gates, but the tree was more than enough to trigger them. As the front bumper folded in and the hood buckled upward, a cloud of white appeared in my face. My head slammed into the bag, throat flooding with dust as my seatbelt caught. It cut into my neck. My spine rippled like a bullwhip. The world spun around me.

I pushed off from the dash and choked—the entire cab of the truck was flooded with air bag dust. I couldn't even see

Riley. From outside the pickup the pop of rifles was obscured by the roar of the house fire. A bullet sliced through the cab, missing my ear by inches as it whizzed like a hornet.

Bail. Bail now!

I clawed my seatbelt free. I reached for Riley and couldn't find her. Then I felt the wash of heat on my face and knew she'd got her door open—she was out, and still in the fight. I kicked my own door open and rolled to the ground, landing on my hands and knees. From the far side of the pickup the familiar pop of a 9mm signaled Riley's engagement. I couldn't determine the enemy's position from the sheltered side of the truck, or where my next point of cover might be, but I knew two things beyond question.

First, I needed a weapon. Something significantly more potent than a Swiss Army Knife.

And second, I had to move.

Staggering to the rear of the truck, I stole a look around the tailgate just as a creaking groan heralded the failure of the mansion's roof. With a shuddering roar, the entire second story of the giant home collapsed, hot sparks exploding outward on all sides. The rush of light was so brilliant I had to turn away...

But it revealed my enemy—at least a few of them. Dug in behind the nose of the Cadillac Escalade, twin starlights marked the position of two riflemen. They were both raining fire on the front of the Dodge, concentrated on Riley's position. I couldn't see her from this angle, but assumed she had found shelter behind the tree we collided into.

They hadn't seen me—not yet. It was time to move.

I exploded from behind the truck as the Victorinox's three-inch stainless-steel blade locked open with a snap. I routed for the back left corner of the Escalade, stretching my wounded left leg and forcing myself through each stride. With every footfall, agonizing pain exploded through my hips and up my spine, so raw and relentless I almost fell.

But the adrenaline arrived right on schedule, as did the battlefield focus honed by years of action on the wrong side of the world's tracks. I forced myself ahead and reached the left rear corner of the Escalade just as a pause in the gunfire marked the termination of my cover.

They had seen me but they couldn't get a shot. They would orbit around the front of the vehicle.

I clenched the Victorinox in my right first, held low and ready, and leaped from both feet just as the first Hound appeared across the nose of the Escalade. He was tall, over-weight, sporting a long beard and a black leather vest embroidered with the gang logo, but no body armor. No protection for his vital organs.

The AR-15 he carried was held in a sloppy low-ready grasp, his point of aim lightyears away from where it should have been. He saw me coming and his eyes went wide. He struggled to raise the rifle.

Then I hit him. Colliding like a battering ram, my right hand rocketed upward just as my left arm caught him across the throat. The rifle cracked, so close to my face that my ears rang, but the muzzle was pointed back toward the road— nowhere near me.

Then my knife blade sank in. Right up to the hilt, pene-trating layers of fat and slicing into his gut. The Hound shrieked and stumbled. He released the weapon and fought to force me off.

But I kept coming. Feet dug in, capitalizing on my momentum, driving him off a sloppy stance and right into the face of the second Hound to cross in front of the Escalade.

The three of us tumbled to the ground as the first guy released his rifle and the second guy opened fire at random. Bullets shattered the Cadillac's windshield and raced across the front fender. I tore the Victorinox free and landed atop the first Hound, driving my knee into his gut and powering back to my feet. Twisting at the hips and slashing with the single-edged blade.

I caught the second guy across his exposed thigh just as he struggled to pivot his rifle on me. The razor-sharp implement sliced right through jeans and deep into his muscle. He screeched and I abandoned the knife, grabbed the rifle with both hands and forced it left as he buckled at the waist and clamped down on the trigger.

Bullets exploded over my left shoulder. I shoved him backwards, my own feet caught up on top of the fat guy beneath me. The rifle slammed into the second Hound's chest, and I jerked hard backwards.

His grip broke. He was thrown off balance, a combination of his wounded leg and my own violence of action overcoming him. The rifle fell into my hands. The muzzle swept down. My finger found the trigger.

I dumped six rounds into his chest before he knew what had happened. He toppled backward without a sound, brass raining over the Escalade's hood. I twisted at the hips, alarm bells screaming in my head—alerting me that I had abandoned the first guy for too long. He might have a sidearm. He might have recovered his rifle.

The muzzle of my captured AR fell over his face just as his right hand appeared from his pocket, a folding knife snapping open. He swept for my leg.

Once again, he was lightyears too slow. I sent three rounds of 5.56 blasting through his face and into the dirt beyond, turning his skull to fragments. The body fell limp, the knife flopped over his chest. I yanked my foot to free it from his grasp, falling back against the Escalade. I gasped for air, rotating the rifle to check the open dust port.

I'd felt something. A barely perceptible alteration in the cyclic slam of the bolt—like a skip on a CD track. A sensation any hardened warrior knows well.

Sure enough, I was right. The weapon had run dry. I was staring at an open bolt and a plastic mag follower, and just as I reached for the release button to strip the empty magazine away, fresh noises exploded over my shoulder.

A shout from Riley, her voice raw with energy and desperation. The twin roar of motorcycle engines. And an instant later, the hissing snarl of full automatic fire—a submachine gun.

I instinctively hit the deck, rolling onto my stomach and looking beneath the Escalade. The noise of the engines drew my gaze just as muzzle flash marked the darkness. It came from an open rolling door at the middle of the metal barn where I'd found Ravi Kumar's new phone number.

A split-second later headlights flashed, and then a pair of dirty Harley Davidson CVO Road Glide STs exploded out of the shadows, barreling right toward me.

45

There was no time to claw my way to the second fallen rifle. No time to do anything but grab the body of the man I'd gut-shot and roll him onto his side just as the explosive wrath of the submachine gun rained hellfire on my position. Small caliber rounds pinged off the Escalade and blew out a tire. Air blasted my arm. I dug into the dirt, face down, and choked on the dust. The thunder of the bikes drew nearer. The gunfire persisted. I thought I heard Riley returning fire, but I couldn't be sure. I twisted my face to look beneath the Escalade just as the Road Glides raced behind it, sticking to the asphalt driveway.

They blazed past the wrecked pickup. Blazed past their fallen comrades. Blazed right past the fish pond and were headed up the second slope toward the gate as I found my feet. I clawed the second AR-15 from the ground, whipping the rifle into my shoulder and centering on the dim tail lights of the second Road Glide.

Its bulky rider wore white. He bore down on the throttle.

He was two hundred yards away and working on three. The AR-15 was equipped with a cheap red dot site, and I couldn't be sure that it was properly zeroed.

I fired anyway, three quick shots at varying levels of elevation, hoping to get lucky as much as I hoped for the rifle to be accurate. I missed all three, and the bikes reached the blown-out gate. They both turned left. Engines howled.

And then they were gone.

I kept the rifle up, crouching next to the nose of the Escalade and sweeping the rifle backward to cover my own six. The red dot crossed over the house fire—the first-floor walls were caving in. I reached the detached garage, the flames hot on my face. I covered the pool deck.

The Gateway Hounds were nowhere to be found, but I knew that couldn't be right. Jerry had three guys with him at the dam. I presumed Carter Custer to be riding astride the second Road Glide, so...

I hit him.

I remembered the shriek of pain as I unloaded Kumar's pistol against the Gateway Hounds at the dam, and I circled the Escalade. I yanked the back door open. I led with the rifle.

The third man lay lifeless in the back seat, dark crimson drenching his chest from a nasty neck wound. Bled to death...just like Kumar.

"Are there keys?" Riley shouted as she sprinted across the driveway, the Smith and Wesson held at her side, the slide locked back over an empty magazine.

"Stay under cover!" I shouted.

It was too late. She met me at the side of the Escalade, her face blackened by smoke.

"Get in!" she shouted. "We gotta go."

"No good." I jabbed a thumb at the blown tire. "Search the bodies and find a weapon. I'll be back."

I rolled the AR in my hands and dropped the mag, inspecting the load. The cartridges looked to be .223 Remington hunting rounds—a far cry from the green tips I used overseas—but at least a dozen remained.

Good enough.

I slammed the mag home, shouldered the rifle, and sprinted for the one building not yet ablaze—the metal pole barn.

The middle door stood open as I reached the end of the asphalt drive and pivoted around the corner. My thumb flicked automatically forward, searching for the pressure switch of a weapon light, but the rifle was equipped with nothing more than the questionable red dot. Glowing like neon, the holographic sight swept across the interior of the barn, passing the dissembled Low Rider, the Confederate flag, the beer fridges, the desks...

And coming to rest on the pair of Harley CVO Road Glide STs remaining in the building. They stood just as I'd last seen them, wheels cocked toward their deployed side stands, dirty paint reflecting the distant firelight. Abandoned. Left behind.

Then I saw something else. I had missed it at first—my eyes registered it as a refraction of the red dot optic. It was red, all right, and LED. But not a weapon sight.

It was a clock resting atop a nondescript white cube wrapped in transparent packaging tape. Wires connected the clock to the cube. The LED numerals displayed eighteen seconds...then seventeen.

My heart lurched and I hurled myself forward, racing for

the nearest bike. Against the back wall the clock flashed down to twelve seconds as I hurled a leg over the Road Glide and landed in the saddle with a slam, the rifle dropping over my legs.

Without really considering it, I had elected to take a tremendous gamble. Modern Harleys don't use keys—they use keyless proximity fobs, just like modern cars. If the fob is close enough, the bike will start. If not...the bike is dead.

I had no prior knowledge to assure me that the Gateway Hounds would have kept the key fobs *on* the bikes. But locked up inside a secure metal building, with four fobs that looked identical and would be difficult to keep apart...why wouldn't they?

I clamped down on the clutch and flicked the ignition switch. The lights of the Road Glide's giant digital display flashed. I stowed the side stand with a slam of my left heel. My right thumb dropped over the starter button. I mashed it.

The Harley thundered to life. With a cough and a roar, the entire machine rumbled between my legs. Temporary elation flooded my body, followed instantly by a flash of desperation as my gaze settled over the right-hand mirror. I saw the clock, displayed in reverse, but still readable.

Seven seconds.

Dropping my left foot on the shifter, I rammed the bike into first, cranked on the throttle, and dumped the clutch. The rear wheel screamed against the concrete. I exploded out of the open rolling door and struck the asphalt, already racing ahead fast enough to demand a counter-steer as I pivoted toward the Escalade. Riley stood behind it, face blackened by my smoke, the Smith 5906 replaced with one of its modern equivalents—an M&P.

"*Get on! Get on!*" I screamed.

Riley hadn't seen the bomb. She had no way of under-standing the nature of my desperation. But she was smart enough not to argue, throwing herself at the bike as I mashed on the rear brake, slowing but not stopping. I lost the AR-15 but found Riley's arm. She belly-flopped across the rear seat, ribs slamming into the tour-pack. She shouted in pain. I rolled on the throttle.

"*Hold on!*"

We hit the drive and the Harley screamed toward redline. I leaned instinctively forward, dropping over the handlebars. Bracing myself.

And then the building went up. The blast was every bit as loud and powerful as I had feared, enough to turn the metal walls of the building into a spray of shrapnel and each Phillips-head screw holding the structure together into an individual bullet. I kept the bike running all the way to the bottom of the hill, not stopping until we were adjacent to the fishpond. I turned back in time to see twisted sections of roofing metal raining down amid a cloud of smoke.

There was no fire—there rarely is with C4, and I knew by the blast signature alone that C4 was to blame for the build-ing's instant destruction. The final Road Glide was history. The dissembled Low Rider on the motorcycle lift was history. That Confederate flag was history.

But most of all—the *evidence* was history.

I swept my gaze across the twin heaps of a burning garage and a burning mansion. An abandoned eighty-thou-sand-dollar SUV. Dead guys and bullet casings everywhere. A scene of carnage, but nothing that would point the way to where Carter Custer and Jerry Withers were headed with their blood money. Nothing that would allow the FBI to trace them once they escaped the country.

If they escaped the country. They hadn't yet, and I knew exactly where to find them.

46

"Find the nearest airport!"

I turned the Road Glide back to the scene of carnage only long enough to collect the fallen AR-15 and allow Riley to get seated properly on the pillion before we were roaring past the fish pond and up through the gate again. I turned left at the two-lane, following the route Jerry and Custer had taken.

Then I dumped on the power, and I immediately understood why Custer had invested so much money into four identical CVOs. My Fat Boy was fast—the Road Glide ST was like a missile. Even riding two-up, the massive 121-cubic-inch engine hurled us along with effortless power, both wheels remaining firmly planted as we streaked toward three-digit speeds. The shark-nose fairing worked miracles at deflecting the oncoming currents of wind, so effective that I was easily able to hear Riley as she shouted over my shoulder.

"Right turn ahead! There's a small airport about six miles distant. Looks to be private!"

That's it.

I screamed through the turn, dragging the right floorboard as I cranked on the power. The bike launched ahead, the LED headlight bar illuminating our path as bright as day. Wind tore at my hair and my left leg burned with pulsing waves of agony, but I didn't slow. I wouldn't slow.

This was ending—right there in the middle of nowhere, Missouri. If I was wrong about the airport, and Custer and Jerry were really headed for a mad highway run to Mexico, the FBI would catch them long before they reached the Oklahoma state line. But I wasn't wrong—a plane would be the most logical option. Custer probably had a standing evacuation plan, which was why he'd torched his mansion and blown the pole barn into smithereens.

A quick flight south. A bag full of cash and a chance to build a brand-new criminal empire in a country rife with such opportunities. But not if we got there first.

"Left in two miles," Riley called. "I checked the satellite view. There doesn't appear to be a fence!"

I saw the airport only seconds after making the next turn. A rough county road stretched out over relatively flat ground, and a few thousand yards off my right shoulder, bright red lights blinked at the end of a private airstrip. There were hangars—maybe a half-dozen of them. A mobile building that might be the airport's office. A sign illuminated by floodlights that marked the airport's entrance.

And parked at the far end of the strip, its cockpit glowing with soft red interior lights, was a single-engine aircraft—a big one, its turboprop already spinning as shadowy figures climbed through an open side door. The aircraft was still nearly a mile distant, and it was impossible to identify any faces.

But what I *did* recognize were the pair of brand-new CVO Road Glide STs parked just behind the plane. Abandoned, their headlights still blazing.

"That's them!" Riley called. "They're getting away!"

Not on your life.

"Hold on!" I shouted. "We're going off road."

I mashed on the rear brake to bleed off a little speed just before I leaned hard into the right-hand grip, banking us off the road and directly into a shallow ditch. The front tire hopped off the pavement and sank into the dirt. I clung to the handgrips and planted my feet into the running boards, adding more power.

The bike was aptly named—it was a Road Glide, not a Dirt Glide. It was built for the pavement, not the trails. But the engineers up in Milwaukee had done one heck of a job designing the bike's suspension, and despite the road tires and the awkward angle we hit the ditch at, the Harley remained upright. It powered straight through the ditch and entered the edge of the field beyond. Tall grass and low brambles ripped against the front wheel and tore past the shark-nose fairing. Some of them whipped back and stung my legs. Riley bounced on the pillion, crying out and struggling to keep her seat. The AR-15 she wielded slammed into my ribcage. My left thigh pulsated with pain.

But I kept going. I cranked on more power. I fixated on the aircraft at the end of the runway, its propeller now whirring to full speed, its door closed. I thought the plane was moving. We were still hundreds of yards from the end of the airstrip, but the path ahead was clear and flat. Just more tall grass and briars.

"Get ready!" I shouted.

"Ready for *what*?"

I didn't answer. I up-shifted and dumped on more power. The massive V-twin obliged, and the back tire dug into the dirt. The last stretch of grass faded into a blur as we raced for those red lights at the end of the runway—a hundred yards. Then fifty. The plane was definitely moving, departing the hangars and taxiing for the airstrip. Gaining speed. Turning toward us.

I braced myself against the floorboards, rising off the seat as we struck the tarmac. A jolt exploded through the bike. Riley shouted. The rifle smacked me in the ribs again. Then all that vibration was gone. The bike ran smooth on the concrete. We were pointed dead at the airplane, it's whizzing turbo prop shredding air three thousand yards away. It was a Cessna, a model 208 Caravan, I thought. Fast and light, easily capable of streaking south into the oblivion of a no-extradition Latin American country.

But it wasn't off the ground yet.

"Put the rifle on my shoulder!" I said. "Aim for the prop!"

Riley didn't need to be told twice. She shifted on the pillion seat, dragging the AR-15 out from under my arm and resting the handguard over my right shoulder just as the Harley reached eighty miles per hour. The yardage between us and the Caravan had shrunk by half. The aircraft was now moving at a steady clip, roaring toward us despite the obvious threat of an incoming road block.

The AR's muzzle passed inches from my face. The snap of the selector switch was audible even over the roar of the wind. I remembered the cheap red dot and prayed that it was accurate enough.

A pair of shots through the prop and into the engine could easily enough set alarm bells screaming in the cockpit.

It wouldn't take much to keep the plane on the ground. Just a little luck.

Or maybe a little providence.

"Shoot!" I called. "You're running out of room!"

Riley opened fire. The rifle barked in my ear, so loud I winced and wanted to jerk away. I didn't move, keeping both hands tight around the grips, back rigid, shoulders stiff. Offering Riley the best shooting platform I could manage.

From four hundred yards away sparks flew from the Caravan's propeller—bullets were striking the blades and being deflected off. I saw the pilot moving in the red light of the cockpit, ducking beneath the dash.

But *still coming.* Defying the risk, maybe because there was another gun pressed into the back of his head.

"*Dump the mag!*" I called.

Riley did. The shots rained in a ceaseless hail, muzzle flash nearly blinding me as the rifle twitched on my shoulder. Further sparks exploded from the propeller. We were three hundred yards out. Two hundred. The plane kept coming. The rifle jerked as a final trio of shots ripped from the barrel. Riley swore as the weapon ran dry.

Then I heard the scream—a metallic grinding, a haze of smoke rising over those red cockpit lights. The plane twitched and semi turned. We were a hundred yards out.

I had to move. I was out of time. I counter-steered hard right, leaning the bike to its limits to swerve around the plane. It was the logical move as the plane twitched to our left, but then the aircraft spun back the other way. Smoke poured from the engine bay. The wings sliced through the air like twin blades, the propeller whipping straight toward us, the air alive with that metallic shrieking grind.

In another few seconds we would collide. The digital

speedometer on the Harley's dash still read sixty miles per hour. The world around me descended into slow motion—it was the old lady in her land yacht all over again, except this time the Caravan's prop was ready to grind us like the blades of a blender.

There was only one choice left. A choice no competent motorcyclist should ever have to make...and yet, for the second time in as many days, here I was—making it.

"Brace!" I shouted.

Then I laid the bike down.

———

47

The CVO Road Glide ST came stock from the factory not with a traditional crash bar, but with a stubby crash arm that stuck out perpendicular to the frame. It was likely the only thing that saved my left leg as the Harley went down hard on its clutch side. Sparks exploded from the crash arm as we spun beneath the Caravan's lefthand wing like a child's toy kicked across a hardwood floor. I felt Riley eject from the back seat just as my shoulder struck tarmac with nothing but a Walmart t-shirt to protect my skin. I instinctually covered my head with my left arm as I continued to cling to the righthand grip, pulling myself into the bike. Trusting the bulky metal beast to protect me from bone-on-concrete evisceration.

The Harley slid for another thirty yards before finally coming to a halt, the built-in tilt sensor having already killed the engine. Bouncing off the fuel tank, I released the handlebars and struck the tarmac on my road-rashed shoulder.

The world didn't spin, it danced. I stared up at a Missouri sky littered with gleaming white stars and gasped for breath, not sure if I was still in one piece. My ears rang. My head swam.

But from across the airstrip the grumbling thunder of a gun-shot turboprop engine reminded me that the fight wasn't over. The Caravan hadn't taken off—it hadn't crashed either. It squealed to a stop facing perpendicular to the direction of the airstrip, engine howling as it dispensed clouds of black smoke. A cargo transport model, the aircraft featured no windows behind the cockpit. I couldn't see anyone moving inside.

But I knew they were there.

Rotating on my shoulders, I grimaced against the pain and searched for Riley. I found her lying on the tarmac fifty yards away, face twisted away from me, body motionless. I didn't see blood. I didn't see anything other than the Smith and Wesson M&P handgun she had carried, now resting between us, spotlighted by the still-running high-beams of the Harley.

I gritted my teeth and pushed off from the bike. I landed on my back with an explosion of pain in my left thigh— reminders that I was already gun-shot, but if I didn't move quickly, I might well be again.

I reached my feet and staggered. I spat blood and probed a loose tooth with my tongue. I looked once more at Riley.

Then I caught the flash of movement to my right. It came as a temporary dimming of the red cockpit lights, an indicator of something—or someone—blocking the pilot's window.

I didn't wait to identify the threat. Launching away from the Harley, I ignored the pain and sprinted for the M&P. I was just stooping to scoop it off the concrete when the first burst of gunfire cracked from the open pilot's window of the plane—not a rifle, but a handgun, spraying rounds at fifty yards. They whizzed over my head and one grazed my arm. I dove for the gun, landing on the concrete with a crash, breath exploding from my lungs. My right hand found the grip and I swept the muzzle up. Stock three-dot sights orbited over the window. I pressed the hinged trigger just the way I'd pressed handgun triggers tens of thousands of times before—a steady, smooth squeeze. The snappy recoil of a .40 caliber Smith and Wesson cartridge shot up my arm, and I reacquired the target. I shot again. A third time. A fourth.

The red lights of the cockpit returned as the body fell against the dash—tango down. I clawed my way back to my feet, dropping the mag and checking the load. Four, maybe five rounds remained. I rammed it home and staggered toward the plane, each footfall on my left leg so painful that my knee almost buckled. Pistol up, grasped in both hands, I opted for the tail of the plane instead of the nose.

Beyond all rationale or reason, the turboprop engine was *still* running. Not fast. The speed approximated a strong idle, the tri-bladed propeller shredding the air.

I knew there were doors on both sides of the Cessna, meaning that Jerry and Custer—who were presumably still inside the aircraft—could bail out on the far side at any time. I bent at the waist to look beneath the belly of the plane. The ground was blank, and I reached the tail just before a starboard side door exploded open with a crash, followed a split second later by the unearthly thunder of a shotgun. Buckshot pellets ripped past the Caravan's rudder, blasting away paint as I scrambled for cover behind the tail. The shotgun slammed as the shooter pumped a new shell into the chamber, followed a moment later by an enraged shout.

"*Sharpe!* Is that you, you scum?"

It was Jerry. I backed against the tail of the plane, looking toward the nose and the still-open pilot's window. If somebody leaned out with a handgun, they would have a clear shot at me.

But if I circled the tail, Jerry would blow me away.

"Who do you think it is?" I shouted, my own anger lacing the words.

My peripheral vision caught a flash of movement from the pilot's window, and I swept the M&P in that direction and pressed the trigger without thinking. A forty-caliber round entered the window at an angle and ricocheted off the steel flight panel. I heard it as a whining whiz, followed by a pained shriek. It was Custer who screamed—I recognized his fried-chicken drawl. He struck the floor and thrashed. Temporary pandemonium overtook the interior of the plane.

Then Custer managed a clear order. "*Git 'im!*"

I clenched my jaw and looked back to Riley. I thought she'd moved since I last saw her. She raised her head, and I made an exaggerated *stay down* motion with my left hand.

Then I turned for the tail of the Caravan.

"You coming, Jerry, or do I have to drag you out by your beard?"

A nasty curse, followed by the airplane's door exploding back on its hinges. I crouched, pistol ready to cut him off at the knees the moment Jerry departed the cabin.

But he didn't drop straight out—he was too smart for that. He jumped instead, hurling himself out from the fuselage and firing at the concrete near the tail all at the same moment. A shower of buckshot exploded against the tarmac, sending concrete shrapnel exploding upward. I bent and shielded my face, scrambling for cover toward the front of the plane. I fired once beneath the tail, knowing I would miss but desperately needing the time. The shotgun crashed as Jerry worked the action. I reached the cabin and bent at the waist to stay sheltered beneath the pilot's window. The engine noise was so loud in my ears I could barely think. Propeller wash blasted my face, and I stole a look through the window, hoping to recover whatever weapon the pilot had fired at me.

I couldn't see it—I could only see the pilot's body, his head split open by a forty-caliber slug.

Two rounds, Sharpe. You've got two rounds.

"Get out here and face me like a man!"

Jerry's voice thundered, raw and crazy, loud enough to be heard over the idling, smoking engine. I danced up onto the lefthand landing gear to protect my feet from a hail of buckshot—and not a moment too soon. Jerry fired again, blasting the concrete beneath the plane.

One ball of buckshot ricocheted upward, zipping into my right calf. It bit like a red-hot hornet sting, and I choked back a fresh surge of pain.

"*Get out here!*" Jerry howled.

I gasped, looking down at my handgun. Looking back toward Riley. She had crawled to the Road Glide and now lay huddled behind it, grasping her left leg.

I saw blood, and the fresh variable added to my dilemma. I could sprint around the nose of the plane and test my reflexes against Jerry's—see which one of us had the quickest trigger finger. I would need to not only be quick but accurate. Nothing less than a heart-shattering hit would stop Jerry from popping off a final blast with the shotgun.

Meanwhile, even a brushing pass of buckshot at ten

yards could be enough to knock me off my feet. The advantage seemed to be on his side.

No. I didn't like the math. I had to change the status quo.

"You want to fight like a man?" I shouted. "Ditch the shotgun. Let's hit the ring—one on one."

A derisive curse. "You think I'm stupid?"

"Nah, Jerry. Not stupid. *Impotent.*" The thought occurred to me just as it was coming out of my mouth, and I knew it would be a winner. The airplane engine continued to choke and howl, oil splashing across the concrete, but Jerry didn't respond.

Pay dirt.

"Riley told me," I said. "Seems you've got a little problem downstairs—a *performance* issue."

The artillery shell landed. Jerry's next curse exploded into a roar. His boots thumped the tarmac. I still couldn't see him.

I dropped off the landing gear and stepped out from under the wing—moving forward, not back. I kept the gun at my side, finger on the trigger, but I didn't raise it. I orbited the nose of the Caravan, allowing plenty of clearance for the propeller. I found Jerry standing thirty feet away, shotgun hanging at his side, his muscled chest heaving. Face flushed.

I grinned. "You shoulda learned in high school, Jerry. Girls talk."

That was enough. His teeth crunched. Spittle sprayed. He looked like a bull ready to charge. I lifted my left hand, beckoning him on. Still sneering.

"Let's have it, big dog. Show me what you got!"

He charged. I charged. Both weapons hit the ground at the same moment—and then we hit.

48

It was stupid. I should have trick-shot Jerry in the throat and left him to bleed out on the tarmac. But if I was honest, I wanted a piece of his sweaty, mangy hide as badly as he wanted a piece of mine.

This monster was responsible for Spencer Meyers' hospitalization. For the deaths of countless migrants, alone in a foreign land, just trying to build a better life. He'd roughed up Riley. His thugs had come after the Purple Crane Campground.

No, a gunshot to the jugular wouldn't do it. This problem would be solved the old-fashioned way.

Jerry's right arm arced toward my face just as our bodies closed within striking distance. I bent at the waist and pummeled him in the ribcage, driving my right hook with everything my battered and abused body had left. Jerry grunted, but he didn't go down. He didn't even stumble. His right knee rammed upward and I caught it in the stomach. The breath hissed through my teeth and I staggered. Jerry retreated, lips lifted in an angry snarl. His right hand dipped into his pocket, and he spat.

"I never told you, Sharpe. I done some time in the Army myself. Dealt with a thousand self-righteous pricks like you."

His hand reemerged with a switchblade. It snapped open, double edged, gleaming under the red glow of the nearby cockpit lights. I gasped for air and retrieved my own knife. It was coated in dry blood. The blade rocked open.

"Surprised you made it through basic," I said. "They usually perform an IQ test."

"IQ test? Is that the best you got?"

I shrugged, falling back into a fighting stance. "I'm gunshot and winded, Jerry. You'll take what you get."

His gaze hardened. Then he lunged. The first sweep of his knife arced toward my face and I leaned back to dodge it. I swept with my left leg, striking for his exposed knee. He danced aside with surprising agility, and the tip of his blade glanced across my chest. Not a deep cut, just a scratch, but I felt it.

I staggered back, leaning on my left leg. Pain from the bullet wound ignited again, and my knee locked. I began to topple.

Then Jerry closed in, knife clutched in his right fist, punching with his knuckles. Instead of swerving the blow I stepped into it, taking it straight to my shoulder, risking his blade so close to my throat but hoping for an opportunity to knife him in the ribs.

Jerry realized what I was doing just as I stabbed at his side. He twisted and the blade of my Victorinox skimmed his flesh instead of sinking into it. I opened up a long gash and shoved, pushing him off me. Jerry staggered and I circled, striking again with my right leg. I hit him in the knee and he shouted. He swept with the switchblade and I ducked it, almost falling. The throbbing in my left thigh was so constant I barely noticed the waves of pain. They faded into the tapestry of the fight, a background fog that I fought through. I lunged again, launching another right hook for his ribs. He leaned to dodge it and caught my left jab on the bottom side of his jaw. His teeth closed with a crunch and he staggered.

I could have gone for his throat, but I risked a gut-stab if I did. I retreated again, wiping blood spray from my face and fighting to catch my breath.

"The truth about men like you," I said, shouting over the chugging Cessna engine. "It's not about IQ. It's not even about that angel hair spaghetti noodle between your legs. You wanna know what you're all about, Jerry?"

Jerry stabilized ten feet away, spitting a broken tooth from his mouth. He turned red eyes on me, no longer looking angry. Now he looked simply crazy. Like a wild beast, thirsty for blood.

And that made my point.

"Tell me, Sharpe!" he barked. "Tell me what a monster I am!"

"Monster is too much credit," I said. "You're just a bloodsucking parasite."

I charged him. Jerry twisted to slash at me, and I ducked low beneath the knife. I drove with my shoulder, slashing with the Victorinox—aiming beneath his ribcage and opening his stomach as though I were butchering a pig. Jerry howled and his knife slashed at my back. The blade opened up a cut over my shoulder blades.

But I kept driving. Another push. Another yard. I struck

his wounded knee with another kick, and this time the joint broke. He screamed. I stabbed upward with the knife, sinking the Victorinox up to its grip in his stomach. Twisting. Jerry writhed and flailed with the switchblade. The weapon glanced off my shoulder. He lost his balance.

I shoved once more, finishing. Sending him staggering backward...straight into the whirring propeller of the Cessna.

The tri-blade struck Jerry first in the back of his head, carving off a chunk of his skull before it sliced off his left arm. As he toppled in a spray of blood, the blade caught him once more across the gut, finishing the job I had started and laying him open. The body struck the tarmac. Blood splashed against my jeans. I stood breathless ten feet away, still choking for air as the plane snorted, then finally cut off.

The whirring blades died, still slinging blood over the concrete. I was transfixed by Jerry's wide eyes, now misted by death.

Then I heard another sound. The snapping click of a cocking handgun. I looked up to see Carter Custer standing behind the open door of the airplane, a polished revolver in one hand. The muzzle gaping at me. His eyes wide with horror, his cheeks flushed pale. His left arm was drenched in blood from a bullet wound in his shoulder. He looked to Jerry. He looked back to me. His gaze hardened.

Then a pair of pistol shots ripped across the tarmac. The first shot landed in Custer's left knee, the second striking him in the skull as he toppled. His revolver fell. The body hit the pavement only yards from Jerry.

I gasped for air, heart hammering. I twisted.

I found Riley lying on her side twenty yards away, stretched out, with her left hand gripping the compound fracture jutting from her left thigh. In her right hand she clutched the M&P I had dropped, its slide locked back over an empty magazine. Smoke rising slowly from the muzzle.

Riley dropped the gun, her face racked with pain but her eyes strangely calm.

"That was for Kaley."

49

The FBI was late to the party, but they turned up eventually. A helicopter landed at the airstrip, followed shortly by a medevac. I'd stemmed the blood flow from Riley's wound, but her femur was splintered —a result of the motorcycle crash. My fault, really.

While the medevac raced her off to a hospital, I remained on site sipping water, quelling my own pain...and waiting for the questions. I'd done this before, a few times. I had some inkling of what came next—bureaucracy and incompetence, the slow-moving gears of a massive agency operated by some of America's finest but led by some of her worst.

Despite my bias against three-letter agencies, I had to admit that the ground team deployed out of St. Louis took me by surprise. The Special Agent in Charge was a chipper young Asian-American woman with a ponytail and a mouth full of gum. She approached my seat, popping her gum and taking nearly a minute to survey me, all without comment.

Then she said, "Well, you look like hell."

"Shoulda seen the other guy," I muttered.

The SAIC grinned, and I relaxed a little. She introduced herself as Special Agent Park, and I couldn't help but think that the name sounded vaguely familiar. Park slapped me on the shoulder and brought me water. She invited me into the helicopter—handcuffed, but treated with respect—for a ride back to the city. Six hours later, with my knife, road rash, and buckshot wounds suitably stitched and bandaged, we sat on either side of her desk and shared a pepperoni pizza while I delivered my testimony.

I didn't fudge anything. I didn't see a point. I began with Spencer and ended with the moment Jerome Withers met justice at the edge of the Cessna's propeller. Park listened without comment, not even taking notes. I knew the conversation was being recorded. At the end she informed me that I would be kept overnight while my story was corroborated by Agent Vaughn, who was currently undergoing surgery. I shrugged and asked for Advil. Park laughed and tossed me a bottle from her desk drawer, then I limped away under the guard of two of her men.

***

DESPITE SPECIAL AGENT Park's good nature, the machinations of bureaucracy won out in the end, and I was held for three days. All without charges, all without consulting a lawyer.

Ah, the joys of three-letter agencies.

In the end, the FBI determined that enough of my story was true to not warrant any further suspension of habeas corpus, and I was released. I hadn't minded the long days spent in a holding cell at the SLMPD jail. The food was decent, the jailer brought me magazines—and besides, the place was absolutely abuzz with grade-A gossip. Apparently, the Gateway Hounds case was turning into a goldmine of juicy investigatory opportunity, and SAIC Park was sinking in her gum-chewing teeth.

Prostitution. Illegal gambling. Drugs. Extortion. Fencing. All the street crimes Riley's investigatory unit was already aware of were now joined by the organ harvesting scheme, which turned out to be far darker and more extreme than even I had imagined. Kumar's laptop was recovered from the Caravan, and at least sixteen murderers were documented within. Using the GPS logs from the Road Glide's infotainment systems—which Jerry and his crew had been stupid enough to use—Park located a surgeon in Chicago who served as the buyer of the illegal human merchandise. Dr. Stavers was his name. He had connections with wealthy elites from all over North America. They paid big bucks—in *cash*—for emergency transplants outside the government-regulated organ donor system. Stavers made millions. Custer made millions. Jerry made hundreds of thousands.

And all that filthy money was cycled through layer after layer of substantially less and less dirty street crime operations, just as I had suspected. "Progressive money laundering," Special Agent Park called it. I wondered if she knew I was the one to coin that term.

It was a king-making bust for the FBI's St. Louis field office, but of course, the corruption ran even deeper. "Judges and prosecutors," Jerry had said. Bought and paid for, a legal shield. Uncovering their names would take time, but Park had a nose like a hound dog and I was confident she wouldn't stop sniffing until she had uncovered the very last bloody bone. Rumor had it suspects at the local courthouse were already under scrutiny.

Who knew how far the trail would lead? Park might become the director of the FBI before it was over, and Riley's career would certainly benefit just as much. At least...if she wanted it to.

I limped out of the SLMPD with a fresh pair of Walmart clothes bulging around the bandages on my legs and back, compliments of one of the many jailers I'd befriended during my three-day stay. The sun was warm on my face as I cocked my head back, looking toward a cloudless blue sky. The cool breeze felt even better on my face.

The rest of me...well. I felt terrible. But that was to be expected. I'd really run myself through the wringer on this one. Mostly, I just wanted a belly full of good food, a warm shower at the Purple Crane Campground, and about forty-eight hours of uninterrupted sleep. Maybe a fifth of whiskey.

But first, I had one more stop to make. It wasn't going to be an easy one. I would have rather put it off.

But my heart wouldn't allow it.

50

I found Spencer Meyers in the same hospital room where I'd left him. He had replaced the news channel with a blaring action movie, and the rest of the room looked substantially different from how I'd last seen it.

There were flowers—a lot of them. Spencer played a new hand-held video game, chewing on a bag of candy as his cast-frozen leg rested atop the sheets.

"What the heck is this?" I said.

Spencer looked up, smacking his lips as our eyes met. He grinned, then that grin faded into a distressed blink.

"Dude...what happened to you?"

I snorted and limped to his bedside, assuming the cheap armchair next to him. I gritted my teeth as I sat, my whole body racked with pain. If three days in lockup had done anything, they had converted my muscles into brittle, inflexible steel rods that dug into my flesh with every movement.

I leaned back into the seat and cycled a few breaths, scanning the room. My gaze settled first on the flowers, then the candy...then back at Spencer. I cocked an eyebrow. He grinned and tossed me the bag. I dumped multicolored sugary glory straight into my mouth and chewed.

It was amazing, but it didn't quite take the edge off my guilt. I swallowed and wiped my mouth, sitting in silence for a moment. Spencer muted the TV and twisted in the bed, shifting his cast-frozen leg.

"I saw the news, man. You took the whole gang out! Wrecked those suckers!"

His face glowed with jubilation, a grin stretching ear to ear. I knew what I had to say would melt that hopeful smile like butter on a white-hot griddle.

"It was a joint effort," I said. "I can't take credit."

"You were knocked down, but you didn't stay down," Spencer said. "That's worth some credit."

Our gazes met. My stomach twisted. I set the candy bag on an end table and swallowed.

"Spencer...I didn't get the money."

Spencer frowned. "Huh?"

I faced him again. "The money I won at the fight ring. The money they owed me...the money for Lily's treatment. I tried to get it, but...there wasn't any cash. All their dirty money was in offshore accounts. The FBI is seizing it."

The puzzlement on Spencer's face persisted. He didn't look disappointed. Just confused.

"I'm sorry," I said. "I'm gonna keep working on it. We'll figure something out."

Another pause. Then Spencer grinned. "You don't know, do you?"

"Know what?"

Spencer twisted in his bed, reaching for a nearby meal tray. He knocked a paper cup onto the floor. He dug out a card and pressed it into my hand, tears bubbling into his eyes.

"Mama got this yesterday… She and Lily are headed to the airport now."

I squinted, scanning the seal emblazoned on the face of the envelope. It was circular and embossed. It read:

United States Senate.

I tugged the card from the envelope and flipped it open. The handwriting was inky black and difficult to read, but I managed with a squint.

Dear Madam,

During a recent phone call with my daughter I learned of your present situation involving your children, certain medical needs, and resulting financial burdens. Having lost my mother at a young age to a disease too expensive to treat, I have dedicated my career in public service to rectifying the American healthcare crisis. Progress in Washington, as I'm sure you can imagine, is slow.

In the meantime, one of my political partners operates a foundation dedicated to supporting families such as yours who are struggling with medical expenses. I've already made a call and you can expect his people to reach out shortly.

I'm so sorry that you've faced this battle for so long on your own—but you are alone no longer. If there is ever anything you need, please don't hesitate to reach out.

Sincerely,

Senator R. H. Park.

I looked up from the card, my exhausted brain struggling to unpack what I'd read. I frowned. I whispered the name to myself.

"Park..."

"They sent all this stuff." Spencer gestured to the flowers, the candy. His grin spread. "The foundation people. They're covering all my bills. They're flying Mom and Lily to Germany for the treatment—they're even helping Mom with some rehab. It's..." He stopped. He choked. The tears wouldn't stop this time. I felt them in my own eyes, also.

"It's amazing," I finished. He nodded. I lifted my fist, and he lifted his. Our knuckles touched.

"Here's to never staying down," I said.

Spencer nodded. "Never."

51

I spent the next two weeks at the Purple Crane
Campground, basking in the Mississippi River
sunsets, grilling thick ribeye steaks, playing my
violin...and happily forgiving myself for skipping my lap
swims.

My left leg always hurt. My back hurt just as much, but at
least the stitches were removed. Scabs on my left shoulder
promised that the skin would regrow eventually. I drank
whiskey every night and slept in until noon, waving to the
neighbors when I eventually emerged from the Airstream.

Everybody knew about my involvement with the recent
FBI takedown of the Gateway Hounds. Supposedly, I'd
declared a one-man war against the gang in vengeance of
Ms. Dottie's ravaged petunias.

I let the rumors rage, simply shrugging and changing the
subject whenever any of the newcomers asked questions—
the full-timers were at least conscientious enough to respect
my privacy. It was fun at first, but by the end of my two-week

respite the familiarity of the campground routine was starting to feel a little too ordinary. A little too predictable.

Despite myself, I was getting restless. When Arty called to update me on the completion of my old GMC, I knew it was time. I cleaned my Airstream top to bottom, stacking my gear on the picnic table outside for later collection. Then I walked the keys to the office and slid them across the counter to Christine.

She stared at them a long moment, but didn't touch them. When she looked up, her eyes watered. I stood with my hands poked into my pockets, not relishing the conversation that was to come. We hadn't really talked since the night I'd told Ms. Dottie the truth.

Ms. Dottie and I hadn't spoken either, but she smiled and waved whenever I passed. It hurt a little. But I understood.

"You're a lot like him," Christine said, at last.

"I take that as an honor."

Another moment dragged by. I shifted my weight.

"Do I owe you anything?" I asked. "What about the broken door latch on the camper?"

Christine shook her head, scooping the keys into the drawer.

"Don't worry about it. Just come see us, sometime. You're always welcome."

I shot Christine a salute and asked her to say goodbye to Ms. Dottie for me. Then I staggered back to the 1994 Harley Davidson Fat Boy parked alongside Slot 12. I grimaced as I slung a leg over. I buckled my half helmet and waved to a couple of my neighbors as I fired up my engine.

They knew I was moving on. They understood, the way only full-timers can. It was part of the cycle. You make friends, you make memories...and eventually you move on.

I rode across the river with the sun setting in my eyes, then turned south on the Missouri side and kept rumbling all the way to Arty's garage. I was excited...and also a little nervous. Arty had mentioned several "upgrades". Last-minute, creative installations he was sure I would love.

I was sure I would love them, also. I just wasn't sure I could afford them. There was only enough cash left in my little lockbox to cover his initial estimate...hopefully.

I rumbled into the parking lot and found Arty lighting up a fresh smoke alongside my parked GMC. The instant I saw the truck basking in the sunset glow a flutter of excitement ignited in my gut and rushed through my chest.

The GMC looked *amazing*. Very likely, better than brand new. Nothing Arty had done was anything less than the very best work a restoration craftsman could manage. The paint was flawless, the trim polished to a brilliant shine. I deployed the side stand and met Arty near the pickup, where we both stood silently for a while just to admire his handiwork.

Every dent was gone. Every scratch erased. Fresh tires shone. The camper shell had been repainted white to match the cab. Arty tugged the passenger side door open, and I looked over a freshly reupholstered seat and reinforced floorboards. He had replaced gauges and even added an air conditioning unit with vents mounted beneath the dash.

Every update was tasteful, blending perfectly with the vintage curves and elegant design of the original. Every surface cleaned, repainted, and refinished. The dash recovered. The rearview mirror replaced with a modern unit complete with compass and thermometer.

"I did a little work on the engine," Arty said, speaking for the first time. He beckoned. I followed him around. He raised the hood.

The engine bay was spotless. Fresh ignition wires ran to all six spark plugs. A brand-new battery rested in the cradle. Brand-new LED headlights were neatly wired in.

Arty pointed with his cigarette. "Electronic ignition. No more tuning. Runs like a dream."

I smiled, nodding my appreciation. I couldn't deny it... Arty had done one heck of a job.

"What do I owe you?" I said, wincing a little as I said it. Arty scratched behind one ear, then tugged on his smoke.

"Quote ran a little short, what with all the upgrades and all. I helped you out where I could. Final bill was like ninety-one hundred...call it an even nine thousand."

I chewed my lip. I'd counted earlier that day and there was only fifty-one hundred left in my lock box. I needed at least a little of that for living expenses until I could scrape up some more cash.

Arty knocked ash off the tip of his smoke, his face turning suspicious. "You short?"

"No, not short, just..." I trailed off. I looked over my shoulder. "Say, Arty. You wanna buy a Fat Boy?"

Arty grinned.

52

The GMC ran better than new. It started up with a flick of the key and purred like an absolute house cat as I rolled out onto the street. The shifting and acceleration were so smooth I could have closed my eyes and envisioned myself rolling out of the sales lot way back in 1967.

A simpler time. A golden age of automobiles.

It was nearly dark in St. Louis and I still had to pick up my gear from the Purple Crane, but before I hit the highway I had one final stop to make. A stop I had been looking forward to all day long.

I pulled up in front of Rusty's Rib Bar and cut the engine off, noting that the door hinges didn't so much as grunt as I stepped out of the truck. An old guy with a Vietnam Veterans hat was just exiting the building, his wife's hand clasped in his. He stopped a moment to view the GMC and whistled softly.

"Nice truck."

"Thank you."

"What'll you take for it?"

I laughed. "Sorry, sir. Not for sale."

He chuckled in return and I limped my way to my favorite booth in the back of the restaurant. Rusty waved but didn't ask for my order. I raised two fingers, and he nodded his understanding.

Just as the food was arriving, a little red hatchback appeared in the parking lot, sliding to a stop next to my GMC. The engine cut off, and a moment later the door popped open. Special Agent Riley Vaughn hauled herself out, dragging a left leg that wore a cast straight up to her hip. She struggled with a crutch, struggled with the door, and struggled to lock the car.

When some beefy guy in a trucker's hat offered to help, Riley said something that made him blanch. Eventually she found her way to the table and slid onto the opposing bench, again dragging the leg.

Her face was a little white despite the sweat trickling down it. She leaned the crutch against the table's end and brushed hair away from her crystal eyes.

"I swear, Sharpe. It'll be a cold day in Hell before I ever get on a bike with you again."

I laughed, sipping tea. Riley's blazing gaze locked with mine. She looked like she might smack me.

But she joined my laugh instead. We dug into full racks of ribs, potato salad, collard greens, and lots of Texas toast. The waitress kept our drinks topped off, and when the platters were removed neither one of us refused the offer of pecan pie, despite our bursting guts.

I leaned back against the wall and sipped tea, enjoying the distant crooning of Rusty working his way through a

Freddie King album. It was as off-tune as ever, but just as pleasant.

"So how about Jimmy's pickup truck?" I asked, broaching the subject of the case for the first time.

Riley snorted in disgust. "A great question. Seems like the FBI should pay for it, but they're baulking. I already sold my Sportster S and reimbursed Jimmy. He was bummed, but I'm sure there's another old Dodge around here someplace."

"That was good of you."

A shrug. "I wrecked it. It's not like I'm going to be riding any time soon...or maybe ever."

Her gaze fell. She poked at her pie. The silence felt suddenly tense, and I knew what was coming. I waited for Riley to make the next move.

"So you're headed out," she said at last.

"Yep. Sometime tonight."

"Where to?"

I shrugged. "I don't know yet."

Riley looked up. She blinked once, very slow.

"Is that...how you deal with it?" she asked. "Staying on the road, I mean."

I looked at my pie, not answering. Not sure how to answer at first. I set the fork down.

"At first, I guess it was. After that it just kinda...became a thing. I didn't have any place to be. I had just enough money to eke along."

"It helped?" Riley's lip quivered. I looked up, measuring the pain in her face and searching for what to say.

How could I explain the last two years? The long days and longer nights. The battle scars—most of them invisible. All the wrestling, the endless carousel of recovery. It was a journey I had experienced in my very bones, and yet I couldn't really communicate it. Not even to somebody who was embarking on the first leg of that brutal pilgrimage.

"Only time helps, Riley," I said. "What you do in the meantime...I don't know if it matters. As long as it doesn't damage you further."

Riley sighed. She shook her head.

"I thought... I mean, I shot Custer..." She trailed off. I gave her time. "I envisioned myself wrapping both hands around his throat *so* many times. Giving him the speech. Dragging him away in handcuffs. I just knew it would fill the void, you know? Give me some kind of closure. But now that it's over..."

She looked out the plastic-covered window, gaze vacant. I reached across the table and placed a worn hand over hers.

"It's not about closure, Riley. I think it's bigger than that. It's..." I hesitated. She tilted her head, waiting.

I withdrew my hand and reached beneath the table. I lifted a little cardboard box and slid it toward her. Riley lifted the top. She squinted.

"A Bible?"

There was some cynicism in her tone. Maybe a little annoyance. I understood.

"My fiancée was a Christian. I never really got it. After she died, I kept her Bible. Over the last couple of years, I've been reading it, and..."

I lost the words. Riley looked up, something between exhaustion and hope in her face.

"You found answers?" she asked, her voice carrying the semi-frustration of a woman who had heard it all before.

I shook my head. "No. But I found some hope. And I think you can, too."

Riley looked back at the Bible. She studied its face for a

long time. I had the bookshop engrave her name into the cover the same way Mia's was engraved. Elegant script. Riley nodded once, replaced the lid on the box, then slid it into her purse without a word.

When she looked back up, she wiped her eyes. Then she dug into the pie like it was the last slice on planet Earth.

I joined her. We joked about Rusty's future in the music business. We swapped jabs about each other's battle scars.

We didn't talk about the case, her career, or what lay beyond the next sunrise. We definitely didn't talk about motorcycles.

We finished the meal, I paid the tab, and we walked outside. I gave Riley a hug, then dug a quarter out of my pocket.

"Call it, Vaughn."

I flipped the coin. It gleamed in the lights of Rusty's Rib Bar. Riley called heads. The coin landed in my palm and I smacked it against my forearm. I moved the hand.

"Heads it is," I said. "Nice call."

I pocketed the coin and headed for my driver's door.

"Wait," Riley called. "What does heads mean?"

"It means I'm driving north," I said, spinning my truck keys on one finger.

"What's up north?"

I grinned. "I have no idea."

ABOUT THE AUTHOR

Logan Ryles was born in small town USA and knew from an early age he wanted to be a writer. After working as a pizza delivery driver, sawmill operator, and banker, he finally embraced the dream and has been writing ever since. With a passion for action-packed and mystery-laced stories, Logan's work has ranged from global-scale political thrillers to small town vigilante hero fiction.

Beyond writing, Logan enjoys saltwater fishing, road trips, sports, and fast cars. He lives with his wife and three fun-loving dogs in Alabama.

Did you enjoy *Knock Out?* Please consider leaving a review on Amazon to help other readers discover the book.

www.loganryles.com

ALSO BY LOGAN RYLES

Mason Sharpe Thriller Series

Point Blank

Take Down

End Game

Fire Team

Flash Point

Storm Surge

Strike Back

Knock Out

Printed in Great Britain
by Amazon

49300508R00189